SAY
YES

SAY YES

LUCIA FRANCO

PAGE
&
VINE

To every reader who fell in love with James and Aubrey and asked for more, Say Yes *is for you.*

Chapter 1

Sleep eludes me as I fight off this horrible headache.

I turn over and curl onto my side. Light from the cracked door spills across the bed and I place a pillow over my face to block it out. Sleeping in a pitch-black room has always helped in the past, but this time it isn't working. The main cause of my headache is stress. I've had so much on my mind lately I've hardly slept.

I yawn and close my eyes, feeling the pull of sleep finally taking me under. I'm nestled under a pile of blankets when a door outside my room slams, startling me awake. I lay in silence for a moment and begin to drift off again, until I hear James yelling from the other room.

"You tell that little fuck he has one last chance to come clean with me or I'm dropping his case, and he can go beg another lawyer to take him on pro bono." A pause of silence. "Reece, I was paraphrasing ... Yeah ... I'm not in the mood. Remind him I was the fifth person he spoke to who finally said yes. Let him know if he doesn't come clean with everything by the time I get back, I'm dropping him. All I need is two minutes with him and I'll know if he's lying."

I swear I can feel James's tension through the walls. He's quiet as he listens to Reece. I hear the clatter of ice cubes falling into a snifter. The glass meets the marble countertop with a sharp clink, and the lid pops from what would only be a bottle of cognac. I know him like the back of my hand. He'll give it a little spin after he pours and take a quick sip before he responds to Reece.

I move the pillow off my face, stretch my arms above my

head, and draw in a deep breath. My body is desperate for sleep, but I want to see James more.

"Thanks, Reece. Just stay on top of it. I'd hate to drop him, but maybe it's time he learned a lesson."

After a pause, James lets out a lively laugh.

"Yeah, she's here. Stop thinking about her like that, you fuck," James says, his tone playful. "Yeah, I'll tell her you said hi. All right, man, yeah. See ya later. Thanks again."

A tired smile tips my lips. I like hearing the two friends banter. James and I had discussed the possibility of bringing other people into our bedroom since we are officially a couple now. Reece has been trying to get us to recreate that hot night the three of us shared a few years ago. We're both comfortable in our relationship and don't feel the need to bring anyone else into it anytime soon.

Quite frankly, I'm not sharing.

James's footsteps echo as he walks down the hall. His shadow appears before he opens the door and pushes his way into our bedroom. He doesn't hit the light switch because he knows I have a headache from hell, so he leaves the door open just enough to be able to see me.

"Val."

I love when he calls me Val. My blood rushes with desire for what's to come at the sound of that nickname. Today I just want him to put me out of my misery. Maybe an orgasm or two will help soothe the worries on my mind and the pounding in my head.

James is standing at my bedside. He places his glass on the nightstand, then leans down to press a kiss to my forehead. My eyes close. I wrap my arms around his shoulders and pull him to me. He climbs into bed without hesitation.

I cuddle up next to James and nuzzle the scruff on his neck with my nose. I draw in a breath and throw a leg over his hip, needing to feel his body pressed to mine. He wraps a strong arm around my back and scoots closer. I guess he needs me too.

"Feeling any better?"

"Mmmmm," I hum under my breath. "Now I am."

"Are you?" he asks, serious.

"Yes, it's a dull headache now, but a lot better. It helps being in your arms."

I release a sated sigh and burrow myself into his chest. Being in James's arms is the only medicine I need.

"I would've come home sooner if you needed me."

Angling my chin up, I press my lips to his. I shake my head. "Not necessary. Everything okay at work?"

James hooks my knee with his hand and scoops my leg around his hip so that I'm partially lying over him. A little purr vibrates in the back of my throat at feeling the heat of his body warm mine. He lays his hand at the crest where my thigh and hip meet and gives me a good tug. A fire burns inside of me at having someone like James—the strong and silent type—hold me like I'm the only thing that matters in this world.

"It would be if this client of mine would get his act together. This kid doesn't seem to comprehend the charges he's facing. He thinks it's a joke and figures since he's got my firm to rep him, he'll walk scot-free. Too bad it doesn't work like that."

"How old is he?"

"Seventeen."

"That's unfortunate," I say quietly. "Hopefully he'll come around. He only has so much time before he seals his future with bars."

James is quiet for a moment. He's stewing over the situation. Attorneys are taught to leave their emotions at the door, but they're humans too, and occasionally, a case gets to them. I can tell this one bothers him.

"Yeah, I hope. I'd hate to see him wind up as another teen statistic, and that's the route he's going down."

I don't like the sound of hopelessness layering his words.

James constantly offers a helping hand and takes cases pro bono as often as he can. He's a good man with a good heart. To see him troubled to this degree bothers me. I want to help ease the tension coiling his body.

I glide my palm over his chest, feeling his strength beneath the expensive material. Pressing into James, I roll against him until he's lying on his back. I rise to my knees and straddle his hips. I lean over and linger above his mouth, purposely rubbing myself over his hard cock. James grips me, his hands splaying my ass cheeks.

"I heard you call out to Val when you walked in," I say, my voice taking on a huskier tone. I know what he needs, and I want to give it to him. James needs his mind taken off work and what he can't control. He needs someone to take the reins and make him forget the world around him.

I'm that girl.

I reach for his black tie and loosen the knot. I pull gently until the satin slides from around his neck. My fingers search for the black buttons of his dress shirt, undoing each one. His hips give a little surge into mine, causing a tide of tingles to flow through me. James slips his hands under the oversized shirt I'm wearing and skims up my stomach. His palms graze my pebbled nipples, teasing me. My body turns lax, and my eyes roll shut as he kneads my aching breasts. I slowly rock against him.

"I did," he murmured.

Val. We made a deal when we officially started dating almost two years ago. When I become Valentina for the night, all cards are off the table and I am at his mercy. Not that I'm not every other night, but on Val nights, it's different. We're different. I don't say no. I wear what he wants me to wear, and I do what he orders. Anything he's voiced about liking or wanting to try, I give to him, something his ex-wife never did. James is relentless when I hand him power over my body. In return, he rewards me with mind-blowing orgasms. It's a win-win for the both of us. Being open with our sexuality is what drew us together in the first place. Happy sex life, happy wife. That's the motto, right? Although I'm not his wife, it's pretty much the same thing. I like to make James happy. He walks around with a goofy grin on his face all the time.

At first, I worried that Valentina was who James wanted and not Aubrey, but he'd assured me that wasn't the case. He said he liked to change things up a little, and I couldn't fault him for that. Who doesn't? I know I do. He was open and honest with me. Val keeps things interesting and fun for us. I never know when he's going to call out for her—it's always a surprise—and I never regret it. Usually, I'm eager for the next time before we're done.

"Only if you're up for it," James says.

Move aside, Aubrey. Valentina's up.

"I'm always up for you," I say, dropping my voice to match the mood. James loves when I go full Valentina on him.

My fingers reach the last button. I push his shirt open to reveal the colorful tattoos on his chest. It's hard to see the actual designs in the shadows, but I know the colorful swirls of ink on his skin by heart. My palms slide up his abs, feeling each rib of muscle, then over to his pecs. For fifty-six, he's in better shape than most twenty-year-olds. James Riviera is hot as sin and he's all mine. I scoot down to undo his belt, but he reaches out to stop me before I can even pull it free.

My eyes snap to his. Without saying a word, James flips me over so he's looming above me. He pulls me in with his steel gaze and I'm lost to him. He lowers his body, settling between my thighs. My fingers thread through his hair while I revel in the feel of his weight on me.

"How about Val visits this weekend," he suggests, and my brow creases in confusion. "We're going to Tahiti. I already have it set up and cleared your schedule with your assistant, and I made sure the cats are well taken care of."

My eyes widen in surprise, my heart rushing fast from excitement. Before I can respond, James says one more thing that makes me a goner for him all night.

"Right now, I only want Aubrey and I want to make music with her body."

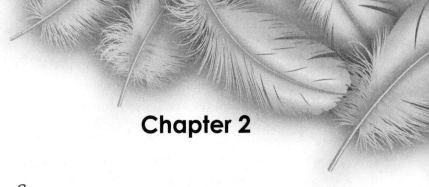

Chapter 2

Since James and I were reunited that day in Chelsea—thanks to Natalie—he's taken me around the world every chance we've had.

We've been to each continent and tried as many delicacies as our bellies could hold. He knew I wanted to travel and see the world, but he also knew how important it was for me to focus on Sanctuary, my non-profit women's and children's shelter. The money I made while working as a high-end escort was enough to set myself up financially for the rest of my life and pay it forward to help those in need. I feel good knowing I could give back. In some way, it makes me feel like Grammy is still around.

My chin is resting on the tops of my hands while I lay on my stomach in our private over-the-water bungalow room. Behind me, James is giving me a hot-oil deep tissue massage. He spared no expense on this trip. It's early morning and the French doors are open wide to allow the breeze to flow through. The spray from the salty sea blends too perfectly with the rich, floral scent of the frangipani flower. I inhale the sultry aroma as I stare at the crystal teal water lapping under the cloudless sky. This is paradise. I could sit here all day.

James doesn't think twice when it comes to needing time to breathe and get away from the rat race we live in. He just gets up and goes. Sometimes he takes me on a surprise vacation for two days, other times for two weeks. I used to worry at first because Sanctuary demanded so much of my time. James told me I had to take time for myself to recoup, and that if I didn't, I would burn out. But I felt bad enjoying the pleasures in life while seeing firsthand how people struggled to make ends meet. I wanted to do more and give more, before I could take for myself. Some of the members didn't have two pennies to rub together when they first walked in, and now they have part-time jobs. Seeing them thrive makes me happy, but it all comes with a price.

Sanctuary has grown so much over the course of two years that I'm opening another one on the other side of town. The second location will cater to single fathers and their children. Call me naïve, but I never knew how many men were left alone to raise their children and are in need of help. Society always assumes it's the woman, but there are just as many men who are raising their children with nothing.

"What are you thinking about?" James asks, pressing his thumb into my shoulder to knead out the tension. I let out a sigh and close my eyes. This feels incredible. He gives the best back massages.

"That you're so good to me," I say, my voice taking on a dreamy tone.

James applies more hot oil and I sink deeper into the bed as his hands spread over my back.

"I'd do anything for you," he says, then leans down to press a kiss between my shoulder blades. "I know you're stressed about Retreat." A small smile tips my lips at the mention of my second shelter. "Right now, the only thing I want you to focus on is us, and what my hands are doing to you while I work out these knots. There's nothing else you can do for the shelter, sweetheart. Everything is finished and ready for the opening."

I let out a sigh. "I know. You're right. I just feel like I'm missing something. It doesn't help that the gala is the same day."

When I'd learned I would be one of the four recipients of the New York City Women of Impact Humanitarian Award, I was both stunned and honored. I was considered a trailblazer who was making a difference in the world. I hadn't seen myself like that, but it felt good to be recognized. I haven't been able to stop thinking about the upcoming dinner, or how I had been chosen in a city housing eight million people. Adding to my stress is that Retreat is opening the same day. I could always move the opening day, but I don't want to let anyone down either.

"That's normal. You've invested a lot of time, money, and energy into it. This isn't just a hobby for you, this is your life and what you love. It's what drives you. I know you want it to run smoothly, and it will. Just stop thinking about it for five minutes."

I bob my head. I really do want that, but my anxiety is still there and wreaking havoc on my nerves.

Exhaling the worries like James said, I focus on his touch, how he pushes the heels of his palms up the sides of spine. His fingers curl along the slopes of my neck and he presses down. Wetness pools between my thighs. He massages my shoulders, igniting a deep need for him. My nipples pucker against the cool sheets. James drags his hands down my ribs, the tips of his fingers grazing my breasts. He reaches my hips and grips them tightly. Friction surrounds my clit and the pressure intensifies.

The only problem with James giving me a back massage with hot oil is that I want sex now.

His fingers are on the back of my neck again, this time threading through my hair. My lips part in bliss. I love having my hair played with like this, and James knows it. His hands cup my scalp, and he massages my head with a sensual tug of my hair.

"James ..." I grin then laugh. "I know what you're doing."

"And what's that, sweetheart?"

I rise up on my elbows and look over my shoulder at him. He's humoring me.

Every time I look at him, my heart does this stupid flip-skip thing that causes the organ to swell larger for him than the cage it's held in. We're an unlikely pair with him being thirty-plus years older than me, yet we couldn't seem more perfect for each other.

It's been four years since we met, and I swear the man hasn't aged. He's still rocking the salt-and-pepper hair with the matching beard, but now he has more tattoos. I know people stare at us a little longer when we're in public together, but I don't care. He's mine, and I wear him proudly.

"Come here," I say, waving two fingers at him.

James leans over me while still straddling me from behind. I cup the back of his head and pull him to me so I can feel his lips on mine. I kiss him once and his mouth opens, allowing me to slip my tongue inside and lay it against his. James returns the kiss ten times better then breaks away to move off me so he's on his back. I scoot closer and hitch my leg up, my knee lying against his heavy sack. I look into his baby-blue eyes for a moment. The desire I have for him is just as strong as the first day we met. He presses his thigh against my pussy. I rub myself on him and notice the tent in his shorts growing. Sensing my arousal, James applies pressure.

"I love you," he whispers. His hand fists my hair and he studies me like I'm the eighth wonder of the world.

"I love you more." I give him my usual response.

My heart beats wildly as an array of emotions fills me. Sometimes it scares me how much I love James. Occasionally I'll wake up in the middle of the night and reach for him, panicking in my sleep that I won't have enough time to love him.

"What's wrong?"

I shake my head. I don't want to tell him my thoughts, even though it's something I think about a lot. I love this man more than I love my own life. I can't imagine a world without him. A world where I don't get to love him the way I want to. The way he needs to be loved.

"Nothing. I'm just really happy I get the man I love all to myself for the next few days. It's just you and me, babe."

He's quiet. His fingers are brushing over my jaw, and I lean into his hand. "I've been wanting to ask you something."

I smile into his palm. "Oh, yeah? What's that?"

"How would you feel if I sold my brownstone and we bought a house together? Say, in Bergan Beach?"

I pick my head up and look at him, my brows drawing tight. Within six months of getting back together, I moved to Brooklyn Heights to be with him. We'd spent two years apart and didn't want to waste any more time than we already had. It only made sense since we were at each other's home every night anyway. He offered to come live with me, but I knew being in Brooklyn was better for him, so I'd packed up the cats and moved in with him.

I kept my grammy's house, though. I can't bear to let it go, but I hate to see it empty too, so I use it now as a transitional home for those in my shelter who've taken the steps to get on their feet. There's no charge for rent, just utilities. They have to start somewhere. Living in New York is extremely expensive—one of the priciest places to live in the world—and I want to give these women the chance they deserve. I don't need the money anyway. There are strict rules they have to follow, along with monthly check-ins. I wish Grammy was here to see what my non-profit idea turned into. I know she would've loved to be part of every phase. She had given me advice shortly before she passed away, encouraging me to do what makes me happy and not what I should do to give me a good paycheck one day. I think she'd be proud I followed my heart, and that makes me feel good inside.

My brows deepen. "Can I ask why?"

"I picked that place out, had a decorator come in and spice it up. We didn't pick anything out together. I want something we both love that's only ours." His tongue slips out over his bottom lip, like he's hesitating. "I want us to have a place to call our own, where we can continue creating more moments. I want everything with you, Aubrey. A marriage, a home. I'm in this for life, sweetheart, and I'm ready to take the next step with you."

Chapter 3

My eyes soften at his words.

I didn't think it was possible for my heart to grow any bigger with love for this man. I'm smiling from ear to ear so hard my blushed cheeks are aching.

"James Riviera, how are you the sweetest man in the world?"

Creases form between his eyes and the muscles in his body stiffen. That isn't something I expected.

"I'm serious, Aubrey. You're my life. I love you. I want us to be more, and I think buying a new home that's *ours* is a step in the right direction."

My palms skim over his chest, then to his arm where he had a map tattooed when we got back together. It was expertly done with a fine needle and spans from the top of his shoulder down to his wrist. Only it's not a typical world map. This one has drawings of places we've visited together, like when we went to Aspen and stayed in his cabin. He had snowy mountains inked for that one. They were our moments, he'd said.

He documents all our moments that are important to us. Every single place he's taken me that's brought us closer together, he's had inked onto his body forever. I still remember the day he came home with his arm bandaged in white gauze and plastic wrap. He hadn't told me he was getting a tattoo and wanted to surprise me. Surprise was an understatement. James once told me he had been saving that arm for a special occasion. I've been wanting to surprise him with a tattoo of my own, I just haven't figured out what I want to do yet. I want it to mean something to the both of us the way his do.

I pick up his wrist and kiss the place where his pulse is. I gaze at it with softness, then thread his fingers with mine. My thumb caresses my favorite inked moment by far—the day he told me he loved me for the first time. We weren't anywhere romantic, or on a special trip. In fact, we were right in the middle of Manhattan getting Chinese food in the dead heat one summer evening when he said it. Our order hadn't been ready for pick up yet, so we'd been standing on the busy street with his back to the wall and me in his arms taking in the perfect Instagram-worthy sunset. The fiery amber ball burned between the skyscrapers as it descended, illuminating the buildings with a breathtaking glow.

This wasn't just an ordinary sunset. Anyone could see as they walked through the concrete jungle. I'd remarked on how incredible it was and that I'd never seen the sun between the buildings like that before. James told me it was called Manhattanhenge, when the sun aligns with the city's street grid to produce—and fit—the perfect setting sun only four days out of the year. It was larger than life, and the heat flowing around the outer rim could be seen when "I love you" came out of James's mouth. It was so natural and just right, and it ended up being the first tattoo he got for us—a sun that overlooks his map. I glance at the warm hues of orange, the soft, buttercup yellows, and shades of red over his pulse and smile softly at the memories I hold so dear behind it.

My knee nudges his erecting cock. "James, I love that brownstone. I love being there with you, I love walking up the street to our home and taking in the flowery landscape that people don't typically associate with living in the city. If you want to sell it, then we'll sell it and buy a new home. I want what you want. But don't think for one second that it bothers me that you had it before I came back into your life." I pause, an idea springing to mind. "What if we get rid of everything your decorator bought, and we go shopping together? We'll create our own little oasis. If you want to redo the whole damn unit and tear everything out, we can do that too, but I'm happy there and I really love it."

His frown deepens. "You do?"

I nod. "I do, but if you'd rather us have a new place, we can do that too," I say, then something dawns on me. My head tilts to the side and I ask, "Do you want to sell because you purchased it during a low point in your marriage and it reminds you of that?"

James has been divorced for four years now, but he spent more than twenty years in that somewhat unhappy and unwanted marriage. Now I can see why he's considering selling it.

"A little bit."

A soft smile tugs at the corners of my mouth. "Then we're selling it. End of discussion. When we get home, it's going on the market immediately. But, James?"

"Yes?" His body relaxes a little, and I clamp my teeth onto my bottom lip.

"I'd like to stay in Brooklyn Heights, or in one of the surrounding neighborhoods ... like Williamsburg, or even Park Slope, and in one of their brownstones. I never thought I'd live in Brooklyn, but now I can't imagine not living there. It's our home, where my heart is, where we have so many incredible moments together. I don't want to leave them behind."

James scoots up to a sitting position and takes me with him. He wraps a strong arm around my lower back and tugs me up until I'm straddling his hips, our bodies flush together. My nipples graze over the soft dusting of hair on his chest. A purr escapes me. I drape my arms over his shoulders and look him in the eyes.

"A compromise I can work with," he says, a hint of a smile pulling at his lips. "I assumed you'd want an actual house one day like most women, the whole white picket fence and all of that."

I grin and brush a hand down his beard. "I think we both know by now I'm not like most women."

He chuckles and the sound causes my belly to flutter. "Thank fuck for that. I love you the way you are, sweetheart, and I wouldn't change a fucking thing."

I'm really fortunate to have a man who accepts all my flaws and sins ... and not give a damn about all the men I fucked when I was an escort. I don't hate that part of my life because it brought James to me, but sometimes I have regrets because of the things I did for money.

"Then it's settled."

"I just want you to be happy," he says, and it makes me mushy for him. He's such a romantic at heart.

"Well ..." I begin with puckered lips and flirtatious eyes. "There is one thing I need that would make me *really* happy."

"Anything," he says against my lips.

My heart is beating so fast for this man that I seal my lips to his in a bruising kiss. He's my every heartbeat, my every breath. God, I love him so much. I tighten my arm around his neck while my free hand holds his jaw. My breasts are pressed to his chest. Our tongues tangle each other's as desire blossoms between us.

"Make love to me," I whisper.

"I already told you, sweetheart, I've been making love to you the whole time."

James reserves his charming side for when he's in a loveable mood like this, but I know deep down he's serious about what he said.

His palm connects with my thigh, and a little zing zaps through me. "Lift up." I rise to my knees and James grips his cock in his hand, angling it at my entrance. He peers up at me with a burning need in his eyes that I feel in my own.

"Now take all of me," he says.

And I do, sinking down on him in one good, long stroke. My head rolls back and I exhale a pleasure-filled sigh. Sometimes we forgo foreplay because I like the feel of him stretching me.

One would think with a boyfriend James's age that sex would

slow down or it would be hard for him to get an erection, but it's the complete opposite. Sometimes it's me who can't keep up with him. He has so much testosterone running through his veins that our lovemaking grows more manic each and every time. There's an abundance of passion flowing from his touch to the way he kisses me with hunger. I'm addicted to him.

"Stay down," he demands with his hands on my hips.

My inner thighs are quivering as I try to loosen up to accommodate his width. Sometimes he slides in and bangs me, other times it's a little tight at first. I wonder if I'll ever be able to fit him without pain.

"Then kiss me and make me forget how your cock is stretching my pussy out and tearing me from hole to hole. You're going to give me a gaping vag one day."

He grins. "Such a filthy fucking mouth."

"You love it."

"Fuckin' right I do," he says, then kisses me. After a few strokes of his skillful tongue, I'm slowly riding him.

James is still in control with his arm around my hips, allowing me to only rise halfway up his erection. I love it and hate it because all I want to do is fuck him wild but he's setting a pace that will drive me into a frenzy for him. It's sublime torture on my clit and I cry out. He's hitting it but he's not. Teasing me until my heart is racing a mile a minute and pleasure begins to set in at the tips of my toes. My nails score his skin and he grows ravenous, thrusting deeper inside my pussy. James groans, and I feel the vibration from his chest against mine.

"It doesn't get better than this," I say.

He chuckles, his warm breath tickling my neck. "You say that every time."

"And every time it gets better. You're like fine wine, James. You get better with age."

"I prefer cognac," he says, and I laugh. "One day," James says, his breath hitching, "I'm going to make you my wife, Aubrey. I hope you're ready, sweetheart, because I'm not taking no for an answer."

"James," I whisper, then gasp when he plunges in deep, holding me to him. My hips angle into his and he leans over with my thighs molded to his, holding us up with one hand flat to the bed. James rears back and slams into me. His lovemaking becomes needy and his hands are groping every inch of my bare skin. This position couldn't be more perfect for us to come together. He's striking my clit and pounding into my pussy while he angles my hips to reach a deeper spot for himself. He's going to leave bruises on my body when he's done from how hard he's gripping me. Everything becomes an afterthought when that first prick of euphoria assaults me in the best way. We don't conceal our lust, instead, we allow any sound to express how we feel when we're this deep into the moment.

My heart is racing double time now. I don't need a piece of paper to know that he's mine and I'm his. We already know that. There's no reason to put a label between us. We have a good thing going. Why ruin it?

Some of the best and longest-lasting relationships are ones without any type of label.

I don't want marriage, and I hope that's something he can understand. I love him and he loves me. That's all that matters.

Right?

Chapter 4

I'm not a fruity drink kind of girl, but I am on vacation.

I like to try all the touristy drinks and foods native to the country we're visiting because I know when I go home, no matter what I do, I'll never be able to recreate it. Manhattan is thriving with just about every kind of cuisine one could want, and while I'm not complaining, it's just not the same.

Tahiti has a drink native to the island called The Tahiti. I laughed over the name at first, until James reminded me there's a Long Island iced tea and a Manhattan Special where we live. All I know is this has pineapple- and coconut-infused juice with a rum only made here, and a sprinkle of ginger. It's delicious. I'm on my third and feeling amazing in my man's arms.

James and I are sitting on the beach under a massive umbrella in a lounge chair together. I'm between his legs lying back against his bare chest. I love to be in his arms every chance I can. When he came out of the bathroom earlier dressed in only board shorts that sat super low on his hips, I had to fan myself. He's too damn good-looking. I told him I want to chain him up in our basement and keep him all to myself. He said he was cool with that.

James has his leg propped against the armrest, his hand on my hip with the tips of his fingers under my bikini bottoms, lounging away with me.

I never want to leave here.

"Want a sip?" I lift the glass over my shoulder. I ask him every time and every time he takes a sip to appease me, even though he despises sugary drinks. I just ask to be nice, really.

"You're almost out. Do you want another one?"

I finish off the rest and place the tall glass on the round mosaic table next to us. My hands find his and I lace our fingers together, shifting so I'm laying my head on his arm. I kiss the inside of his bicep and snuggle up to him, breathing him in. He smells like suntan lotion.

"James, if I didn't know any better, I'd say you're trying to get me drunk."

I feel him shrug. He has no shame, and I love that about him. "Two words. Drunk. Sex."

I giggle. Alcohol does two things for me: I'm giddy, and I want to have sex. I pause in thought. Actually, make that three. Sometimes I like to drop it low and shake my ass.

"Drunk sex in the ocean?" I suggest.

"You're too wild for the ocean when you're drunk. I may accidentally drown you."

I laugh and pick up my head to look at him. Laughter dances in his blue eyes. "You make me that way. It's all your fault."

He smirks and I feel it in my belly. "You're welcome."

Reaching higher, I drop a quick kiss on his lips and sit up. I try to pull back, but he cups the back of my neck and holds me for a longer kiss. Sometimes I can't concentrate when he does that. Like when his thumb is pushed up under my jaw.

Grabbing his hand, I break the kiss and pull up to stand. I'm a little tipsy but not drunk.

"Come on, let's go swimming. I want to feel the water on my skin."

James's eyes roam the length of my body, making sure he doesn't miss an inch of skin. He makes me feel so beautiful. So wanted. So loved.

"Sweetheart?"

"Yeah, babe?"

"When we go snorkeling later, you're not wearing that."

I glance down. I did pick a red skimpy suit to wear for him since I know he likes this color on me. My top is two sizes too small, making my C cups look even bigger, and I'm wearing a Brazilian-style bottom that's very cheeky. Since I've gained a few pounds over the years, I think I'm leaning toward D breasts, though I'm not entirely sure since I don't usually wear a bra at home anymore. Everything I wear when we go out already has proper lining.

"What's wrong with my bathing suit?" I ask, trying not to smile. "I picked it out just for you."

"You're testing me. I'm two seconds from ripping it off you."

I giggle again and take a few steps back toward the ocean. "You have to catch me first."

Turning around, the sand is hot under my feet, so I run on my toes toward the beach. The light crystal blue water reminds me of James's eyes. Just as I reach the shore, James wraps an arm around me from behind and lifts me up, throwing us both into the water.

I'm giggling as I go under and hold my breath. The water feels refreshing. I wish it was like this back home. New York doesn't have light teal water beaches like this. They're murky and gray, and the water is always so cold.

We come up for air, both of us smiling. I reach for James and wrap my legs around his waist. He automatically tugs me closer. I can reach the ground, but this is more fun.

"I caught you," he says, his voice low.

My heart does a little flip. He caught me the moment we met in Bryant Park. We both know that.

"You did," I say.

"If I didn't already set up a full day of sightseeing for us, we'd be making our own waves right now."

"Real suave, James. That might be the most cliché thing you've said yet."

"I have my moments," he says. "I can cancel ..." He lifts a brow in suggestion.

I almost want to say yes, but I don't. I playfully slap his shoulder. I know he's not serious. When we're on vacation, we make the most of it and see and do everything we can.

"No! I want to see the waterfalls and snorkel with the fish. I want to feed the sharks and stingrays. I want to do couple's massages with you, and after dinner, I really want to see the Polynesian dance. You're taking me to do all of that." I try to be firm, but he can see right through me.

James is smiling from ear to ear. He moves the wet hair stuck to my cheek and leans in to place a kiss on my neck.

"Okay, okay, okay. Whatever you want to do, I want too." He lifts his wrist and checks the time. "We have about an hour before we have to be at the dock for the boat I chartered. As much as I want to make love to you again, I think we should eat and get one more drink. We have a full day planned."

"And change my suit. I want to grab some shorts too."

"We'll get your shorts but don't change the bathing suit. You're fucking smoking in it."

"You don't care?"

One corner of his mouth turns up. "No, sweetheart, I was just playing. Let people look at you. I want them to. I know who you'll be coming home with at the end of the night."

"Damn straight, big daddy."

James lets out a raucous laugh then pulls us under water to kiss me.

***

Cardi B's "Money" starts blaring in our bungalow.

I frown as I try to uncover where I placed my purse. I know that's my phone, but I don't remember setting that ringtone for anyone.

"Who's that?" James asks as he buttons his shirt.

"No idea."

I grab my cell phone from my clutch and read the screen. I shake my head as I answer the phone. "Real slick, Natalie."

It takes her a second to comprehend what I'm talking about, then she bursts out laughing. "I forgot I did that!"

"Now your dad thinks you like to fuck in big tall heels, but you don't really need the D because you just really want the money."

She's still laughing. "Oh my God! I'm dying!"

I turn to gauge James's reaction. He's slipping on his Tag watch and rolling up his dress shirt sleeves to his elbows. I love this look on him. Casual yet dressy. The distressed jeans and partially buttoned shirt. The way the tattoos tease his arms and chest works well with who he is. We'd been sightseeing and snorkeling for most of the day. Now there's a golden tint to James's cheeks.

I can't believe I snagged myself a fucking hot silver fox.

I still can't believe he's my best friend's dad either.

"What's my ringtone when I call you?" I ask.

"'Milkshake' by Kelis."

The beginning of the song begins to play in my head, and I smile. Natalie is hysterical.

"What's up, bestie?"

"I hope not my dad's—"

"Nat! Stop it."

She sighs dramatically and chuckles. "When do you two lovebirds get back? I have breaking news."

I frown. "Are you all right? Is everything okay?"

James looks at me with concern. He lifts his chin, wanting to know what's going on.

"Everything's fine," she says. "I just have something I want to talk to you about in person."

"You're pregnant." I deadpan, and James's eyes widen.

"No, you raging lunatic." I shake my head at James so he knows she's not pregnant. "I'm living my best IUD life. If I could find a doctor to perform a hysterectomy on me now, I would. No little monsters for me. I plan to spread myself thin."

I shake my head, laughing under my breath. James still doesn't know Natalie is the one who got me a job as an escort at Sanctuary Cove, and he never will. I'm happy she hung up her knee pads and isn't hooking anymore.

"But are you okay?"

"Yes, I just want to make sure I see your face when you get back."

"Ah, okay. We'll be back late the day after tomorrow."

"I'll be there the next morning with bells on bright and early equipped with guava and lime mimosas."

"Oh, what are we celebrating?"

"My vagina's freedom. I gotta run, Ram Jam. Don't forget to make sure he wears a rubber. You can't trust anyone these days."

Natalie hangs up, leaving me laughing at her sarcastic, vulgar sense of humor. Nothing she says shocks me anymore.

"What's the ringtone when I call you?" James asks.

A huge smile lights up my face. "Call my cell and find out for yourself, Big Daddy."

James retrieves his phone and dials up my number, then meets my gaze when "Doin' It" by LL Cool J blares from my phone.

"That's what plays when I call you?"

I nod proudly.

"Every time?"

I nod again.

"I fuckin' love you," he says, and plants a kiss on my lips, then takes my hand and guides us to dinner.

Chapter 5

James has his arm around me while I drag my nails back and forth over his forearm. We're sitting on our deck under the night sky sipping Remy Martin. James ordered a special bottle for us and says we have to finish it. We're about halfway through, but neither one of us is drunk. It's a soothing, warm body, relaxing high when sipped slow.

After a romantic dinner with the full moon slipping behind the darkening ocean, we walked a short distance with my high heels hooked on two of my fingers and James holding my other hand. I could walk the streets of Manhattan in five-inch heels, but on the soft sand, I basically had two left feet.

We watched the Polynesian dance show. I was entranced the entire time, and I think James was too. They thumped the tops and the sides of the barrel drums with their thumbs and heels of their hands, then they blew into conch shells to produce a sound I'd never heard before. James said if you hold a conch shell to your ear, you can hear the ocean. Mini tiki torches were posted every two feet or so in the sand. The flames were small, but enough to come together to create a sultry mood and color the women's exposed skin in a coppery radiance. The best part was the large, vibrant feathered headpieces they wore that I imagine are heavier than they look. Matching straw skirts that sat extra low on their hips and a basic triangle bathing suit top finished the ensemble. Every time the skirts swayed, a rustle blew in the air.

I've seen some pretty eclectic dancers on the subways in New York City, but the precision and speed these girls popped their hips and rolled their bellies was fascinating to watch. I swear they hit every beat and didn't stop until it was over. They encouraged the locals and tourists to go on stage to dance with them toward the end and managed to carouse James up. I wish I'd brought my cell phone to dinner so I could record a video of him to show Natalie. The way he was smiling from ear to ear, how his eyes glittered with delight as he danced in the sand barefoot with the girls made me so fucking happy. James Riviera makes me high on life and it made me realize just how much my love for him grows by the minute.

"Thank you for this, for tonight."

"For what, sweetheart?" he asks.

I look at him. "For bringing me here. For noticing when I'm stressed and trying to help. For being you. For having a big heart. This might be my favorite vacation we've taken yet. You're so good to me. Sometimes I feel like I don't deserve you."

James doesn't say anything. He reaches for me, cupping my cheek, and kisses me softly. My eyes close and I draw him in. His lips are pressed between mine, but we don't move our mouths. We hold steady, cherishing the other's touch. It's the simplest of kisses yet makes me feel the most, like he's grateful for me and that I matter to him.

Breaking away, James's steel eyes search mine. He's breathing a little deeper, heavier. "I was going to tell you I want Valentina tonight." He pauses to shake his head. "But I don't. I just want you. Always and forever, just ... you, Aubrey."

Be still my heart. James takes my breath away. I swallow hard, feeling the pulse in my throat beat chaotically. I love this man so much.

"Come on. I have something planned for you," he says.

James takes my hand and walks us to our bungalow about twenty feet away. We step through the French doors and my jaw drops in surprise. My eyes widen as I take in the room, wondering how he made this happen while we were sitting on the front deck.

The lights are turned down low, and there are white candles lit along the walls. There's usually a tropical aroma that follows us on the island, but in our room, there's something deeply seductive and alluring about the scent that pulls me in.

My eyes land on our king-size bed. I shoot a quick glance at James who's watching me. There are white feathers and red rose petals sprinkled on top of the down comforter. I've never seen a blend like that on a bed before. It's beautiful but sexier than anything else.

I turn toward James. "When did you do this? When we came back, none of this was here."

He steps closer until he's an inch away. "I had the resort set it up for us. I gave them instructions and told them when to come. I shut the door so you wouldn't hear them while we sat outside together."

I shake my head, blinking a few times in disbelief. I can't believe how thoughtful he was to set this up. "This may be the most romantic thing you've ever done."

He cups my cheeks and gazes into my eyes. "I told you, Aubrey, you're my world. You make me feel young and what it's like to be happy again. You're my light, what I look forward to every day I wake up. There isn't a thing I wouldn't do for you."

Emotions well in my eyes. I'm overcome by his love. James has been beyond good to me, even while I was working at Sanctuary Cove, but something about this moment, tonight, has shifted a part of my heart to lock into place. I'll never forget this. James can be a total mush ball, but he never gets this mushy like he is right now.

Apprehension suddenly fills my mind. I know James loves me and he'd walk over hot coals to see me happy, but tonight makes me wonder if he's hiding something terrible from me and he has to break the news, because why did he go all out like this? My lips form a thin flat line. My jaw trembles.

"Sweetheart, what's wrong?" James grabs my arms, his frightened eyes look back at me. "Tell me what's wrong."

"Is there something that you're afraid to tell me? Are you sick? Is that why you're being sweet to me and had this set up?" My voice shakes. I feel so stupid asking that, but I can't think straight now that my heart's a frantic mess. "Because I need to know if you have a terminal disease and need to buy two caskets because I can't live without you, James. I just can't."

I feel like I'm about to hyperventilate. James stares back at me in complete silence. His jaw is hanging open and his blue eyes are unmoving. I knew it. I guessed, and he didn't expect that.

My stomach is in knots. Now I'm always going to associate Tahiti with James telling me he's sick.

"Uh, Aubrey?" he says, scratching the side of his head. "There's nothing wrong with me. I don't know where you got that I was sick from, but I'm not. I'm healthy as a horse."

My eyes shift back and forth between his. "What?"

"I'm not sick." He drops his arms. "I just want you to know how much you mean to me and that I really just fucking love you so much. I can't believe you thought I was sick."

I roll my lips between my teeth and cringe inside. My eyes drop to the floor as my cheeks bloom with embarrassment. I feel like a moron that a small giggle makes it past my lips. Closing my eyes, I laugh at how dense I am sometimes. Natalie likes to say it's a good thing I'm pretty when I say something really ignorant. I bet if she were here, she'd say it again.

"Baby, I'm so sorry." I put my hand on his chest. "I feel terrible."

"And that's why you laughed," he says with zero emotion. No smile. No personality.

Oh, no. James is hurt and that makes me feel like shit. I hate that I sometimes laugh at the wrong moments.

"I laughed because I'm dumb. I'm really sorry, James. I never once doubted your love for me. This was just so sweet that when you started talking, I thought you were preparing me for something bad."

He doesn't say anything, and it causes my pulse to spike. God, I fucking ruined it.

"James? I really am sorry."

"I guess my emotions are a little more hands-on this trip." His Adam's apple bobs as he swallows. "But that's because I'm so proud of you after watching how hard you've worked these last couple of years. I know we've been together a while now, but I've never felt a love like this. You hold all the power inside of me, and I can't do anything about it. My fucking heart won't stop burning at the sight of you. If this is what real love feels like, then I never want to have the chance to experience it with anyone else ever again. What I feel for you scares the shit out of me. Every move I make, everything I think about, it involves you in some way. I guess the way you make me feel turns me into a sap, but that's what you do to me, Aubrey." He pauses. "I can't turn off what I feel for you. It just keeps growing."

I'm speechless.

I'm also a fool.

I definitely didn't know he felt like *that*. I knew how he felt about me, but wow.

A very small smile curves my full lips. My eyes drop to his throat where his pulse hammers away in his neck. I lean in, pressing my lips over it, and allow my tongue to do a lap. I find the buttons on his shirt and begin to slowly undo them. James's hands slide onto my hips and he gives me a little tug. Without lifting my head, my eyes shoot to his. I'm a little nervous, but I want him to know his feelings are not one-sided.

"Tomorrow," I say, and my voice takes on a velvety smoothness, "you and I are going to this little tattoo shop here we passed a few times when we were strolling. I'm going to get my first moment. I've been waiting for the right time, and it's now." I swallow and lick my lips. "When I say I love you more, it's because I can't imagine you can feel more than what I already do." Sudden shyness attempts to pull at my lips. My cheeks are a little flushed.

His hands roam my loose and flowy dress, inching it up with the tips of his fingers. The need in his touch and the way his fingers leave a trail of heat in their path rocks me down to my core. He has a way of making me fall even harder for him. To be loved so profoundly is a feeling one would never understand unless they lived it. This is what life is all about and the meaning behind why we're here. We were meant to meet that day in Bryant Park.

I can tell James all night long that I love him, but I'd rather show him how I feel.

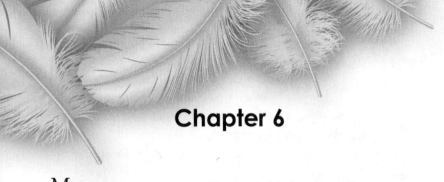

Chapter 6

My hands move to his shoulders and slide his shirt off.

It falls to the floor in a soft heap. I lean forward and press my lips to his chest. He cups the back of my head as I inhale the cognac and crushed cigar scent that clings to him. He smells like money and masculinity. My fingers reach for his belt buckle as I slip out of my high heels. James pulls down the straps of my dress where it falls next to his shirt.

"Never doubt what I feel for you." My voice drops to a throaty whisper. I look at him. "Never doubt it's any less than what you feel for me. You're it for me, baby."

Rising up on my tiptoes, I palm his cheeks and bring his kiss to me. One hand finds my lower back, the other is threading through my hair, holding me to him. His tongue slides against mine. The way James kisses me this time, while it's the same, it's completely different. It's deeper, harder, more intense. He's not holding back and showing me how he truly feels.

He tears his mouth from mine. "Do you trust me?"

I nod without hesitation. "Of course."

"Lay on the bed facedown."

I do as he says and lay on the feathers and petals. I hear him rustling behind me and turn to watch him over my shoulder. James in a designer suit is heart-stopping, but James naked is ovary combusting. He's a big man all over, strapping and brawny. I like the power his presence wields.

James picks up one of the many candles in the room and climbs onto the bed. He straddles my legs. His heavy, thick cock grazes the back of my thighs.

"This is going to be hot for a second, but it won't hurt you." James blows out the flame. "The wax turns into massage oil."

"Are all the candles like that?"

"Yes."

I nod in eager excitement. Hot oil is drizzled down my spine and over my ass. I hiss and fist the sheets, my hips rising back of their own accord. It doesn't last long, just long enough to spread a soothing warmth over me. I relax again.

"Does it hurt?" James stops pouring.

"No, not at all. I just didn't know what to expect the first time. It feels good actually."

"I wish you could see yourself like this," he whispers, then places the candle down on the bed and begins to massage my back. Fingers spread out, he applies pressure and glides up my back to my neck. He gives my shoulders a good squeeze before moving back down. The tips of his fingers browse the sides of my breasts, over my ribs, to my lower back.

"Oh, wow." I nearly purr, my hips moving again. My toes curl. "This feels incredible."

"I'm going to do your entire body."

He applies more oil to my back, then moves down to my ass. Wide hands palm my cheeks as he caresses me in slow circles. He takes his time, dragging his thumb up the inside of my ass, before moving in an outward circle and repeating the motion.

"Can I do you next?" Fuck. I can barely speak.

"Another time. This is for you, sweetheart."

After he does my entire backside down to my ankles, the desire hovering above my tingling skin makes me painfully needy for him. My body is hot, but in a good way, like the oil enhances my craving for him. I hope James is ready for me soon. He had to know what a massage like this would do to me.

James turns me over and I immediately start laughing. The

oil turned into a glue. He looks at me with a puzzled expression.

"The feathers and petals are sticking to my back," I answer his unasked question.

Laughter spreads across James's face. "I didn't prepare for that."

"You can pull them off when we're done and then we can dip in the ocean," I suggest, and his eyes light up. He likes the idea.

James takes his time and starts at my feet, making his way up my thighs. I realize the oil is scented with vanilla bean and a dark tropical smell, which only heightens my senses. I watch James as he's so careful with my body and how he applies pressure to the thicker parts of me. In the two years I've been with him, I've gained a fair amount of weight and he swears he loves it. I went up four full sizes—five, depending on where I shop. "More cushion for the pushin'" he'd said when I'd grumbled about it. I laughed.

My hips are more rounded, my thighs are a little bigger, and my ass is heavier with more bounce. Somehow my stomach has stayed flat. Most of the weight went to my boobs. I'm curvier than when I first met him, and I've never felt sexier in my life. James has a way of making me love my body. He treats it like a temple, worshiping me every night, bringing out the confident vixen in me.

Pleasure spreads throughout my body as his fingers press and knead my inner thighs. I lift my knees and slowly open my legs to expose myself to him.

"I want you to put it on me here," I say, touching my pussy.

James's blue eyes flicker against the flames. They remind me of sapphires. I'm already so wet and ready for him. I dip two fingers inside. He watches as I pull them out and use my glossy desire to circle my clit. My back bows and I suck in a breath.

Bracing myself, I hold my breath as I watch him get another candle and blow out the flame. He returns to the bed and slowly drizzles the hot oil all over my pussy. My eyes fall closed and my head presses back into the sheets. It's a shock at first that quickly leads to an overflowing stream of pleasure. My lips part and I gasp as it drips into my tender folds.

James makes eye contact one last time before the oil breathes warmth into me, alighting my flesh with intense sparks of desire. He rubs it in and I draw in a long breath, clenching the sheets in my fists. His fingers show attention to my clit, and it almost sends me over the edge. I cry out from the friction, desperately wanting to orgasm but don't. I turn my face and the rose petals are soft as silk as they graze my cheek. My back arches in response, nipples puckering, knees falling open as wide as they can go when his fingers begin to delve carefully around my pussy. My toes dig into the mattress and a moan escapes my throat.

"James," I gasp, reaching for him. My heart is burning with fire. "I need you inside of me right now."

He doesn't respond, just leans down to press a kiss to my stomach, then moves onto my arms.

I watch his face as he focuses on what he's doing. The lapping ocean waves outside are our only sound. It's peaceful while there's a passionate storm brewing inside between us. James is tense, his shoulders are bunched tight and his brow is creased.

Placing my hand on his bicep, I ask, "Can I pour the oil on you so you can feel what I do?" His nostrils flare and he nods with a set jaw. I look at him once more and he answers my confused look.

"I'm trying not to lose control," he says.

A murmur forms in the back of my throat. "I like when you do, though." My gaze drops to his straining cock. The tip of his head is a shade of deep violet and there's proof of his arousal dripping from the tip. I lick my lips watching it fall in a thin stream to the bed.

After he finishes with both my arms, I sit up. Between the warm oil, the smooth taste of cognac streaming through my veins, and the touch of his skilled hands, I'm hungrier for him than ever before. I want to devour him.

"I'm not done," he says.

But I can't handle anymore. I'm about to jump his bones.

James gets a fresh candle. He lifts it to my face for me to blow out the flame, then hands it to me.

James is kneeling in front of me, mimicking my position. "I don't want to hurt you," I say, suddenly hesitant as I look at the steaming oil and his jutting erection.

"There's nothing you can do that would hurt me, unless you leave me."

My eyes snap to his. I shake my head. If I wasn't so worked up inside, I'd be angry he even suggested such a thing.

Palming his cock with one hand, I hand him the candle to hold for a second as I scoot back. I lean down to take him in my mouth, flattening my tongue and relaxing. I taste his arousal as I suck him good and deep before pulling back.

My heart is in my throat.

His head is tilted back, and there's a maze of veins straining in his neck. Through the colorful ink, his chest is blushed with desire and the vascularity in his body is pulsating. It sounds funny to call a man beautiful until you witness it. James is beautiful when he's in the throes of passion. He's abandoned reserve and moves on feeling.

"I love you, James." I find myself whispering as I look at him. My heart is so full, bursting with love for this man I never should've been able to love in the first place.

His head comes up and his eyes open to reveal a depth of emotion I wonder if I've ever had in my eyes when I've looked at him.

Leaning forward, James grabs ahold of the side of my neck and plants a hard kiss on my lips.

I break away, breathless. "I don't want to hurt you," I say

again.

"If you're concerned, you can pour the oil in your hand and rub it on me. But it's not going to hurt."

Nodding, I direct him to lie back, and he does. His legs are spread wide, his thick thighs dusted with fine hair. Our eyes meet one last time before I lift the candle and turn it over slowly. I watch in fascination as the oil drizzles down his engorged cock. A loud moan rolls out from his throat and his body vibrates. The tip of his cock produces a small pearl of cum. I place the candle on the table next to our bed, then wrap my hand around his width and lean down. I run my tongue over his pleasure, tasting the saltiness. His back bows and he palms the back of my head, his thighs coming up to encage me. He releases me and I twist my wrist and squeeze, stroking him as I suck the head of his cock, the only place the waxy oil didn't touch.

"Stop," he demands, his voice like gravel and he fists my hair. James pulls my head up as he sits up. "Get your ass over here," he says, his voice low and so fucking sexy.

One of the things I loved about James when we first met was the sound of his voice and how New York he sounded. When he's aroused, it's so much deeper and stronger, more lax on the Rs and tighter on the vowels. He thinks it's funny that I like hearing him talk, but I do. He's sexy.

Scooting closer, James gets up on his knees then sits back on his feet. My heart is racing, pounding with anticipation. I climb over his hips so my knees are pressed into the mattress as I straddle him. James reaches out for my waist to guide me to him. Grasping his cock, he angles it at my entrance but stops me from sliding down on it. He looks into my eyes and I hold my breath.

"I want us to last all night. We don't come until we can't handle anymore, and when we do, we come together."

I dig my teeth into my bottom lip and nod. I like this idea. I just hope I can hold out.

"We're not fucking, Aubrey," he states. "Tonight, we're going slow. I'm going to show you how much I love you."

Chapter 7

I swallow hard as James guides his cock into me painfully slow. He gives good foreplay, and he knows it.

"We're going to feel every bit, so we never forget who we belong to."

My lips part and I fall more in love with this man as he inches his way into me. I'm not sure my heart can take anymore. The way it beats, how it's pulsing in my throat, how when I look at him, I know he's the love of my life.

Once he's fully seated inside of me, my thighs loosen, and I soften against him. My hands come up to cup his face. Leaning in, I hear him draw in a breath before our lips meet. Sometimes I feel like the only way to tell him how much he means to me is by kissing him with everything that's in me. Slow, with a side of control. Everything can be felt with a kiss.

James guides my hips to move with his. This is where we both make perfect sense because we connect in the same fashion with the same splitting control. My hips slowly rotate over him, my clit hitting the hair on his mound. James drives in and holds my ass in place. We move at the same pace, the same tenderness, the same passion. It's a deeper connection for us, one that we never speak about.

"James," I whisper against his lips. My forehead is pressed to his, my hands cupping his curved shoulders. I move one hand to the back of his head as he holds my hips steady and thrusts inside of me. He's so fucking wicked on my soul that I want to beg for him to always take me like this.

"Yeah, sweetheart?" he responds in a raspy voice. He knows what he's doing.

He moves my hair that's sticking to my damp face. My jaw angles up toward him, my back arching so my nipples are pressed against his chest. Our mouths don't touch. Desire lights my body up like a diamond under the sun. I'm shaking, toes curling, fingers struggling to hold on as utter rapture grips me.

"Nothing ... nothing feels this good," I tell him, eyes closed in ecstasy. "How are you holding on?" My entire body quivers. I'm struggling to not finish.

"Look at me."

I open my eyes and find a slight curl on James's lips. His gaze says everything.

"I know your body like a book, Aubrey. It belongs to me. Your pussy, your body, your heart. It's all mine."

Coming from his words alone wouldn't be a first for me.

A saucy huff rolls off my lips. I should've known he'd say that. James bends back slightly to pull out. He watches his cock leave my pussy only to plunge back in without shame. It's one of the sexiest things I've ever seen him do. He's shaking under me now and I know if I move my hips just a fraction, he'll lose control and come. If I breathe too deeply, he'll come.

I grind my hips forward and ride James, feeling the ridges of his cock and taking him in me the way I know he loves. Gritty sex is James's middle name. There's a deepness inside of him that only I can reach.

Rising up on his knees, he leans into me until my back is on the mattress again. Red petals and soft, white feathers breeze around us like it's snowing. He's driving into me like he's determined to show me who's in charge.

"Baby," I say, and he knows what I mean.

I straighten one leg so it's up against his leg and then hook the other around his hip, pushing him farther inside me. We gasp in unison as he slips in deeper at this angle. It's tight as a fist for James and just the right angle for me to come soon.

My hands roam his broad backside, groping every inch of him I can reach as he carries us to a higher level. James is hammering into me with finesse. We're both dewy from the damp air when we finally climax together. Nails score his beautiful ink but never tear him, and my toes curl around the rose petals. An unabashed moan rolls off my lips. James is coming inside of me. I can feel his cock twitching and his warmth filling me. The walls of my pussy suck him until he's completely emptied inside of me.

"I have no words."

I say the first thing on my mind. His cum leaks out between us and I can feel the stickiness of it on my thighs and dripping down my ass. We're both breathing hard, panting. I have a feeling he's about to pull out, so I hold him for a second and just look into his eyes. I smile as he meets my gaze and use my thumbs to trace his lips.

I bring my mouth to his and he cups the back of my head at the same time, rolling us to the side. My legs sandwich his, and his wet cock slips out of me and lays against my thigh. He has no shame between the sheets, and I love that he's so free. I glance between us and smirk at the way his cock glistens, laying there like I completely used him.

I guess I did.

"You're welcome," he responds, and I giggle.

"That was incredible. I can't believe you remembered when I mentioned the candles to you. That was like forever ago."

He smiles proudly. We had ordered some sex toys online on a whim. Since we'd already had so many things in our cart that I wanted to try out first, I figured I'd get the candles next time. I'm glad he took it upon himself to get them for us.

James shifts to fully turn his body toward mine. He twirls my dark hair around one of his fingers and gives it a little tug.

My gaze shifts to his chest that holds a giant lion's face inked into his skin. I look into its black eyes. They lure me with interest and in a strange sense remind me of James. The lion's mane is full of vivacious colors mixed with black lines that are intertwined. I look at it and feel alive. I feel inspired. I feel wild passion. But most of all, I feel James. A silent but strong man who is all mine.

"Aubrey?" he says, and I look up at him with a lazy smile. "Do you ever think about the future? Like, our future?"

I swallow a little rougher and turn onto my side to prop my elbow up and place my jaw in my hand. "Yes."

"How come you never talk to me about it?" His brows start to form a frown but he masks it.

"My future only has you in it. You're all I see. I didn't feel like there was much to talk about."

We're both quiet for a moment. He twirls my hair again.

"You're young. You probably want babies. As much as I'd love to have a child with you and see you become a mother, I think I'm past my time. I don't want to be eighty when my child goes to college. I'll be lucky if I live that long."

I don't say anything because I don't know what to say.

The truth is, I'm torn myself. We've been wrapped in this bubble we both created that I never really thought about if I truly wanted kids or not with him. I used to think I didn't want children. I want to be angry that James is basically telling me kids aren't an option, but I'm not. Sure, I'd love to create a family with the man I love, but in all honestly, the selfish part of me is fine with just having him, and only him, to myself for the rest of my life.

Chapter 8

"I know children are a deal breaker for some," he says. "I feel like it's better to get that out first and go from there."

I peer up at him, surprised by how okay I am with the idea. "Is it strange that I'm okay with not having kids? Women are expected to want to start a family when they get married, but I never had the desire to. For the longest time, I felt ashamed for not wanting children. It doesn't mean I don't like kids, or that I'm too selfish, or inadequate. I just never really considered having them, I guess because it wasn't high on my list." I pause, then ask, "Does that bother you?"

"I think people want it both ways. You see the pros and cons and want both. Do I want you to reason with me about having kids so I feel like maybe you do want our child? Yes. I'm a man, and I want you to have my kids, but I'm also relieved you don't."

I muse over our conversation, my nail tracing the tattoos on his chest.

"I want kids, but I don't. I think I'm leaning toward the cool aunt title more than anything, I just don't have any siblings to make me one." I stop and think about Natalie and how she's basically my sister and could make me a cool aunt. But I have a hard time seeing her ever having kids. Even though she recently told me she's living her best IUD life, people change. I chuckle. "I'm trying to picture Natalie with kids. I don't know why it makes me laugh. I feel like kids would run her life, not the other way around."

James grins and rubs his eyes with the heel of his hand. He

doesn't realize that I caught the spark in his eyes at the thought of becoming a grandfather. "That'd be something."

I think about it more. Would I feel like I'm missing out on something? As a woman, yes, but as a person, no. Maybe we could just get a dog one day and be dog parents.

I trace the black lines of the lion's mane, pulling on some of his chest hairs. "I don't think I'd feel any sort of loss or longing if I don't have kids. I do a little now, but I think that's because I've accepted what I've known all along. It hits differently when spoken out loud."

"Look at me," he says, and I shoot my eyes up to his. I can see the legitimate worry plaguing his eyes. "Tell me you aren't going to resent me for not wanting kids."

I do better. I lean in and give him a hard kiss, then I look at him. James cups my cheek. "I will not resent you," I say slow and clear. "And if I ever change my mind, I'll tell you."

He blinks a few times, still holding on to me. "If you see a future with me, does that future involve us getting married?"

My heart drops and I roll onto my back. I stare up at the ceiling. I had a feeling this topic was coming soon. James has been more lovey, hands-on, and attentive, showing me exactly how he feels. I didn't think he wanted to get married again and was content with the status of our relationship. He'd been with his ex for over twenty years. The last thing I thought he'd ever want was to be tied down. Maybe I was wrong.

I'm not sure I ever want to get married, and I'm a little nervous to tell him. I love James more than anything in the world. I don't need a piece of paper to tell me I'm connected to someone, or to vow my love for them. What James and I have is real, whether I'm legally his wife or not. Most people think the point of a relationship is to get married, but not me. Some people reach a deeper connection because of that paper, while others find it pointless to have that label when nothing is changing.

"I only ever want to be with you for the rest of my life. But I don't think we need a piece of paper to prove we're committed to each other."

As soon as the words leave my lips, I hold my breath.

Fuck. This is harder to talk about than whether or not I wanted kids, and talking about that terrified me. This is making my stomach twist into knots. My throat feels tight. I don't want to lose him, but I'm not going to lie either. This is a conversation of truth.

My lips are flattened. My lungs ache from holding my breath. I'm worried I may have made a huge mistake, but I couldn't lie either and give him false hope. Not over something like this. He's asking about marriage, not which restaurant I want to dine at.

James is staring. He's thinking too deep and it's making my stomach cramp from anxiety. I should've made sure we brought the cognac in when we came inside. I can see the wheels spinning in his mind, and I don't like it.

"You don't want to get married? Is that what you're saying?"

My teeth dig into my bottom lip. "Yes," I say quietly. "I don't want to get married."

His brows deepen the longer he studies me. His eyes though, the crystal blue are sharper than broken glass. It cuts my heart in half seeing James hurt. I feel this hole opening between us. James isn't happy, and his lack of response is spreading the gap wider.

"You don't want to get married," he repeats, a statement this time instead of a question. All I can do is shake my head while I look into his eyes full of disbelief.

James pulls away and my biggest fear is brought to the center of us. He's sitting on the edge of the bed, his eyes scanning the space around us like he's looking for something he lost. My pulse skyrockets in my neck, thumping so hard my skin feels hot. Even with his back to me, I can feel this distant energy burning inside of him. A nauseating feeling spreads through me like wildfire. James wasn't prepared for my response, and I wasn't ready for his.

"James," I say, sitting up and reaching for him.

Wrapping my arms around his waist, I scoot closer and hug him from behind. He grabs my wrist like he's prepared to tell me to stop so he can get up and walk away. Only, he doesn't move. His hold tightens and relief exhales from my lungs. I close my eyes and rest my head on his back. His thumb gently strokes the top of my hand.

We're quiet for a moment. His hurt over my refusal is felt tenfold and I feel so guilty. I love James. The last thing I want to do is upset him.

"Just because I don't want to get married doesn't mean I don't want to be with you."

"It does, Aubrey," he says, and he shakes me off to stand.

Oh, God. My heart plummets with my jaw as he walks away. I'm going to be sick.

"We don't need that piece of paper between us. It's going to ruin a good thing," I say, my voice urging him to understand me. I climb to my knees and pull the sheet around my body.

James remains quiet. His silence lengthens the tension, and it only makes this that much worse. I call his name, but he doesn't turn around to look at me. He just folds his hands behind his head and arches his back until his muscles are straining.

"You really think that's what breaks up a good thing? Sweetheart, you're smarter than that."

James's back flexes as he speaks to me. Dread fills my veins, fearing the worst.

"You're mad at me," I whisper.

James finally looks over his shoulder at me and I'm speechless by the hardness in his eyes.

"Yeah, I fuckin' am. I want you as my wife, Aubrey. I thought you wanted it too."

Chapter 9

"Why can't we just leave what we have alone and not jinx it?"

He shakes his head in annoyance and looks away. "Who says we're going to jinx anything?"

I blink, a little hesitant to proceed. The last thing I want is to get into an argument over this while we're on vacation.

"I love you, James, but we don't need a certificate to confirm it. I've read countless stories about how people change before the ink even dries. I'm not saying that would happen with us, but I don't want to chance it either. Isn't what we have good enough?"

"No, it's not. Good enough is knowing you're mine in every sense of the way. Peace of mind. Peace of heart."

I deflate. My shoulders sag. How could he not know I'm his in every sense of the way already? "But you already know I am. What's the paper going to do?"

"It signifies that you're mine and I'm yours in the eyes of the law and everyone."

"Why does it matter what the law or anyone else thinks? Shouldn't the only thing that matters is how we feel?"

"I want to be able to call you my wife."

My heart melts for this man. "You still can," I tell him. I'd love it if he did.

James shakes his head. "It's not the same thing and you know it, Aubrey." He sounds like he's been defeated, and it kills me. "You won't have my last name."

"It's the twenty-first century. A lot of women don't take their husband's name anymore."

"Call me old school. I'd like to introduce you as my wife and not my live-in girlfriend. I want you to have my last name. I want to marry you. There's a security behind the marriage, you know."

I'm taken aback by his brash tone. I thought we already had security. Never once did I second-guess us. I exhale slowly, trying not to allow the hurt to take over completely because he's offended that I don't want to marry him, but I can't help that it does. We're both passionate people, so the hurt we're feeling spreads to anger, and that's not a good thing for us. Neither of us likes to back down.

"You can't possibly think there's a security behind marriage after your last one." I spit out before I could stop myself. I clench my eyes shut and wince, regretting it.

James's arrogant chuckle under his breath causes chills to run down my arms. "How'd I know you'd say something like that."

It was immature of me to use that against him. We don't have the same relationship he had with his ex-wife.

James walks over to the dresser and yanks the drawer open to pull out a pair of gym shorts. He steps into them then slams the drawer shut with his knee and levels a quiet stare at me. He's waiting for me to change my mind. My heart is cracking down the center the longer the silence spans between us. I remain quiet. The guilt is eating away at my stomach.

The truth is, I can't give him what he wants.

Bending down, James reaches for a shirt I left on the ottoman this morning and throws it to me. It falls into a soft heap right in front of me. I don't reach for it because I can't seem to steer myself from looking at him. His eyes probe me longer, deeper, like he's begging me to change my mind so he can make me his wife. Still, I remain quiet. He exhales a breath through his nose and I feel the frustration flaring from him. I love him so much and I'd give him anything else he asked for, but I can't give him that.

I swallow thickly as he props his hands on his hips. The

colorful hues of his inked arms flicker against the low lighting in our room. My gaze lands on one of the tattoos he'd gotten on his untouched arm from the day we met in Bryant Park. He says it's his favorite.

"Do you have no desire to get married? Or does the idea of marrying me repulse you?"

"Repulse me?" I repeat. "You think marrying you repulses me?"

My eyes flare, instantly filling with tears. I'm shaking over his asinine words. Men are so dumb sometimes. I need to count to ten, but I'm beyond hurt that he thinks he repulses me. How could he even think that? He has to know what he means to me. James is taking this the wrong way.

My heart is a burning ball of fire right now confined inside of my chest. I grab the shirt and let the sheet fall to my hips to slip it on. It's inside out but I don't really give a fuck. I jump out of bed and march right up to him with determination.

Lifting my chin, I say, "If marriage to you repulsed me, would I even be in a relationship with you? Just because I don't want to get married doesn't mean I don't want you."

"What's the reason then, Aubrey?"

"There's no reason."

He takes a step closer to me and a little gasp crests in my throat. I ache to lean into him. To hug him. I'm so drawn to James. How could he question any of it?

"There has to be."

I purse my lips together, anxiety filling me instantly. There is, but now isn't the time to bring it up. Not when the tension is increasing by the second.

"You won't ever marry me, will you?"

His voice is a clamp on my pulse. I'm reminded of the day I walked away from us the first time all those years ago in his home. How he looked when he threw his glass across the room—the way it shattered against the wall—knowing there was no changing my mind. He feels rejected, again.

I don't say anything. It's not possible when I'm pressing my lips together, fighting the tears climbing up the back of my eyes. My lungs are straining for air, my chest taut with what feels like skin being stretched. I can't bring myself to utter the words.

Stepping around him, I walk through the French doors to the patio to where we were sitting earlier in the night. I pick up the glass I was drinking from and toss the rest of the contents back, then I refill it. It burns good going down my throat. Hurts a little, but I like that bite, feeling like I deserve it.

The wood creaks under James's footsteps. Instinctively, I refill his glass then reach out to my side to hand it to him blindly.

He takes it and stands next to me. We're staring at the slow wake of black waves brushing up against our private bungalow together. I can feel the tears balancing on my eyelids about to spill over. Blinking rapidly, I sniffle them back. Unspoken words remain floating between us that thicken the salty air.

Pressing the glass to the center of my chest, my voice is flat as I say, "We don't need a label to make it official, James. Look where your marriage got you. Look where it got my parents. Even my grammy lost my grandpa. They waited until he left the Naval Academy to get married, only for him to pass away a few years later. The only people I know who were married—including you—and look how it ended. It's like a bad omen. I only have you and Natalie in my life. I don't want to chance losing you guys too. That's what I feel like comes from having that dumb paper. You're my family," I add, my voice breaking a little.

James lifts the glass to his mouth and tosses back what is equivalent to three shots like it's nothing. His throat bobs once. He's not handling this well.

He hands me the glass and I place it down next to mine. "I never intended to marry Kathleen, and you know that. I never loved her the way I love you. This is different. I thought you knew that."

I wish I could cave, but the way I see it, I'm doing us a favor.

"We don't need a piece of paper to dictate our relationship."

Chapter 10

James turns toward me.

Eyes illuminated by the soft lights on the deck, he takes my hands in his and lifts them to his mouth. He kisses the back of my knuckles and rubs the center of my palm with his thumb. The fine lines around his eyes are tight with worry. He makes me feel like this is a deal breaker for him.

Licking my lips, I swallow hard. I pray to God it's not. I don't think I could handle it. In fact, I know I couldn't. Just the mere thought makes my stomach knot with dread. I wouldn't survive it a second time. I barely did the first time.

My heart does this odd little flip and my eyes widen from the way it dips into my stomach. I hate the way it only happens when anxiety is consuming me the way it is right now. It's worse when my stomach and heart join forces to produce a nasty panic attack I have to talk myself down from.

But the way he's looking at me confirms my fear. Inhaling and exhaling quickly, I blink rapidly, trying to mentally ease the tightness in my chest. Maybe I'm overthinking and I'm wrong. The thought of James leaving me cripples me to the point that I'm breaking down inside. I'd marry him if I absolutely had to, but I really hope it won't come to that. Then every day I would live in some state of fear that something was going to take him from me.

My knees are shaking. I'm weak and on the verge of fainting when James wraps an arm around my lower back and pulls me to stand against him. He nestles against me and holds our hands pressed to his chest. The warmth of his touch is soothing, and I feel a settling in my soul that only he gives me. James is my rock. My silent warrior. He didn't ask me for anything, he didn't expect anything. Now that he was, I was rejecting him.

I sniffle, upset we're at odds over this, and press myself into him. James holds me tighter and I love him more for it, but I can't help but fear he's going to leave me now. The feeling is too gut-wrenching to ignore, no matter how hard I push the thought from me.

"Can you at least consider it, sweetheart?" James asks. "Marriage is something I really want with you. Nothing is going to happen to us. We're only going to get better. I promise you that. If you think for a second it's ruining what we have, we can get divorced and go back to dating. But please, all I'm asking is for you to think about marrying me."

"You don't know that, James," I say, my heart is in my throat. "You mean too much to me to risk it."

"I would do anything for you," he responds, his words like knives jutting between my ribs.

James's voice is one of the things that drew me to him. Deep and in the back of his throat, his vibe exudes old New York and that ups his smoking hot factor by a margin.

But when he's deep in his emotion and basically asking me to marry him, he's fucking savage on the ears.

"You know that, right?"

I nod. "I know."

"Maybe I *am* old fashioned," he continues, "but I want to know that the rest of my days are sealed with yours. You're my world, my light. You give me a reason to wake up every day. Be mine forever in the way that matters most to me."

My heart is racing a mile a minute. I'm standing in nothing but a sleep shirt that just barely covers my ass. I'm completely naked underneath while James is only in a pair of basic shorts.

And I'm fairly certain James did just ask me to marry him ...

in a roundabout way.

I blink again, unsure what to say. I don't want to ask him if he just asked me to marry him. I won't set myself up like that, but I'm not sure what he meant by that either.

"If it doesn't work out, then we can say we gave it a shot. We can be that couple that never learns and keeps marrying each other."

Fuck. He did.

James turns so his back is to the wall now and pulls me to lean on him. Our legs are pressed together and there's a cool breeze drifting across the back of my thighs. Rising up on my tiptoes, I wrap my arms around his shoulders and bury my face in his neck. I draw James into me as a soft moan escapes my throat. My nipples harden in response and I shiver. God, I love the feeling this man creates inside my heart for him. If love had one specific feeling, this was it. This type of mood, this attraction and undeniable chemistry, is only meant for one person. Only for one person to evoke from another. My other half. James Riviera.

His embrace awakens a desire in me that spreads warmth throughout my body like a damn tidal wave. My shirt lifts, exposing my bare flesh. His palm skims over my rounded ass. He gives me a firm squeeze at the base of my cheek and my eyes roll shut. Little flames pop over every inch of my skin and my head falls to the side. I can feel his hand itching to move higher. I want him to. James knows I love when his dominate side comes out to play.

His thick erection strains against my stomach. He's hot and long, and feeling his frame fit perfectly against my curves makes me want him even more. I've joked to him before that we fit like two puzzle pieces, but we really do.

His hands roam my thighs in a feather-soft touch. Arching my chest into his, I slip my hair over my shoulder as his teeth find my tender flesh. Our bodies create this sultry friction that intensifies with the breaths we take. We're both fighting for something we believe in. Both wanting to give each other what they desire.

His lips brush over the shell of my ear and my pulse quickens. I catch the faintest scent of cognac that reminds me of a crackling fire. My skin flushes with need. He knows my body like the back of his hand.

There's something deeply intimate about being alone with James under the dark sky that amplifies the enormity of tonight's conversation. In the dark, we're vulnerable. Our desires are exposed. His hands tell me what to feel and his kiss silences my fears.

A salty breeze glides past us and my hair feathers around us. I'm hoping we're done talking about the topic of marriage seeing as tomorrow we leave for home. I don't want to go to bed fighting with him, and I definitely don't want to end the trip on a negative note.

I need James's lips on mine so I can show him we don't need a paper to claim what we are. We've been doing that. We know what we are. He is mine, and I am his. Always. End of story.

His prickly beard tickles me as he moves closer to where I need him. He peppers kisses along my jaw, causing me to produce little gasps. Just as I reach for his mouth and my body curls alongside his, I feel his resistance.

"James."

I whisper his name like it's a plea and open my eyes. The way he's looking at me causes a knot to lodge in my throat and render me speechless. He's about to say something I'm not prepared to hear.

"Marry me, sweetheart."

Chapter 11

My lips part.

I'm speechless. I don't blink. I don't breathe.

James doesn't just ask me to marry him hoping for a positive answer in return. He asks me like it's the right thing to do.

All I can do is stare at him in total silence as my heart viciously pounds into my ribs. I'm not all that shocked he'd go there after I told him how I feel about marriage; persistence is James's other middle name. I'm more shocked by how much I want to agree with him.

The truth is, I know it's the right thing ... I just can't do it. I'm scared.

"Marry me, sweetheart," James says again, though he's not as sure this time. There's a deflated tone to his words that kills me. "Say yes."

His arms tighten around me and I find myself leaning into him. I take a deep breath. I want to give him what he wants, but I'm scared. The loss would be too great to endure.

Dating my best friend's dad is one thing. Marrying him is another. I almost lost both Natalie and James as a result of us dating. Granted, it was behind Natalie's back at the time and the furthest thing from a normal relationship by any means. Still, it took Natalie over two years to finally agree to James and I being together. I have a hard time believing she'd accept marriage without issue.

Just like I don't want to risk losing James over a stupid piece of paper, I don't want to lose my best friend either. Being her stepmom is out of the question and just seems so wrong. It would drive a wedge right between us.

James's arms loosen and my heart begins to fall as he pulls away. I glance up and take in the shadows moving through his eyes as his body stiffens defensively against mine.

He's watching me, waiting patiently for a sound in response. I don't give him one. I can't even tell him no.

"What's the real reason?" James doesn't bother hiding the pain in his question. "Can you at least give me that?"

Tears fill my eyes and my jaw bobs. I wish he'd never asked me to marry him.

His arms unravel around me completely. The air leaves my lungs in a slow withdrawal as he lets go. My life, everything I love, suddenly feels gone to me.

James takes a step to the side and puts a small amount of space between us.

"James." I pant, winded as panic sets in.

My stomach drops.

I'm going to be sick.

I'm losing him.

My eyes search his. He's quiet as he moves to the side again, detaching from the concept of us. I can feel it in my bones, in my heart of hearts, and it scares me what might come next. What he could say or ultimately do. That's not what I want for us, or for him to experience.

"James, please."

I reach for him and place my hand on his forearm. He waits, looking at me expectantly. I need him to know ... I don't know what I need him to know other than I love him, and that I need him to not hate me, that this doesn't have to be a deal breaker for us.

"You know you're it for me, right? That I love you more than anything? That nothing will weaken how I feel?" I say, my voice shaky.

There's a slight drop in his shoulders. James doesn't respond. He doesn't move. He stands still like it's both a serious struggle for me to be touching him and for him to be in front of me. I think that's harder for me to handle more than anything. Light begins to fade from his eyes. I wait, listening to the ocean softly lap against our bungalow, and wonder how we got to this point.

"Right? You know I love you more than life," I tell him again.

Gently, he pulls his arm away so I'm not touching him anymore. His body is partially turned away from me now, and that just makes it worse.

"James?"

I don't know what I'm asking for. I don't think he does either. What I want is for him to see that I love him, that we aren't going anywhere, and that nothing needs to change, but he doesn't. He's purposely not looking at me, and I can't stomach it. His avoidance could mean so many things.

My heart is breaking by the second. But so is his. I thought we were stronger than this.

Though his eyes are lowered to the ground, James straightens my shirt so my backside is covered. We're alone out here. No one could see us unless they came onto the deck of our private pavilion. He didn't have to cover me—he chose to.

A tear slips from the corner of my eye. He takes a step away from me like he's ready to leave, and my throat tightens. It feels like there's hundreds of miles between us now and not a few inches. He takes another step and my knees start to buckle.

I can't handle this and need to rectify it.

"Wait," I plead, and James stops. "Don't leave me, please."

Finally, he looks at me, and I almost crumble to the ground.

James is fucking shattered. Worse than me. Absolutely gutted.

My chest feels like it's caving in while being torn apart with two bare hands. I'm struggling to breathe while James looks like he's dying inside. I see the way he looks at me. It screams devastation.

What did I do to the man who has done nothing but love me for who I am? Who didn't try to change me but let my wings flap with the wind? Who's tried to make me smile every single day by showing me how much one could love another human?

I broke him.

I want to reach for him, but I'm scared he'll refuse me. All I can do is grab the hem of my shirt and tug on it like it's supporting me. I can't ask him for anything, not after I quietly rejected his proposal.

James subtly shakes his head in disbelief. He takes two steps toward me and this time I reach for him, needing to feel his arms wrapped around me, hoping it'll give me a sign that we're going to be okay. He palms the back of my head and threads his fingers through my hair. I lean in and meet him halfway. He presses his lips to the top of my head, then steadies himself.

"Contrary to what you think, I can't leave you. Not even if I wanted to."

A soft whimper escapes my trembling lips, followed by a louder one. My back is vibrating with emotion while my heart rips wide open. I'm shaking in his arms while he feels as steady as a rock. I know he's not steady, though. I know he's breaking inside, just like I am. We're two peas in a pod.

James cups my jaw and tilts my head up, bringing my eyes to meet his. Steel baby blues shift back and forth between mine. James studies me. His brows deepen together like he's trying to figure out where he went wrong, how his calculations were off.

He shakes his head again before blowing out a breath of surrender onto my lips. "Not even if I wanted to ..." James presses a hard, brutal kiss to my mouth. He breaks it just as fast, leaving me breathless. "I guess I'll just have to deal with it."

Letting go of me, James steps back then turns around and

strides into our room.

I guess I'll just have to deal with it.

The wind picks up and whips around my bare legs, veiling me with loneliness. My toes curl into the deck floor and I can feel the pressure of the ocean push up into the wooden planks that hold up our room. Like it's knocking into my chest and filling my lungs.

With a hand to my neck, I fall into the chair I sat in earlier.

I became what he divorced.

He's settling for me even though it makes him unhappy. Settling had been the crux of his previous marriage, and why he'd been so miserable. Why he'd been a member of Sanctuary Cove. The sole reason we met and connected is now the same reason we're on the verge of a messy breakup, because this isn't just a conversation about what we're eating for dinner. The conversation doesn't end tonight. It's not over. This is our future fused together by two rings and a piece of paper.

Fear is two hands pressing on my throat. I'm terrified I'm going to push him in the direction of another woman just like his ex-wife did. She didn't satisfy him sexually, and now I don't satisfy him emotionally. Emotionally, sexually, physically connecting to another person, these are the three basic needs for a relationship to stand strong. You can't have one and not the other. It doesn't work like that, because then you'll always be searching for what you don't have in someone else.

With James and me, there was no searching. We were satisfied in every area of our relationship. Until tonight.

Glancing to my side, I eye the bottle of cognac we left open and grab it by the neck.

I don't bother with a glass.

Pulling up my leg, I rest my elbow on my knee then bring the bottle to my lips. I take deep pull after deep pull until my throat burns and I feel like I could blow flames from my nose. I drink until the last bit of amber liquid that was left is gone.

I toss the empty glass bottle onto James's empty chair and pray to God history doesn't repeat itself.

Chapter 12

It feels like someone's using a feather to draw figure eights on my leg.

I inhale an exhausted breath. My eyes are heavy as I rouse from a deep sleep. I try to lick my lips, but I can't move yet.

The airy feeling is back again, tickling my inner thigh. I'm half-asleep trying to piece together where I am. I listen to the world around me. There's a bird chirping, water curling into itself, followed by the sound of trees swaying in the wind. The sheets are cool as I sweep my arm across them feeling for James. Last I remember, I was sitting by myself outside until I could swear I saw the sunrise just peak above the horizon, nursing a bottle of liquor.

I take a deep breath and force myself to wake up. Opening my blurry eyes, I blink a few times, licking my dry lips. I see sunlight spilling into the room from a window that had been left open when it all comes crashing back to me.

"Marry me, sweetheart."

There's a tightness surrounding my heart as I recall his proposal and my rejection.

I glance down and find James has laid his head on my stomach, his body perpendicular to mine. He's drawing on my leg with his finger. My knee is bent up and I realize I still don't have panties on. Threading my fingers through his tousled hair, I watch his eyelashes flutter. I can feel his quiet sorrow and it kills me inside. I never want to hurt him, and I know I did last night.

I've never shied away from James before. Countless times I've woken with his head between my thighs or with him inside of me saying he couldn't wait. The mornings were mine to have him any way I wanted, while the evenings were his. But I suddenly feel like I'm too exposed after the way we left things last night and I shift my legs until they're closed.

This is the first time I didn't wake in his arms.

We didn't make love as the sun came up.

He didn't tell me I'm his forever, and I didn't tell him he's mine.

And I fucking hate it.

"When did I come inside?" I ask, my voice still full of sleep. I want to get up to get a drink of water, but I can barely bring myself to move. I'm too tired and I think I'm a little depressed from last night.

"You didn't. I carried you in," James says. "You fell asleep out there."

"Oh." I frown.

James wraps an arm around my waist and hugs me the same way he does a pillow. He turns his head to look at me and lays it back on my stomach. Emotions climb the back of my throat. Our eyes meet, and regret and sadness spill from both of us.

"My mind is a little hazy. I don't remember being carried in."

"How's your head? Do you have a hangover?"

I think about it for a second. Bringing my hand to his jaw, I run the back of my knuckles down his beard and then over the golden curve of his shoulder until my nails are gently scratching his back.

"My head is fine," I say. "The benefit of good alcohol—no hangover."

He doesn't smile. Instead, he laces his fingers with mine and scoots our joined hands to my side. There's a quiet reserve floating around him this morning. I know James well enough to know how he feels, and right now he feels alone and like he's settling again. He doesn't like rejection. I know this because I'm just like him. We bleed the same emotions, the same feelings, the same humor, the same sexual desires. We're each other's other half. What one feels, the other does too. And what he's feeling fucking kills me.

He's waiting. Being patient. Watching me. The morning sunrise casts a gorgeous radiance across his eyes creating the palest blue. They flicker with the hope I had a change of heart.

But he knows I didn't. He's too perceptive for that.

"What's the reason, Aubrey?"

I swallow thickly from the sound of dejection in James's voice. He sounds like he didn't sleep.

"I already told you."

He levels an unfiltered stare at me. James is not going to stop until he gets the answer I'm keeping from him.

"The real reason, sweetheart. And not the bullshit excuse that you think a fucking piece of paper is going to ruin what we have. I deserve better than that."

The rawness in his words cut through me, but it's warranted. Our connection runs deeper than that to come up with something so trivial. A reason like mine is a joke to him, and probably to most people as well. It would've been a joke to me too, but who knew this is what love would feel like? Once the imaginary love line is crossed, there's no turning back. The further you get, the deeper you're pulled in. Even when we weren't together, there was no denying the force being pushed at in our hearts.

"I don't understand why you think two people who are clearly fucking madly in love with each other shouldn't take the final step and get married. It's preposterous to me."

I shake my head and avert my gaze, stopping to stare at the French doors. No matter what I say, it won't make a difference to James. He doesn't understand why we don't need a paper to keep our bond strong. There's nothing stronger than what we already have.

I'm ashamed though, because in a way, in some closed off

chamber of my heart, I agree with him, and that's not fair to either of us.

My throat is sore and scratchy as I speak. "Do you really think Natalie would be okay with it?"

I can feel the weight of his stare on me while I gaze mindlessly out the window listening to the rippling waves. The sun is fresh above the water right before its peak. It's enchanting and pulls me away from the torment between us. I can't bring myself to look at James because I'm so torn and upset inside. It's messing with my emotions. I want to give him what he wants, but it terrifies me.

Warmth blooms under my cheek. I'm avoiding him and I sense he gets that. A chuckle echoes along the corners of our intimate room. I frown and finally look down.

James is smirking in disbelief and beholding me with stupefied eyes. "You're kidding me, right?"

"I'm dead serious."

He pops his head up and places his chin in his palm. "You and I live together. When she visits, she sits on the bed we have sex in every day. You think she'd object to us getting married?" We're both quiet. "Tell me my daughter is not the reason you won't marry me."

Humiliation invades me. My reasoning sounds like total bullshit now and messes with my feelings. I'm saddened that in all the days we've been together, this is our first real fight, and it's over marriage.

"Did you forget how she reacted to us dating and how long it took her to come around? She's going to be ten times worse over marriage. I'm not going to lose my best friend completely when there's no reason if everything is fine the way it is, which it is."

"It's not fine the way it is," James spits out, then rolls out of bed to pace the floor.

My eyes widen as hurt consumes my heart. I lower my voice and say, "Wow. I had no idea you were so miserable."

"What makes you think she'd react the same way, anyway?" he challenges, throwing his arm in the air. A colorful blur of inked hues crosses my gaze. Frustration drips from him when I don't say anything. "You don't know. You're just scared to take the plunge because you think you have bad luck and it's the reason all the good things in your life are taken from you. Guess what? You had shitty luck before you met me, and you already took a risk with me. Yeah, it fucking backfired on us because it wasn't under normal circumstances, but look at us now. I'm the one good thing that has made it this far with you because it was meant to fucking happen." James pauses, his eyes wild. "I'm not going anywhere, sweetheart. We're only going to get better from here on out. I just wish you'd open your eyes so you stop wasting time trying to fight it and we enjoy what we have."

James is good. His argument guts me. Damn that devil on my shoulder, he was so fucking hot as he did so too.

"I'm serious, James. I can't do that to her. To us. You really think she won't care? You're wrong, and I won't do that to her."

James does that sarcastic chuckle again under his breath as he strides toward the bathroom. It grates on my nerves and makes me want to chase after him, but I don't. He made a good case in a matter of seconds and crushed any reason I feared would tear us down with one breath.

James stops and places his hand on the wall before he turns into the room and looks around the corner at me. His brows angle toward each other like he's struggling worse than I am. My face has tears streaming down my heated cheeks. I wish he'd come to me and kiss them away. I wish he'd tell me we'd find a way to make this work. Because right now, this feels hopeless, and even though he said he's not going anywhere, it feels like he's already gone.

"Hypothetically, say Natalie doesn't have an issue and we could get married tomorrow, would you marry me?"

The silence in the room is deafening. My vision blurs further as the seconds tick by. I watch the hope in James's eyes reduce to grief, and it kills me. Breaking this man does something to me I can't explain. My brain is saying to be smart and follow the evidence so I can break the cycle, but my heart is saying yes. Like why is he even asking me? Of course, I'd say yes.

But I don't say anything at all, and neither does he.

I watch James's fingers tap the corner of the wall. He presses his lips together, his eyes boring into mine, and with a firm nod, he looks away. "Okay," he says, his voice low. "I understand."

Chapter 13

For the last two days, the only times James has spoken to me was to ask me for a reason.

He says my reasons aren't legitimate and I need a better one if I'm going to win my case.

He'd ask me before the sun rose when he'd just woken up. His voice groggy, thick with sleep and making my body come alive. The rawness in his tone that comes with age and patience just gets to me, especially when he's passionate about something. These last few mornings have been torture on me.

I couldn't bring myself to have him the next morning after we'd arrived home. I wanted him desperately, I needed to feel him inside of me, but it felt wrong. Twice I turned over to reach for him and stopped myself. How was I supposed to have what I wanted with him if I wouldn't give him what he wanted with me?

I knew the moment I touched him I would pounce, so I'd quickly climbed out of bed and made my way into the bathroom.

This is the longest we've gone without each other since we got back together, and now we're in this weird state of limbo. Sex is something we connect with and find reprieve from the real world. It isn't just out of necessity to have sex with our other half, it's part of who we are and what connects us as a couple. We physically and mentally and emotionally need each other. Not having every part is sucking the life from me.

I'm standing in our bathroom wiping off my mascara when James rounds the corner. I freeze, holding my towel tighter to my chest as my gaze drags down the length of his body. There's something about a silver fox in black sweats that makes me question why I ever once loved gray sweats on a man. Gray is for boys who like to play with their pecker and braid their pube hair. Black is for men who like to throw you to the bed and take you from behind, all while holding your hair and fucking you into oblivion.

Masculinity oozes from him as he strides toward me with a swagger that makes my heart race. I'm in my prime and want sex all the time. I can't not look. I finish blotting away the smudge under my eyes and drop the cotton ball on the counter. Our gazes don't waver. I don't turn around to face him, but I hold my breath the closer he gets to me. Placing both hands on the counter to brace myself, James steps up right behind me as if this past weekend didn't happen. He moves my wet hair to one shoulder to press a few kisses to my neck and wraps both arms around my waist. The warmth of his body presses against my back and my eyes roll shut. I'm at home in his arms and never want to leave.

"Stop fighting me," he says against my throat. He gives me a little bite then kisses it. "Give in to me."

My lips twitch. He's persistent.

"Be my wife. Say yes."

"I've missed you, James," I whisper, feeling a little emotional.

"I'm right here, sweetheart, for you to have and to hold."

I chuckle and lean into him. I needed that little moment of humor. His breath strokes the curve of my neck, making goose bumps prickle my arms. I miss the feel of his lips on mine and need them. I hope he needs mine too.

I turn my face up to his and cup the back of his head. I pray he doesn't reject me as our eyes meet.

He towers over me, which isn't easy at my height. James stares down at me as I hold my breath, testing me to make a move. His eyes are shaded by thick black lashes that makes them so easy to get lost in. He laughs when I tell him he has bedroom eyes.

James leans in and I produce a little gasp right before his lips find mine. He doesn't hold back and I'm glad he doesn't. I need him to break this awkwardness between us because I'm not big enough to.

James plunges past my lips. My knees nearly buckle at the stroke of his tongue against mine. I moan into his mouth as I thread his hair through my fingers, giving him a firm tug. I press back just as hard with my lips to show him how much I fucking love him. We devour each other in a fiery kiss that leaves us both breathless when he abruptly breaks it.

James shakes his head and gives me a disappointed frown. "Just fucking marry me already."

Each time he asks me to marry him, it hurts more.

He slips his hand through the opening of my gray towel and glides his palm along the deep sweep of my hip. His touch speaks confidence and it's something I learned I was attracted to when I first met him. James is a man who knows what he wants, and he isn't afraid to show it.

I press my chest against his. James doesn't give me any room to breathe. His hands roam over my bare body, loosening the towel. He's stoking the desire I only have for him to a no-return zone. Going without James is like going without water.

I reach between us and palm his cock. My fingers wrap around his erection and I press my forehead to his shoulder looking for support. I dig my nails into his length and he jerks. His hips surge into my hand and my lips part with a not-so-surprised needy sigh. He's as hard as steel and it turns me on high. Desire wets my pussy and I clench my legs together.

I push the elastic waistband over his hips when James rips the towel off me. I give his ass cheek a good grab and yank him to me. There's a nice roundness that I like. James grabs my face as he lifts one of my thighs. He bends his knees to get down and angles the tip of his shaft at my entrance. He surges into me without hesitation and rises to his full height, forcing me to strain on my toes. I gasp loudly and clench my thighs, my toes curling in response. The pressure, the tightness, the pain and longing, the sensations are overloading my senses and taking over. My mind goes blank. All I can do is focus on us and what we're doing.

He spreads my thighs wider and dips again to get deeper, grinding up my clit when he stands. My body shakes in response and I can barely hold myself up. My pussy softens for him and leaks on his cock as I pulsate around him. He's going to make sure I don't forget who's inside of me.

The type of connection James and I have can't be replicated.

I reach for the counter behind me. I'm already weak and my elbow bends. James places a palm on the small of my back then clutches the back of my neck with the other. He pulls out and pushes back in like he needs to be in me. His heavy sack slaps into my ass and he lets out the sexiest groan.

My nails dig into his skin. James is frantic, gripping harder, and I respond like I always do. He pulls me to him and lets out a deep sigh when he buries his face in my neck.

"Say yes ..."

I clench my eyes shut and dig my teeth into my bottom lip until I taste blood. I want to say yes. And I think he knows I want to and it's why he keeps asking me.

"At least give me a reason," he begs. "No one is going to love you more than me. I can promise you I'll love you harder than anyone else until my very last breath."

I don't give him a reason. Not even after he makes sweet love to me for the next two hours, making up for what we lost the last few days.

I don't finish, though. Not once. I can't. I'm depriving myself because I feel guilty over my decision.

Chapter 14

"You better not be fucking my dad!"

Grinning, I sit up higher at the sound of Natalie's voice and feel a spark of excitement burst through me. I've missed my bestie. She said she'd be here bright and early the day after we got home, but shit happens.

Natalie steps into the kitchen carrying a brown paper bag and places it on the island. Sounds like a bottle of some sort. My gaze takes in her appearance. She's wearing the cutest toffee-colored Boho lace-up sandals I might have to borrow from her. It's late summer here in the city, so her tattered ripped shorts and graphic tee aren't going to keep her warm when the temps drop once the sun goes down completely. Always fashionable, though.

I close my laptop. I was taking my time tying up some loose ends before Retreat opens, but I can finish later.

Truthfully, I've been avoiding James. He's been in his home office all day and now into the evening. It's uncharacteristic of him and I'm not sure what to think of it. In fact, we haven't spoken since he made love to me this morning. Granted his office in the basement has a full working kitchen and bathroom allowing room for me to work alongside him, I purposely sat in the kitchen on the main floor in hopes we'd see each other when he came upstairs. At five o'clock I could count on him to come and make a drink, and that's what I'd banked my plan on. Now that it's after six and he still hasn't shown himself proves to me he's vexed.

I shelve my thoughts and hop off the chair to give Nat a hug. "Hey, girl." I smile.

Natalie places a hand over her heart. "Oh, thank God. I thought I was going to walk into a sex fest or some sketchy shit."

I laugh at her dramatic sense of humor. "I'm pretty sure the last thing he wants to do is fuck me right now."

She puts up a flat hand. "T-fucking-M-I, Ram Jam. That's my pops you're talking about."

Like I didn't know.

Natalie continues. "Sex talk about my dad requires alcohol. Good thing I'm always prepared."

She reaches into her brown bag and retrieves a bottle of Dom Pérignon and a bottle of Espolòn tequila. I like her style. "For real, though, what happened? Is everything okay?" she asks.

"What makes you think something is wrong?"

She gives me a droll stare. "Don't insult me. Just tell me if I gotta kill him." She hitches her thumb over her shoulder. "'Cause you know, chicks before dicks and all. Fuck that he's my dad. I only just started liking him. You're my ride or die."

I bark out a series of laughs and she smiles as she unravels the wire then removes the foil from the champagne bottle. I love my best friend. When Natalie gets heated about something, a stronger accent comes out. That flare can't be replicated.

I grimace as Natalie bites down on the cork of the champagne bottle to loosen it. All I see is a row of blinding white teeth she pays top dollar for. "You're going to crack your teeth doing that."

She shrugs. "I'll just buy new ones. Cum wears down the enamel anyway."

My eyes widen and for a split second, I'm gullible enough to believe her serious tone.

"Hello to you too." I laugh, and she smiles from ear to ear.

As much as I'd love to talk about it, I really don't want to. It involves her, and the last thing I want is to end up fighting with Natalie too. I've hardly been able to focus on my actual work since shit hit the fan with James. If life went south with Natalie too, well, there's always the bottom of a bottle to look forward to.

"What are you doing here? I thought you were coming over tomorrow."

Her face scrunches up like she's been snubbed. "It is tomorrow."

What? My brows furrow only for them to rise to my hairline. I shake my head.

"Thank God you're pretty," she jokes, and I laugh with her. "Now tell me what happened. I could smell your pity cupcakes when I walked through the door."

I guess I'd been so stressed about James and our future that I got my days mixed up.

My smile fades. "I'd rather not talk about it."

Blue eyes that resemble the hottest part of a flame glare at me. I give it to her right back. This isn't something I ever planned to talk to her about anyway. I just wanted to hang out with her.

"What? I'm just not in the mood. When I'm ready, I'll talk."

We have a staring match like we're seven years old. Her firm gaze could make a grown man cower, but she's my bestie and I know her just like she knows me. This is what we do. I push her to talk, and she pushes me right back. Normally it wouldn't take long for either of us to give in to the other, but this time I can't open up, because it could be the end of our friendship.

Natalie props a hand on her hip and shifts to the side, waiting. Her eyes are still boring into mine and I struggle not to laugh as she tries so hard to make me open up. She only has so much patience to give. I mimic her action with a smirk and she rolls her eyes and shakes her head. Her arm falls to her side in forfeit. We've done this before.

"Yeah, this isn't how we work. I'll be right back."

Natalie spins around, her long platinum locks have a tint of strawberry blonde to them this summer. I tried going blonde once. Not a full golden hue, I just wanted some summery sunset tones to add to my darkest brown color. The stylist fucking ruined my hair to the point it was melting off. I wanted to slash her tires for it. After that, I never dyed my hair again.

"Where are you going?" I ask after her.

She turns around, walking backwards. "James wants to talk to me. He called me a couple of hours ago and said to slide by. I told him I was already coming to see my favorite wannabe stepmama. So when I'm through with him, be ready."

A chill runs through my spine. Instant paranoia pales me. Natalie jokes, but she doesn't realize how close to the truth she is. I shake my head.

As she takes the stairs down to the basement, I wonder when James called her and why. Not that I really care, but after how things have been lately between us—

An exaggerated scream echoes throughout the brownstone, followed by my name. "Aubrey!"

Making my way downstairs, my heart rate increases with each step I take closer to James's office. I'm not sure how he's going to react to seeing me. But one thing I do know, I'm dying to see him. My heart misses him. We're both working just steps away from each other and yet it feels like it's miles.

Reaching the bottom step, my pulse is hammering in my neck as I wonder what I'm going to walk into. Natalie is leaning on the doorjamb with her hip cocked to the side and her arms crossed in front of her. Large gold hoops poke through the openings of her hair. She turns her head toward me and drops her arms to stand up straight.

Eyes wide, she lifts her hand. Her words rush out of her mouth.

"Why is he watching this? What happened to the pact we made? Just because you're getting boned on the regular doesn't mean you can forget about our deal."

Puzzled, I turn into the room, avoiding James's gaze and look at the television.

"Really, James?" I turn toward him with my arms crossed in front of my chest and lift my brow. "*The Silence of the Lambs*?" Natalie and I had made a deal to never watch that fucking creepy movie ever again. I'm still traumatized over the John who wore a Hannibal Lector mask and asked me to rub lotion on him or I'd get the cock again.

James is leaning back in his leather chair a little too proudly. Even though he didn't go into the actual office today, he's dressed in a white button-down shirt with sleeves cuffed to his elbows, matched with dark slate gray dress pants. He's barefoot, and his hair looks unbrushed.

My nostrils flare. Why does he always have to look so fucking mouthwateringly delicious? He makes the floozy in me flare to life and want to pounce. Like right now. Just at first glance, he made my heart drop and my pussy wet for him. I swear, the older he gets, the hotter he gets.

He's not wearing a full-on grin, but I can sense the one underneath his salt-and-pepper beard threatening to spill from his skilled lips. James's eyes are fixated on mine, challenging me. I have a feeling he's not going to stop until I say yes, and there's a small part of me that's secretly happy about that. Not because I want to lead him on, but because I have hope that one day I can say yes without the anxiety of losing someone clouding my vision.

My fears may seem irrational to someone else, but Grammy taught me not to judge others until I've walked a mile in their shoes. Having only her to raise me, I learned to keep my family close and do what's necessary to cherish them. James and Natalie are my family regardless of a piece of paper. The risk of losing them is greater than the risk of marriage.

Chapter 15

"Turn it off, James, or you'll be paying for mine and Aubrey's therapy," Natalie demands.

James responds by lifting a shoulder. His lips twitch. "What's wrong with this movie? It's considered a classic to some."

"To who?" I scoff. "Serial killers? Men who like to skin women alive and wear their flesh like a fashion statement? I don't think so."

He waves his hands out, palm side up, and this time he grins because he can't help it. My heart palpitates and I briefly wonder if he feels what I do.

"You know I don't judge what goes on behind closed doors, sweetheart. My door is always open."

"Don't make me regret telling you about my Johns."

I had told James I came clean with Natalie about my escort days. He can never know it was really his daughter who introduced me to the lifestyle. It would kill him. I also told James that a John is why she and I have PTSD and can't watch this movie now.

"You told him about all of them?" Natalie chimes in. "Even Ram Jam?"

I offer her a loose shrug and her eyes widen further, then I turn back to look at James. I didn't have anything to hide, and he wasn't judgmental.

Leaning on his elbow, his eyes glisten with delight. "The most memorable bedtime stories ever told."

Natalie fakes a gag like she's revolted. "You guys have the weirdest fucking foreplay. Christ Almighty."

My cheeks heat at her words. What Natalie doesn't know is that when I'd told James about my test Johns and clients, he turned around and recreated a sexual fantasy from each one. I thought it was a sweet gesture. He didn't need to because my past honestly doesn't bother me, but James had insisted he wanted this with me because what he had planned needed to be experienced.

I told him it sounded like a good deal. I'd be stupid to say no to a hot tumble of passion and guaranteed sublime ecstasy.

And I was right. It was the best sex ever.

James had turned Ram Jam into a lick-a-thon with my pussy. My thighs tremble slightly at the memory of James dominating every nerve in my body with the caress of his tongue. Each orgasm I had that night was more breathtaking than the last. I lost count of how long he'd spent with his face pressed deep in my core.

Each encounter I had with a John, James reenacted all of them, making those moments his.

And he had left the best for last.

James isn't watching *The Silence of the Lambs* to taunt me; he's watching to remind me—him, us—of what we have together.

James had rented a log cabin in Washington our first winter together as a couple. But it wasn't just any cabin. This cabin was meant for people with an acquired taste for darker things. Set deep in the woods with massive trees surrounding the property, there was nothing but foliage for miles to hear my pants and screams.

James had tied me up and suspended me in the air by a ring in the center of the main room. Two rows of rope were looped through each other, one went around my waist, the other between my legs with a knot pressing right below my clit. My legs were bound separately with rope down to my ankles. I had been entirely and completely at his mercy. There is just something so illicit about it that entices me even now.

He'd stroked and pumped my pussy with his fingers, not stopping until he had my full submission. Once he'd garnered it, he placed a blood-red satin blindfold over my eyes, leaving me in complete darkness. James then lathered my skin in an oil that warmed through touch, unlike the cold lotion I'd used with the test John. James had rubbed and kneaded my sensitive skin in all the right places. The rope shifted from his deep massage, causing the ribbed outline to push against my tender clit again.

The lust between us had intensified and the scent of my sex filled the room. James then used a feather flogger on me next. He spanked my pussy until I dripped in his mouth with pleasure, then he flattened his tongue across my pussy lips, devouring me until I couldn't focus on anything but the intense gratification flowing through my veins. I had cried out in fucking delight as I came in his mouth.

Afterward, James had lowered me to the floor and yanked my hips up so I was on my knees, and he drove straight into my pussy from behind. Ruthless. Savage. He—

"Earth to Aubrey."

My eyes flash to Natalie's. Never one to hold back how she feels, she wears her expression and doesn't give two fucks about it. One corner of her mouth is twisted up as her eyes search mine. I want to laugh, but I don't. Instead, I blink, wondering how long I've been standing here lost in my thoughts and feelings.

I glance over at the love of my life. My chest aches with guilt. I met James because he was searching for something his wife wasn't giving him, and he found it in me. James wants to marry me, but I don't want to ruin what we have.

Would he search for what I'm not willing to give him in someone else?

Chapter 16

"Aubrey." Natalie attracts my attention again.

"Yes? Oh, I was just thinking about something I forgot I needed to submit for Retreat by tonight."

I see James frown from the corner of my eye. He knows I don't have to submit anything since he acted as my attorney and reviewed every document.

He knows I'm lying.

Warmth creeps under my cheeks and my skin prickles with anxiousness. My eyes shift between both of them. "I'm gonna go." I hitch a thumb awkwardly over my shoulder. "I'll see you in a few, Nat." I turn toward James. "Turn that movie off, please."

I leave before either can respond, taking two stairs at a time to the first floor. My heart's racing fast, my fingers are tingly from my shot nerves. A million thoughts are running through my head, but the loudest of them is what the fuck am I doing.

I grab James's fleece sweater off the back of the couch, then reach for the bottle of Espolòn. On a last thought, I rummage through Natalie's bag and find what I'm looking for. I know she won't care. Hell, she'll join me when she's through with James. Quickly, I write a little note on a Post-It for her to meet me on the balcony, then pocket the joint and lighter, then take the stairs to the second floor where our bedroom is located. I pass our room and make my way down the length of the hallway to a door that's bolted shut. Above our room sits a private balcony.

I unlock the door and climb one last set of stairs to our little tropical patio that overlooks the city. I park my ass on one of the lush lounge chairs and inhale a breath, then exhale. It's one of those nights.

I uncork my clear liquid and take a heavy swig of it. There's a subtle burn and it makes the hair on my arms rise. I haven't had tequila in so long I forgot what it tastes like. I usually drink James's cognac. I take the burn though for the next hour or so, until Natalie finds me.

"Hello? I'm looking for Miserable Mattie," she says from behind me. She's such a sarcastic ass.

I release a little chuckle up to the cloudless sky. I'm much looser now after working my way through a quarter of the bottle. I smile lazily over at her. She observes me with humor in her eyes and takes the lounge chair next to me.

"Not even a chaser ... I'm so proud of you." She palms her hand over her heart in mock pride. "You've come so far."

I laugh and give her the middle finger. When we first met our freshman year of college, Natalie would give me shit for taking shots the way I did. I had to sip them and always chase with a fruity drink.

"I know how to open my throat hole now," I say, reminding her of her old advice. Who the hell says throat hole? My bestie does, that's who.

Natalie grins from ear to ear. "I see you've stopped with the bitch drinks too." She laughs and shakes her head, then her expression turns serious. "If we're gonna talk sex, then I need to catch up to you." She holds her hand out and waves her fingers at me. "Hand me the damn bottle."

I give it to her then reach inside my pocket and pull out the joint and lighter and hand them to her too. It's been a while since we've smoked.

"Nice." She lights up—both her face and the joint—and takes a hit.

"We're not talking sex talk," I tell her. "I don't want to talk about your dad."

"Oh, great. Because I was going to go home and bleach my ears out if that was the case. I'd rather get brownout drunk with my bestie the night before I leave for Italy."

My jaw drops and I turn my head to look at her. I almost laugh over her brownout comment. We'd searched the internet once for an answer as to why we could only remember some parts of a drunken night but not the whole thing. Apparently, it's called a brownout, and we found that hysterical.

"You're going to Italy tomorrow? For how long?"

Natalie shrugs and exhales a dense cloud of smoke. She hands me the white rolled baby blunt. "I'm leaving in three days. I don't have a return date. Figured I'd see where the trip takes me and go from there. Italy is known to have the best food and lovers in the world. Why wouldn't I go there?"

I smile. "Like father, like daughter." I take a deep pull myself and watch the white cloud of smoke appear in front of me. "So, you're leaving me too?"

"Don't get dramatic. And before we talk more about the *Chronicles of Natalia* and what her next phase of life is, I want to know what happened. This isn't you. In fact, I haven't seen you like this since Grammy passed away. I know, it's heartless of me to compare, but you look like someone died. Now tell me what the fuck is wrong."

I swallow hard as tears climb the back of my eyes. I don't look at her, I can't. I know if I do, the waterworks will come. Considering the amount of mascara I wear on a daily basis, I look scary when I cry. Natalie's been trying to get me to try lash extensions for a while now. She swears by them and says I'll never wear mascara again. Now I wish I had tried them.

I blink a few times to pull back the emotions, and then I take another hit and hand the smoke back to her.

Don't be a little bitch. Don't be a little bitch. Don't be a little bitch. I give myself a pep talk.

"What's the weather like in Italy right now?" I ask.

"Oh, we're gonna play like that? Cool. Take a swig and I'll answer. Tit for tat. I'll just get you drunk and make you confess."

My lips twitch at the sarcasm in her voice. I do as she says, and she does too. One for one. I guess she's really on a mission to get drunk with me. Tequila fixes everything.

Natalie doesn't answer my lame question, and I'm grateful. She just hangs with me until we smoke the rest of the joint and have a few more sips each. We listen to mostly old-school New York hip hop as we chill and watch the sky further darken. My best friend knows something's wrong and just sits with me, offering her silent support. Even though I don't talk for a good hour, I know she's got to be buzzed by now. I'm drunk *and* high, and she matched me *and* caught up, yet she seems normal.

"Whatta Man" plays through the speakerphone next and it makes me think of James. I listen to the lyrics, thinking about James. I got myself a good guy and I'm stupidly risking his love. Every bone in my body says to give him what he wants because that's what he'd do for me.

"This must be my old man's theme song, judging by the corny as fuck look on your face." Natalie jokes.

I turn my head to look at her. Oh, yeah, I was right on the money. Her eyes are glossy, and her pupils are basically all I see, which makes me bark out a laugh.

"It's his ringtone." I pause and release an annoyed sigh. "Whatta fucking man is right."

She doesn't flinch. Natalie just studies me with a softness to her. She's waiting, and if I know her, she'll wait all night for me to talk. She may even move her trip back if I don't start flapping my lips soon.

I swallow then quietly break it down for her.

"When you said I look like someone died, it's how I feel."

My heart races so fast at the thought of telling her the truth. I sit up and lean over, placing my elbows on my knees, and stare at the ground. My fingers are tingling like they're numb. I shake my hands out and stand, suddenly feeling really hot. I pace the balcony on bare feet and look ahead at the twinkling office lights. They make the concrete jungle feel optimistic.

"I'm not going anywhere, so you better open up those pretty little lips and start talking. I got all the time in the world, plus this is my dad's house and he'd never kick me out."

Exhaling a dramatic, loud breath, I prop my hands on my hips and level a stare at her. Natalie glares back, challenging me the way a bestie should. Despite the cool air, the liquor sends a fire through my veins and my nerves aren't helping. I blink a few times, then it all comes out before I can stop myself.

"I'm so nervous to tell you. I don't want to fight with you, and oh my god I have PTSD just thinking about it. I wasn't even going to talk to you about this, but the tension is eating us both and it's just getting worse, and that's the last thing I want. I don't want to fight with him and lose you both at the same time, and I feel like that's what's gonna happen." My chest rises and falls fast, the pressure of the moment causes sharp pains around my heart. "The last thing I want to do is jeopardize our friendship because you mean the world to me, Nat. We've been there, and it's honestly the last thing I ever want to go through with you again."

Everything comes out like I've had ten shots of espresso. I'm freaking out inside, and my ears are ringing. But Natalie is just smiling like I'm her form of entertainment for the night.

I lick my lips and keep going, even though I feel like I'm going to cry. It's now or never. Sometimes my nerves cause tears to shed. Angry tears, happy tears, PTSD tears. I groan inwardly wondering when I became a sensitive little hussy. Lifting my eyes to the midnight sky, I exhale, trying to blink away the emotion and sort out the millions of thoughts running through my brain.

"How the *fuck* did I get myself into this situation?"

"Because you fucked your best friend's dad. Duh," Natalie replies.

I chuckle at her dark sarcasm. Looking down, she's just smirking at me from the lounge chair. She's good at making the situation lighter, which in turn makes me slightly more comfortable sharing. Slightly, being the keyword.

"I blame you." I joke. "If you hadn't offered to make me a millionaire floozy, then this wouldn't have happened, and I wouldn't be having a panic attack. It's killing my high."

"Do you regret it?"

"Well, no."

I have no regret about being a high-end escort and the things I did for money.

"Then you can't blame me for shit." She laughs. "You got what you wanted." Natalie stretches her bony arms out. "You're welcome."

I don't know why, but it makes me blurt out what I've been stressing about incessantly for days.

"James wants to get married."

I wait for the aversion to appear in her eyes, but Natalie doesn't react the way I expect her to. It's the opposite, so I repeat myself just to make sure she heard me.

"James wants to get married, like rings and all. He even asked about kids."

She continues to smile, and it's similar to the one James gives me when he finds my manic moments adorable.

"What's wrong with you and your father and that stupid matching fucking smirk on your face? I tell you your dad wants to marry me, your fucking best friend, he wants to make an honest woman out of me, and you just sit there and smile?"

She full-on belly laughs and it totally changes my mood—in a good way.

"I'm gonna punch you," I threaten her.

Natalie's eyes are positively bursting with laughter. "You are *so* dumb."

"Can you elaborate before I have a fucking heart attack?"

Chapter 17

Natalie moves her legs off the lounge chair and sits up.

She gestures for me to take a seat. I hesitate and inhale a heavy breath before sitting down in front of her. Leaning toward me, she makes sure she's looking into my eyes. I roll my lip between my teeth and bite down, unsure how this night will end. My nerves are through the roof.

"Were you honestly worried to tell me my dad wants to marry you?" she asks, then breaks out in a chuckle. "Okay, now that I say that out loud, I guess I can see where you're coming from."

I nod. "It brought me back to the past—"

"Nope. Hush. We're not going there—"

"I know, but I don't want to do anything to ruin us, you know? That was awful, Nat, and I'd do anything to prevent that from happening again."

She offers me a sweet smile. "Glad to know you're all about that chicks before dicks life, but this is different. Listen, that day in the restaurant, when I gave you guys my blessing, it didn't come with terms. That wouldn't have been fair of me. In fact, it'd be kinda fucked up. Am I the reason you won't marry him?"

"How did you know I won't marry him?"

Natalie gives me a droll stare. "Why do you think I'm here? Daddy called about his princess. Thanks for taking my spot, bitch."

I clench my eyes shut and cringe. "Please don't call him Daddy."

We both laugh for a moment until I sober up and say, "He called you about this?"

"He did. It was pretty cute. He was just as nervous to talk about it as you. When he told me he asked you to marry him—not once, but like three times—and you said no each time, my jaw dropped. I can't believe you said no."

My eyes widen. I'm going to get wrinkles from how much I'm lifting and dropping my brows. "He told you that?"

"Oh yeah, when my dad's motivated over something, there's no stone he won't turn over to find a positive outcome. He has no shame in his game when it comes to something he loves. Can't fault him for it. It's admirable."

My shoulders slouch, the guilt beginning to settle in my bones. "That's kind of cute of him."

"Trust me, when he asked me to come over because he had something he wanted to tell me, that was the last thing I expected. I wasn't mad, though, and I certainly didn't reject the idea of you guys getting married. Honestly, I was really ecstatic until I heard you said no. What the hell is wrong with you?"

She isn't angry, but more so frustrated because I'd rejected his proposal. It makes me feel a torrent of emotions for holding back, and especially for causing James to suffer in silence. Natalie clearly has no issue and I'm not sure how to respond to that.

"It's not just you, though." I tip my head to exhale up at the sky. "I feel like we have a good thing going on. Why put a piece of paper between us and ruin it? We're basically married now, anyway. Why do we have to change anything? I feel like that's asking for trouble. You know how they say don't wake a sleeping baby?"

"No, I hate kids, but keep going so I can hear this nonsense."

Natalie isn't sold. I can see it in the way she's glaring at me. I'm searching for answers from every corner of the earth when she and I know deep down the only place I'll find them is in me.

I sigh. "It just means don't ruin a good thing."

"First of all, my dad's a lawyer. He loves to live by the law.

Marriage, in his eyes, is making it official. Making it official gets his jollies off. It's basically something no one can ever take from him or you. It's something only you two can have. What makes you think it'll ruin you guys, anyway? What if it binds you together even more?"

I stare at Natalie, wondering where this romantic side of her came from. She's usually so far removed from the idea of marriage and commitment, yet here she is giving some pretty good advice. I bet she reads my old sappy romance novels I left behind at her apartment. I bet she wants the white picket fence and two-point-five kids. Maybe even a dog since she hates cats.

"I'm scared, Nat. I've lost so many good things in my life. My parents, Grammy. I almost lost you and him. You guys are all I have left. The same way James would move mountains to get what he wants, I'd do it to prevent anything bad happening."

"You didn't almost lose me. We were on a mini break." Regret softens her words.

At times like this when everything seems impossible to have, I love my best friend even more for reminding me hope isn't lost. Our bond is strong, but that doesn't mean we're unshakable. Shit happens and it's all about how we react to it. We've lived and we've learned. Since day one we've been there working out our problems as a team, just like now.

"You didn't lose those people because of you. Your parents were in a car accident, your grammy, well, you know. They were unfortunate situations, but they're not your fault, and there was nothing that you could have done to stop them from happening. You know that, right?"

My eyes drop to the ground and I let out a defeated sigh. I know I didn't personally cause their deaths, but they left my world in the blink of an eye because of a split-second change in events.

"Why would I risk tomorrow when I know what the outcome will be? We have a good thing going on right now. Why can't it just stay that way? That paper is pointless. We don't need it."

There's a flare in her eyes now. Natalie reminds me of James when he's confident he's about to win an argument.

Shit.

"That paper is not pointless to him. Can I ask you something?" The tone in her voice seizes my heart. Hesitantly, I lift my gaze to her. "Do you want to marry him? Tell me the truth."

I don't have to think about her question—I already know my answer. The organ beating behind my ribs nearly breaks through them. Marry the love of my life? The thought of walking down the aisle to marry James is a rush unlike any other. It makes me giddy thinking of him as my husband, but that doesn't mean it should happen. No one gets to eat their cake without consequences.

"Of course, I want to marry him. I fucking love that man so much. I wanted to marry him yesterday, but you know what's stopping me now."

Natalie is beaming from ear to ear like a total fool. Admitting I love her dad isn't scary—she can see the proof herself when he and I look at each other. Telling her I want to marry him is a totally different emotion that chokes me up. Wrecking his heart is not on my list of things to do, and neither is losing a bestie.

Tears fill my eyes, and I swallow hard before telling her what's been on my mind since the first time James brought up marriage.

"I'm scared, Nat." My heart rushes with anxiety and the knots in my stomach are cramping together. The truth is always hard to admit. "I'm afraid of loss. Everyone who's ever meant something to me has died. What if that paper ruins us?"

"What if it doesn't."

I blink and stare, thinking about James dressed in a designer tux standing next to the officiant with Natalie across from him. I'd want our wedding to be small and intimate, so it's only about our love and the people who mean the most to us. My gut is saying to take the risk, but my heart is marked with wounds that hold me back. His face flashes through my mind again, and this time not only do I see his devastation, I feel it.

"You know he's so madly in love with you he'd do anything to be with you, right?" She pauses, and for the first time since I've known her, she looks reluctant to continue. "I never saw him look at my mom the way he does you." She lowers her voice. "I always thought they were in love. They laughed, they smiled, they kissed, the usual affection every married couple and parents have for one another. But as I get older, I realize they didn't love each other in the same sense my dad loves you, that's for sure. The smiles are real, the kisses aren't forced, and the laughs are genuine. It's a bone-deep type of love." She squints her eyes as she thinks about her next set of words. "Isn't it funny how things work out? You think you know love until someone comes around and changes your entire perception of the word, making you reexamine every aspect of your life. It takes you by surprise and makes you wonder why that is, and how you went so long without it."

James wants a marriage with someone he loves more than life, and he wants that with me. My eyes clench shut at the veracity of my thoughts. It makes my heart swell with pride that he'd want me to be his wife.

Opening my eyes, I steal a look at Natalie. I think she's realizing how honest her confession is. It takes strength for her to let go and admit her father loves me in ways he didn't her mother.

Natalie continues, though her tone is gentle. Sympathetic. "If I was a reason you were holding back from marrying him, and we already confirmed the loss of your family doesn't mean you'll end up like them too, what's really going on?"

We're both quiet for a moment until I look away with embarrassment. I have a great man who wants to make me his wife, he wants to give me the world, and I said no.

"Me. I guess it's just me." I let out a dramatic sigh over my stupidity. "I'm dumber than a box of rocks. Marriage terrifies me."

She offers me a somber smile that clenches my heart. Melancholy doesn't complement her.

"Yeah. This isn't any regular relationship, so there's no manual to reference. Look at how you met him up until now. Sometimes weird shit, like marrying your John who's also your best friend's dad, is meant to happen. You beat the odds once. What makes you think you can't do it for a lifetime?" Natalie picks up the tequila bottle and takes a swig, then hands it to me. "Cheers to you becoming Mrs. Aubrey Riviera. I'll never call you mommy, so don't get any ideas."

The shot doesn't make it down. It gets stuck in my throat and I choke. *Mrs. Aubrey Riviera.* My eyes widen as tequila spills from my mouth and burns my nose. It hits the ground with a splat. I reach out and Natalie takes the bottle, then moves next to me.

"Lift your arms above your head," she says.

I don't question her, I just do it. The burn of the tequila effectively sears off the skin in my nostrils, while simultaneously making me feel like I have a horrible case of strep throat. I turn my face into my bicep and cough into it. My eyes are watering, and I squeeze them shut.

"Bend over and put your head between your legs."

"What?" This time I manage a brief confused-as-fuck look at her.

Eyes wide, Natalie yells, "Just do it!"

Chapter 18

I do and she scoots closer so she can pat my back and rub circles over it.

"My mom used to do this to me when I had croup as a kid. This angle is supposed to help when you're choking and can't breathe. Take small breaths and focus."

I'm perched on the edge of the lounge chair with my knees spread wide and my body bent over, my arms still in the air. I feel like an idiot sitting like this. I can't tell if this is helping or not with how far I'm leaning over. I feel like I'm blocking my airways, not opening them up. Once the coughing subsides and my eyes aren't watering anymore, I sit up.

I look at Natalie. "You know the first thing I thought of when you told me to put my head between my legs? Marilyn Manson."

"What the fuck for and why?"

"I heard he had some ribs taken out so he can suck his own dick."

She blinks, and remains quiet for a second, then lets out a hilarious chuckle. "This is why we're besties. It's shit like this that comes out of your mouth that just confirms we're soul mates. Wait—did you think I was telling you to get yourself off?"

It's my turn to giggle. "No, he just popped into my head for some reason. I felt like I was bent over really far and he just appeared in front of me, pasty white face, piranha teeth and all." I pause, thinking about how weird this conversation is now. " I wondered if he could actually do it or not."

"That'd be some sick shit, but after all the Johns I've had the last couple of years, I wouldn't be surprised if he could."

She's not even phased. I'd seen a lot in my escorting days, but Natalie's been around the block a time or two more. The stories she's told me are not something you can make up off the top of your head.

I sniffle, feeling like a hundred-pound cement block has been lifted from my chest. "Now that I've poured my heart out to you, tell me why you're leaving me."

Natalie's face softens. She has this innocent, sweet look like she couldn't squash a bug when in reality she eats men for breakfast and spits them out.

"Only if you promise me you won't reject my dad again because of me." She waves her hand in the air in a dismissive motion. "Listen, you're stuck with me forever, whether you have a piece of paper between you guys or not. It makes no fucking difference to me. So why not make it official?"

My lips twitch. I glance down. "You really think he's going to ask me to marry him again after I shot him down multiple times? Fat chance." Before she can respond, I divert the conversation back to Italy. My heart can't handle another ounce of anxiety over rejecting James. "So, Italy? What part and why?"

"Italy is calling to me, so Italy is where I must go," she says, and I'm grateful she takes the hint to change the subject. "I don't have a specific spot. I'm just going to backpack it and see where it takes me. The plan is to eat my way through the country and see if Italian men really are the best lovers in the world."

My brows rise. "You're going to backpack it?"

Natalie rolls her eyes. "No, but it just sounded better. You get my drift."

I nod. She'll have a driver or plane on standby, a wad of cash, and a black American Express card. Oh, and a luggage full of designer clothes.

"Considering the number of men you've fucked over the

years, you'd think you'd die happy never having to spread your legs again."

"*Au contraire*," she says with a light French accent and holds up one finger. "I discovered what I like and what I don't like, but also that there's literally someone out there for everyone. I'll find my man in the land of cuisine and attractive blokes," she says. "If not, I'll just move on to Greece. They're basically cousins of the Italians. I'm bound to find a few."

I study her, finding it comical what she wants to do. "Are you just going to put out a want ad or something? What's your plan of attack?"

Natalie purses her lips together. "My milkshake brings all the boys to the yard ..."

We giggle together. "How long are you going for, really?"

She shrugs. "Until I get my fill?" We both laugh again but she sobers up. "The older I get, the more I realize we only get one life to live, so why not live like tomorrow isn't guaranteed? I know not everyone can do that, but I can. I don't want the opportunity to pass me by."

"Your idea of living life to the fullest is eating Italian food and no-strings-attached sex."

"Basically." She winks.

I love how Natalie's not ashamed in the least. She is who she is, and she loves herself for it. I find it an admirable and endearing quality.

"In some odd way, it suits you," I say.

"Did you ever have a feeling inside of you that you can't explain but you know it's right? That's how I feel about going to Italy, well, about traveling in general. New York will always be home, but I kind of want to see the world."

"You're going to get wanderlust like James."

Her blue eyes light up like that's her goal. I could totally see that being her kind of lifestyle.

Standing up, Natalie fixes her shorts and smooths out her shirt. "I'm gonna go. My plane leaves in three days and I still need to go shopping."

"That soon? What if James asks me again and then wants to get married three days later? You're not going to be here?"

The annoyance in Natalie's glare makes me chuckle under my breath. "'Thank God you're pretty. I'll just fly back ASAP. Duh, Ram Jam."

Natalie grabs the mostly empty tequila bottle and chugs the rest then dumps it in the garbage. I shake my head and stick the remains of the joint in a pile of sand we use as an ashtray and walk her out.

"I'm going to start praying for your future husband now."

"Good. My future ex-husband is going to need all the prayers he can get when I'm done with him."

A giggle erupts from my throat. "You're already calling your divorce. That's great. Who gets the kids?"

"Psh." Natalie pushes through her lips. "Won't be an issue because I fucking hate kids."

"You're a real piece of work." I joke as we step off the last step onto the first floor. My gaze flickers around the room. I pretend I'm not looking for anyone specific, but I really am. It's quiet and I don't like how empty it feels. The only light is coming from the living room around the corner. I can picture him sitting in his Chesterfield chair with a cigar in one hand, and a crystal tumbler in the other. Quiet nights lounging in his leather chair are his favorite. My heart aches to be next to him, but I'm too embarrassed to see him now.

"You love me," Natalie says, taking me away from my thoughts.

"I wouldn't want you any other way."

Our smiles match each other's. Natalie grabs her purse then a water bottle from the fridge before she heads to the door. I follow next to her.

"Tell *Daddy* I said bye-bye."

I don't conceal my gag. Not only did she call James daddy, but she said it in a sex operator's voice.

"I hate you sometimes. Don't forget to FaceTime me while you're living your best life."

"Oh, I'll be living my best life surrounded by balls the size of lemons that country produces, while you'll be with ones that look like prunes under the Tuscan sun." She pauses for a second and gives me a smirk. "P.S. I wasn't supposed to tell you what James told me. So, hush, hush, like a good girl."

I stare at her long and hard. Her harmless smile is anything but. Kill 'em with a honey-sweet voice and southern belle smile while throwing digs at them. I know her, though. Inwardly she's struggling not to laugh because she's that girl who laughs at her own jokes.

Finally, I speak. "I can't wait until the day you have to introduce me as your stepmom."

That one breaks her and she throws her arms around me chuckling. We hug each other tight for a moment longer then break apart. Pressing a kiss to each other's cheek, we say goodbye and part ways.

I shut the door and stand there for a moment contemplating what I should do. If I should go to James or just go to bed. After all the alcohol I consumed, plus the smoke, my emotions are delicate now and I feel like I'd cry easily in front of him. That's the last thing I want him to see.

Chapter 19

I bite my lip and make my way to our bedroom.

I decide on taking a bath because I'm not quite ready to go to sleep yet. I need to unwind. There's too much vulnerability swimming through my veins to talk marriage with James again. I'd just end up a bawling muffled mess. Plus, he's kept his distance today, so there's not much driving me to do that.

I turn on the water to start my bath, then I undress and tie my hair up. I want him to know marriage isn't off the table, but I need time to process it. I went from not wanting to marry to saying yes in the span of a couple of hours. That's a lot for my heart to bear and my mind to process.

Stepping into the steaming hot water, I sigh as I sink down. My eyes close as I listen to Demi Lovato's voice croon out a heartbreaking ballad. Her brutal honesty somehow manages to trigger an arrangement of emotions to burst inside of me. James Riviera is the only man who has ever done it for me. It would almost be hypocritical of me to not marry him, really.

I wave the water between my fingers, watching the bubbles fizz. Could it be possible we'd be even more in love and happy together? Like Natalie said, James loves to live by the law, so a marriage certificate would mean a lot to him. Seeing him happy would make me happy too.

I know he'd do it for me if the roles were reversed.

I let out a long, tired sigh and sink further into the water until it hits my neck. My eyes are growing heavy when I hear the wood floor creak below me. This brownstone echoes and we can hear everything. I know exactly where that creak is too—in the kitchen near the small bar. The decanter clinks together and I can hear the faint sound of liquid being poured twice.

Hope branches through me. I sit up a little higher and hold my breath, knowing he's headed up to me.

The door pushes open and James steps inside, gently kicking it closed behind him. Blush tints my cheeks and my teeth dig into my bottom lip at the sight of him. My heart desires him in ways that turn me into a stage five clinger, and I'm not ashamed in the least. My eyes openly drag down his body. He's wearing sweatpants that sit low on his hips and nothing else. I run my tongue over my lip, staring at the space between his hips. His manly appeal makes him so fucking gorgeous. James is in excellent shape. I love how hard his body is. The fact he doesn't look like a twenty-year-old makes me ache even more for him. There's just something about a man, an older, real man, with a good career whose wisdom and confidence are his sex appeal.

His observing eyes meet mine.

"Hey, you." My voice is relaxed, easy.

His face softens. "Hey, sweetheart."

My heart is about to pump out of my chest. In the quiet of our bathroom, we both feel that pull between us.

James places two glasses on the counter then picks up the accent chair and carries it to the tub. I sit up and rise to my knees just as he's about to take a seat. Suds trickle down my body, his heated gaze follows the lavender-scented soap over the swell of my heavy breasts and along the slope of my belly.

I don't give him a chance to speak. Extending my arms upward, I reach for James, and he responds to me immediately. He drops to his knees. I grab his cheeks and pull his mouth down, planting a hard kiss to his lips. James clutches my waist and kisses me back with just as much force. I wrap my arms around his shoulders and press my chest to his. I'm soaking wet but it doesn't faze him. Our tongues tie together, sliding against each other's in a slow, languid kiss. He moans into my mouth, and it makes me ache for him. Our love is insurmountable.

"I don't want to fight with you," I say quickly, breaking away. "I feel like there's this wall between us and I don't like it."

"Sweetheart, shhh," he says. James cups the side of my face and I lean into his palm. His blue eyes stare into mine. "There's never going to be a wall between us, Aubrey."

My eyes water. "Promise?"

"Yes." He hesitates for a split second, then says, "I respect your decision and won't bring it up again."

A breath hitches in my throat. My ribs feel like they are being laced together and pushing the air from my lungs. How can I tell James I want him to propose again? Guilt takes hold of me. I'm the definition of an ungrateful woman, one who held onto the past and ruined what was right in front of her. Here I am worried he'll never ask me to marry him when he asked me a handful of times already.

"I want you to know that marriage isn't off the table," I say, my voice shaky.

Cupping my cheeks, he tilts my face up to his so I'm only an inch or so away. There's a hint of lavender surrounding him that fuses gently to the cognac on his lips. James looks into my eyes. He's all I see and all I want in this life. I find myself pressing closer to reach him.

"I will forever want every part of you," James says. "I will forever love you more than anyone ever could. Never doubt that. You were right about something, though. We don't need a piece of paper to prove what we have. We are only what matters."

I don't know whether to cry or smile or do both at the same time. "What did I do to deserve a man like you?"

"Not deserve but complement. When two people have an unconditional love like ours, that's a complement to each other."

I can't tell if James realizes I've had a change of heart. I need to tell him again just to make sure he knows I do want to marry him. If he wants the paper, then there is no reason why I shouldn't give it to him when he so obviously would give it up for me.

"You heard what I said, right?" My brows angle in worry between my eyes. "That marriage isn't off the table."

His lips twitch, and he nods. "I'll think about it. Gotta make sure you really are wife material."

A matching smile tips my lips, I pull in a gasp and giggle. James steals a quick kiss, then says in all seriousness, "I love you, Aubrey."

"Not more than I love you," I say. "I want all my moments to be with you for the rest of my life."

Chapter 20

"It's been thirty-seven days, sixteen hours, and four minutes since the day you were here, and he still hasn't asked me to marry him again," I whine to Natalie over the phone. "He's never going to ask me. He's going to make me ask him, I just know it."

I almost laugh at myself over how ridiculous I sound.

"He's doing it on purpose," she says. "I thought he would've this morning before your shelter opened, but I guess not. I wish I could've been there with you today. Congrats, Ram Jam. That mouth of yours is still paying it forward."

"You're such an ass." Shaking my head, I laugh.

Today marked the opening of my second non-profit shelter, Retreat, a place for fathers with children. I decided to keep the men's and women's shelters separate since more than half of the women had noted on their questionnaires that they felt more comfortable amongst other females. Respecting everyone's wishes has been a struggle since I want to help everyone, but we've managed pretty well so far. I had planned to open one final shelter, a place for runaway teens, but James had suggested we do one for families too. His desire to be involved melts my heart. I love him more for it. I guess teamwork really does make the dream work.

"What's taking him so long? He isn't getting any younger, you know."

"I'm sure he's aware. He still doesn't know I told you I spoke to him. How sweet. He's really respecting your wishes and not pushing it."

"Fuck my wishes. Since when has he really ever done that?" I mean ... he has and hasn't ... like in the heat of the moment when I'm screaming his name.

"This is different, sis."

I groan, gripping the phone tighter. She's right, and that annoys me. "I know. Maybe I should drop hints. But obvious ones."

"Don't embarrass me."

A smile draws across my face. I wouldn't go that far, but it was fun while the thought lasted. Exhaling a breath, I wince at the inflamed skin over my ribs. I gently cup my side and hold myself, wondering what James will say. After this morning's opening of Retreat, I told a little fib and said I had a doctor's appointment I couldn't miss.

"Do you think James will like the tattoo?" I ask Natalie for the tenth time since I got it. She saw it the moment the artist was finished. I had quickly FaceTimed her before it was wrapped up.

"Yeah, I actually think it's gonna give him a raging boner."

I shake my head. Any chance Natalie gets to be vulgar, she jumps on it. "I hope so. At one point I felt like she was under my damn boobs with the needle gun."

"It's gorg, Aub. He's gonna love it. Maybe be a little jealous you didn't take him with you for your first tattoo. Put a robe on so he doesn't see it through the slip."

"Good idea," I say, then stand up to retrieve the silk robe. I'm waiting until later tonight to surprise him with it. "How's Italy treating you?"

"I'm rich, young, and single, fucking my way through Italy with limoncellos running through my veins. What's your question again?"

She's a rare breed of person. "You are literally the worst, and I love it."

"Oh, speaking of lemons ... this man came up to me on the beach today, and to make a long story short, he said I haven't had the best limoncello, even though I claimed the one in my hand was the best, to which he replied I haven't had *his* lemons yet. Thank heaven he was gorgeous, or I would've taken him to church for that one."

I laugh. We both hate lame-ass pick-up lines and would try to beat each other with who had the worst ones in college. I could just imagine her facial expression when he said that to her. It would've been priceless.

"I would've loved to have been there for that. What did you say?"

"I told him when you've had one lemon, you've had them all." I feel like she's right next to me as we're having this conversation. "He asked me to come to this place called South of the Lemon Tree."

"What's that?"

"A restaurant that overlooks the Amalfi Coast."

A dreamy sigh rolls off my lips. "I've been wanting to visit Italy, especially that coast. Your Insta pics are stunning. That's one place James and I haven't been to yet together. So, when do you leave?"

"For what?"

"To meet the lemon guy."

"Yeah, that's not happening."

My jaw drops. "What? Why not?"

"Because he sounded like a fucking creeper and talked about how amazing his lemons are?" Natalie says with such sass. "Any man who talks about his junk like that gets kicked out of my bed."

"I think you should go. Humor me. He could be one for the books. You never know unless you try. What else do you have going on?"

"I don't know. Watching this amazing sunset alone on my wraparound balcony in peace? Don't you have somewhere to be?"

I glance at the clock and see I have a few more minutes before I have to put on my dress. "We have the New York City Women of

Impact Humanitarian Awards dinner tonight. All I have to do is put on my gown and I'm ready to ride."

"Take pics for me. What are you wearing?"

"An emerald green sequin frock James picked out for me. It's floor length with a thigh-high slit and a deep plunge neckline. My boobs barely fit though, they look massive."

"I'm sure he loves that."

I chuckle. "Oh, he does."

The bedroom door opens, and James struts in wearing a black dress shirt, a black fucking bow tie, and matching suspenders that connect to tux pants. My tongue runs over my bottom lip. He looks like sex on a stick walking my way.

"Damn, baby," I say in awe. James's confidence is in his stride, the quiet way he holds himself, and how he doesn't smirk like a know-it-all. "We're gonna be late." He gives me a dirty smile that heats my blood in the best way.

"Annnnddd that's my cue," Natalie says. "I have a date with the lemon man that I apparently need to get ready for."

James leans over and I tilt my head back to give him a kiss. "If you don't want to go, then don't," I tell Natalie.

She hesitates. "It's not that."

"Then what is it?"

"I just feel like I shouldn't be drinking alone with him."

I frown. "Why's that?"

"Because I have this feeling that he would give back just as good as I give. I'd want a second serving."

"And the problem is ...?"

Natalie huffs obnoxiously loud into the phone. "It's not like me to have seconds." She pauses. "I want to do filthy, nasty things to him, okay? Like leave a mark on him so he always remembers me. That's my cue to *not* engage."

"There it is." I chuckle, my voice a little higher but full of laughter. "Despite his corny comment, you still want to hook up with him."

"I have eyes, okay, and they like what they saw ... a lot."

She's so annoyed with herself that I can't stop smiling. Natalie isn't the type to fall hard, but she does love the pretty boys. I can tell this guy is on her mind and that she actually wants to go see him. She just needs a little push.

"Listen, I have to go and ravish your dad before we leave for the dinner, but I think you should go and live in the moment and have fun. Text me tomorrow, ho."

I disconnect our call, not giving her a chance to respond, and put my cell phone down. I rise in my five-inch heels and walk to where James is standing in front of our dresser putting on his cuff links. I catch his reflection in the mirror and wonder if there will ever be a time when he doesn't make my heart rush for him over the simplest thing. He already looks like a walking wet dream and smells like the devil is testing me. I don't need much of a push at this point to pounce on him.

Stepping close to him, my fingers slide over his to lock in the first cuff link. Before I can reach for the other, James uses his index finger to tip my jaw up toward him.

"It's taking everything in me not to rip your clothes off right now and have my wicked way with you," I blurt out before he can say anything.

Everyone loves a good compliment, and James doesn't hide the fact he likes what I said. The smile that lights up his whole face stirs a need inside of me. He palms my waist and slides his hand over my hip.

"The feeling is entirely mutual, sweetheart. I don't know what I'd do without you. Every day of my life I wake up next to you feeling grateful. Watching you devote your time and energy to Sanctuary, and then to see first-hand how hard you worked to bring Retreat to life, made me fall deeper in love. You inspire me, and I find that a hell of a turn-on."

I'm speechless. No one has ever told me I inspire them. That admission hits me right in the center of my chest.

The longer he stares into my eyes, the harder my heart beats for this man. James looks at me like I'm the center of his world. This is what we search a lifetime for to find in a partner.

Leaning in, I press my stained lips to his, the prickly fine hairs of his mustache tickling me. I expect his hand to cup my ass and give me a rough squeeze, like I know he loves to do, but James surprises me. He presses his body to mine. His thick tongue languidly strokes and tugs, taking control. I whimper into his mouth, the blitz of desire assaulting me in all the right ways. James slips his hand through the opening of my robe and cups my pussy, making sure one of his fingers is painfully teasing my entrance while there's pressure on my clit. I move against his hand, aching for more. He knows exactly how to touch me to make me weak for him.

I grip his shoulders. "James." His name is a prayer on my lips. "I need you."

His kiss is deep and slow and leaves me breathless. There's nothing like a man who appreciates a good kiss.

"We have twelve minutes until we leave. Turn around and bend over. We don't have time for you to get fixed up again, and I don't have another pair of tux pants."

"We can wait until after," I suggest with a flirtatious bat of my eyelashes. "Allow the temptation to build."

"Too late for that, sweetheart."

"I love the way your mind works."

Grabbing my jaw, James growls then plunges his tongue into my mouth for a quick kiss. "It's going to be so good, sweetheart."

"The best twelve minutes of my life."

Chapter 21

"You look beautiful," James whispers. "I know I never got to meet your grandmother, but I'd bet my life's work she's looking down on you and smiling, proud of you the way I am, and what you have become."

We're sitting in a room with a few hundred people illuminated by chic chandeliers that shimmer like diamonds. I turn to look at him, a tint of blush colors my cheeks. His words were low and only meant for me to hear. He's holding my hand as the names of the four honorees are being called, including mine. I still can't believe I'm among the women being honored tonight when there are others just as worthy, maybe even more than me. My thumb strokes over the top of his hand as I gaze into his eyes. I love this man so much. I just hope he knows that.

"Thank you for being here with me." My words are soft and intimate.

"There's nowhere else I'd rather be."

A demure smile curves the corners of my lips. I feel myself falling deeper in love with him. I never knew love could feel this way.

"Aubrey Abrams ..."

"Get going, sweetheart." James smiles at me.

I glance at the stage and my eyes widen when I realize the honorees are already up there.

In quick succession, James cups the side of my neck and presses his lips to mine. My eyes automatically roll close at the touch. His thumb is gently resting on the front of my throat then sweeps over to the side. He breaks away and says, "They're waiting on you. Get your ass up there."

I nod quickly and blink a few times to gather my bearings. Standing up, I exhale a breath and smooth down the front of my gown. I smile at James one last time before I make my way toward the front of the room then up the few steps to the stage.

A shiny trophy-like award is handed to me. It's black and in the shape of a tall rectangle. Though I'm still filled with disbelief, I smile at it. It's heavier than I anticipated, and the corners could scratch glass. I glance at the gold-plated tag and read the inscription as the applause dies down.

The award's committee had informed us we would be going in alphabetical order to give our acceptance speeches. Lucky me, I get to go first. Licking my lips, I take a deep breath before stepping over to the podium. I gaze into the crowd of designer suits and custom dresses and allow the reality of the moment to sink in.

My full heart is content. My gaze drifts around the people in this room I find common ground with. We're all trying to make a difference in the world.

"Some of you may not know that my grandmother raised me after I lost both my parents. Giving back is something she instilled in me at a very young age. She was my best friend, my mom, my dad, my sister ..." Tears fill my eyes. Nearly five years later, and I still get choked up thinking about Grammy not being here anymore. I miss her every day. "We may not have been able to afford heat every winter, but that never stopped her from offering a helping hand. She always said it could be worse and I needed to count my blessings.

"As I grew up, I wanted to be just like her. I still do. She taught me to follow that driving need in my heart, to go after what makes me happy, and that's what I've been doing ever since. My need to help others has never wavered. When she died, I lost a life, but in opening Sanctuary, and now Retreat, I've gained so many more. I think she would've been proud of the shelters she helped me build even after she left."

The last thing I want is to be that person who talks too much and has to be ushered off the stage, but I have a few more things I must say.

I look at James and meet his steel blue eyes. I grip the award a little tighter in my hand as I speak.

"My grammy isn't the only one who's influenced me. There's a man here with me today who means the world to me. He's my best friend, my confidant. He's my biggest cheerleader and *extremely* patient with me. I'm a better person because of him, because he encouraged me to grow into the person I am today. He not only helps to continue my grammy's wish with me, but he also wants to be there knee-deep in the planning. I will forever be indebted to him for that. Rome wasn't built in a day, but when you have the right people on your side, it feels like it can be. My only wish is to inspire at least one person who walks through my doors the way he and Grammy have me. Feeling hopeless doesn't mean all is lost. When you help yourself, you improve the lives around you."

Taking a deep breath, I prepare to end my speech. There's a bubbling need inside of me to claim James in front of everyone and show the world he's mine.

"James Riviera, my—" I pause for a split second with my heart in my throat. The word husband wants to slip off my tongue like it's the most natural thing in the world. Like I'm supposed to say it, and that shocks me.

"James, my love, you are my world. Thank you for wanting to create a future of moments for people you've never met. You didn't have to, but you wanted to, and that means more to me than you could ever know. This award is just as much yours as it is mine. Thank you."

I gather my dress with one hand and rejoin the other women as the next honoree gives her speech. After the last woman addresses the crowd, I make my way back to the table where James is waiting for me. I only see him. The applause fades away as harp music fills the room.

James stands as I approach. I hand him my award and he places it on the table, then closes the distance and pulls me to him, planting a huge kiss on my lips in front of everyone. Heart to heart, I forget the world around us for a moment and respond to his love, showing James that he is my everything.

Breaking the kiss, James pulls away leaving me breathless. My lips tingle as I gaze into his eyes. He doesn't say anything, but he doesn't need to. It's all right there for me to see what I mean to him. I can't wait to be alone with him tonight, and not even in a sexual way. His presence is my salvation.

"I fucking love you so damn much." James grins. "I love this woman!" he shouts to the room, and my cheeks instantly burst with heat as a smile stretches across my face once more.

"James!" I whisper sharply under my breath.

He gives me an unapologetic shrug. He doesn't hide who he is, and I love him even more for that.

Taking my hand, he laces his fingers with mine and sits next to me until the dinner is over.

Chapter 22

"Tell me when you had time to plan this?" I ask James.

As soon as the dinner had ended, James whisked me into a Bentley and had the driver take us to a private airstrip where a plane was waiting for us. He wouldn't tell me where we were going no matter how many times I'd begged, but he'd assured me it was somewhere I wanted to go.

And he wasn't wrong.

Aspen holds fond memories for us. It's where we both fell hard for each other with so much on the table to lose. Where we found balance and unison. Aspen is where we'd realized we were unapologetically in love with each other. I'm delighted he planned a surprise trip like this.

"I had a little help." James beams from ear to ear as he guides me inside the log cabin I've dreamed about revisiting. It looks exactly the same, like we were just here yesterday. The cozy first floor is decorated in forest greens and brassy gold hues.

Happiness swims through my heart as I take in the space around me. This place screams home to me.

"Who helped you?" I turn around and James stares like the answer is obvious. "Natalie," I state. I can't believe that dirty little ho didn't tell me.

"I planned this a few months ago, but Natalie only knew about it recently because I asked her to pack you a bag. I didn't trust her to keep it a secret from you."

"You asked her to pack my bags? I'm scared to see what she put in there."

James laughs and walks over to where I'm standing. I wrap my arms around his broad shoulders and his hands encircle the small of my back.

"I caught her before she left for Italy and told her to go shopping for you. I've been hiding your suitcase in my office." There's a pensive weight to his stare now. "I know you've been wanting to come back here. I have too, but I felt like it needed to be a special occasion for us. Today, with the opening of your second shelter and the award's dinner, it felt like the time was finally right."

"It's *our* shelter, baby." I correct him and drape my arms over his shoulders. What's mine is his, always.

James shakes his head. "No, sweetheart, that's all yours. I'm just along for the ride."

"How did I get so lucky with you?" I want to smush his face against mine and kiss the fuck out of him.

"Well, I wouldn't necessarily call it luck ..." We both see the dark humor behind his comment. James continues. "I need you to do me a favor and close your eyes. I have one more surprise."

My cheeks are starting to ache from smiling so hard. I'm giddy with excitement. "Another surprise? James, you're too good to me. It is enough just being here with you. I don't need anything else but you naked and on top of me."

His eyes glow with need. I wiggle my hips against his, along with a few brow raises, and his smile stays until his eyes fall to my mouth.

"It's never enough when it comes to you. Don't you realize that by now?"

James turns serious, squinting as he studies me.

"Do you think there are other couples out there who are as happy as we are?"

"I'd like to think there are, otherwise, that's a sad life to lead. I have to grab something really quick. Don't move."

I agree with him, then I loosen my arms and take a step back. He returns a few seconds later and steps behind me, placing a satin ribbon over my eyes. Tingles work down my arms in anticipation. The last time we were here he'd used one of his work ties to pin my wrists together and played my body like a violin.

"Is it too tight?"

"No."

I feel James step in front of me and take my hands into his. Lifting them to his mouth, he presses a kiss to the top of both.

"I didn't plan this part ahead, so I'm going to improvise and carry you. I don't want you to trip up the stairs since you can't see."

James scoops me up as if I'm light as a feather and holds me to his chest. We make it up five steps when he says, "Did you gain weight?"

My lips purse together. I know he's playing around. James has been trying to thicken me up more. With my weight gain over the years, he's turned into such an ass man and can't get enough. My ass is a magnet for his hand now the way his tongue is a magnet to my pussy.

Placing my hand on his chest, I notice he must have removed his tie and unbuttoned his shirt halfway before blindfolding me. I skim my hand over his bare chest until I feel his nipple under my fingers. My thumb circles around it before I pull it between two fingers and pause. I fight a giggle.

James stops walking. I think we're midway up the stairs. "Aubrey," he warns. "You know what that does to me."

"It goes straight to your dick?"

This time I can't help but laugh. Sometimes I revert to a seventeen-year-old. I start twisting slowly and feel the tips of his fingers dig into my body.

I continue, and since I can't see him, all I feel is a cool breeze skate across my neck before his teeth latch onto the top of my breast just above my dress. I hiss in a breath.

"I can play dirty too, sweetheart," he says with my skin between his teeth.

I give him one good crank and let go, but he's just as quick and sinks his teeth deeper. I flinch then gasp before letting out a laugh.

James pulls back and says, "That's going to leave a mark."

We finish making our way upstairs. I remember this place well and know he's taking us into the master bedroom. The door creaks as he opens it and the scent of burning wood blankets me. Warmth fills the air. I sigh dreamily at the sound of the crackling fire behind us.

James lets go of my legs and helps me stand.

"Don't move," he warns.

"What do you have up your sleeve?"

James reaches around me to untie the sash. My eyes adjust to the low lighting. I glance around and realize I'm standing near a thick pile of blood-red and hunter-green blankets on the floor. There's a woven basket holding two glasses, champagne, and some snacks. Familiarity fills me.

"James," I whisper. My gaze bounces around the space, taking it all in at once. "What did you do?"

Chapter 23

From the blankets to the fire to the bottle of cognac, James has recreated one of the evenings we spent with our naked bodies flushed together in ecstasy. The weather had been brutal that night, dropping to a mere three degrees, but that didn't faze us as our passion built toward the most glorious climax. I consider it a favorite and one of our most romantic nights.

James steps closer to me. There's something in his hand I briefly take note of before he places one hand on my hip and looks into my eyes. I'm all he sees and that makes me hotter than the fire behind me.

"I never knew I could love someone the way I do you. You're it for me, Aubrey. I love you more than life itself and will do anything to see you happy. I'll make it my mission to show you how much you mean to me. I met Valentina first, but I fell in love with Aubrey, and I'm going to love them both more than anyone else could."

My eyes are round and huge, and my lips are slightly parted. James places one foot behind him and steps back, bending his knee. My pulse skyrockets, my breathing is labored. Chills pepper my arms.

I thought ...

Oh, God.

My heart is pounding against my ribs.

I can't think straight, and I'm a bit in shock.

I didn't think he was going to ask me again. I really thought I had lost my chance.

Tears fill my eyes instantly, and I flatten my lips tightly

together.

James lowers to one knee and presents a black velvet box to me. I meet his gaze and look at him, the man who will become my husband one day. The other times James had asked me to marry him, there'd been no ring. I suspected he had one with him, but when I rejected the notion of marriage, I'd just assumed he didn't take it out.

He also never got down on one knee until now.

He lifts the top up and I draw in a loud breath. I cup my mouth. Nestled inside the cushy pillow is a large diamond engagement ring. It looks nearly flawless as it dazzles against the glow of the fire. There's a row of thin diamonds encrusted around the outer edge hugging what has to be at least four carats. I stare at the way the diamond sparkles against the metal. He didn't go for platinum. He didn't go for gold. He went for rose gold, and I know without a shadow of a doubt it's because I wear my mom's necklace and the one Grammy got me all the time. They're both rose gold. James knows how much they mean to me. He also didn't go for a traditional princess-cut diamond. He went for the pear-shaped cut, the least common engagement ring.

We most definitely aren't like everyone else.

"Please, sweetheart, put me out of my fucking misery and just say yes already. Say yes to forever with me."

Tears are streaming down my cheeks. I can barely focus over the pounding of my sprinting heart to formulate words. The only thing I can do is nod and give him my shaking left hand as my answer. I'm standing in the cabin where we found love in the most unusual way. And now, four years later, James is on one knee asking me to be his wife.

I think my response shocks him. His wide eyes stare at me with hope, and his beautiful lips that worship me like a queen part with disbelief.

"You're ... you're," he stammers. I can't recall a time when

James faltered his words.

I nod my head and smile at him. "I was a fool to say no the other times you asked me."

He stares at me with profound awe. He's not even blinking. I giggle at him, then wiggle my fingers.

"I finally say yes, and now you're going to make me wait?"

James falls to the side and catches himself with his hand. He's sitting back on one foot and staring up at me with his baby blues. His hand is shaking as he runs it through his hair. It's a little longer than usual, but I like it on him. The way he's acting is adorable. I gather my dress and attempt to bend down so I'm eye level with him, but James raises his palm for me to stop and gets back up on one knee.

"I feel like I'm going to have a heart attack. You're really saying yes? Don't play with me, Aubrey. I'm old."

A laugh rumbles in my chest. My lashes fall to a half-moon as happiness settles around us.

"Yes. I'm saying yes, James."

I find it endearing how stunned he is. He blinks rapidly and looks between the jewelry box and me, then attempts to take the ring out. He plucks the ring from the box and it almost slips from his fingers. A breath hitches in my throat as he fumbles to catch it. He's nervous. I never thought I'd see the day. I fight the grin tickling my lips.

"Goddamn nerves."

He takes my left hand in his, and just as he's about to slide the delicate ring over my finger, I pull my hand away.

"Wait!"

James snaps his gaze up to mine and pales. His skin almost matches the gray hair on his head. I realize I need to make this quick. He's probably thinking the worst right now.

"You have to promise to never divorce me. Under no circumstances are you allowed to even utter those words, James

Riviera. And don't even think you can use your special lawyer skills and say it in ten different ways, because it won't work on me. If we get married, this is it. You're with me for life." Emotion fills my throat. My heart flutters. I allow the panic in my voice to be present. This is real. "I'm not playing. Can we include it as a clause in our vows or something when we get married?"

James shakes his head then drops his attention back to my hand and the ring he's holding. Not letting another second pass him by, he pushes the ring forward and slides the stone where it belongs. The thing is larger than my knuckle.

A little sob escapes me. I can't believe I'm going to marry the love of my life.

I look at our hands. James is looking too. I belong to him, and he belongs to me. He raises the top of my hand to his lips and presses a gentle kiss. James stands, looking into my eyes, my left hand still in his.

"The only reason I would ever divorce you is if that ring ever comes off your finger."

I can't stop the blush that sweeps over my cheeks.

"Then I guess we have a deal."

A massive smile lights up my face. Excitement I didn't even know was possible to experience explodes like fireworks inside of me. I'm suddenly excited that I'm going to be his wife one day.

"You know, that ring is basically a contract between us," James says matter-of-factly.

My cheeks are burning from smiling so hard. He finally throws me a beaming smile, and it's a good one. James likes contracts. Once they're signed, there's very little that can be done to reverse them, he says.

"Can I just start calling you hubby now?"

His mouth flickers with humor. "Two months ago, you rejected the idea. Now you want to start calling me husband early?"

I give him a shrug. "Why not?"

James barks out a laugh. "I'm going to make you the happiest woman on earth, sweetheart."

"You already do."

I close the distance between us. James cups my cheek softly. He leans in and captures my lips with his. I open for him and allow his tongue to slide against mine. My eyes close and I press my chest to his, kissing him back with the same slow intensity he's kissing me with.

There's no rush to this kiss.

We kiss like we're making sweet love to each other.

Chapter 24

My arms loosen from around James's neck. Flattening my palms, I glide them down over his chest and catch the sparkle of my engagement ring.

"I know you keep saying you're going to make me the happiest woman on earth, but I need you to know I intend to do the same for you. Marriage was never a goal of mine, but now that I'm going to marry you, it scares me because of the love I already have for you, and how much more I want to give you."

"You know what would make me really happy?"

"What's that, handsome?"

"You on your back naked with nothing but that ring on your finger, and me deep inside of you. Aubrey, I gotta get in you."

I want that too.

"In front of the fire?"

"That's where I'm going to have you first as my fiancé." He pauses for a second. "I was thinking when we do get married, we keep it small and intimate. Just a thought."

I love that he's already daydreamed about our wedding.

"I want what you want. But can we please make love first? I'm dying here, baby."

"If I didn't love the way this dress looked on your body, I would've ripped it off you already." His fingers grasp the zipper and start a slow descent down my spine.

James and his dresses. I smile to myself knowing he's about to see my new tattoo.

"You love every dress I wear."

"Because you look fucking incredible every time." He lets out a breath. "I can't wait to call you mine forever," he says, then kisses me again.

I've been his since day one.

The zipper reaches the bottom, and my dress falls in a whoosh at my feet, followed by my slip. He growls and I feel it in his chest. I went without panties or a bra, and he's pleased. James's palm skims my bare body, creating a trail of warmth but stops when he reaches the Saniderm bandage that was placed over my tattoo. He pulls back and turns my body to inspect what he touched.

Startling blue eyes land on the delicate ribbon of feathers that decorate the length of my ribs and come up under my arm to cup around my breast. They were detailed with an extra fine needle like his tattoos. I almost showed James the moment I got home but I wanted it to be a surprise. Little did I know he had his own surprise planned too.

James angles my body to read the words entwined with the feathers: *I love every moment with you.*

"I got it for you," I whisper.

James is quiet. The pad of his index finger carefully moves over the letters I picked out with him in mind.

"When did you do this?"

"Remember when I said I had a gynecologist appointment today?" His eyes lift to mine and he nods. "I lied." His brows raise. "I wanted it to be a surprise for you. I hope you're not upset with me."

James stands to his full height and my heart beats a little faster. His penetrating gaze weakens every nerve in my body and the aura surrounding him gives me chills. With his shoulders pulled back and his chest slightly pronounced, he slips a hand around the small of my back and yanks me to him. His erection strains against my leg.

"Upset? No. I'm fucking turned on. You did that for me?"

he asks, and I nod. "Does it hurt? Your skin is raised around the outline. You should probably take the plastic off soon."

"It's tender right now. I went to your girl. She said it's going to feel like third-degree burns for the next few days."

"Sweetheart," he says, his hand moving toward the back of my neck, "I didn't think it was possible for you to be any sexier, but that just put me over the edge." He swallows thickly and I see his Adam's apple bob. "I fucking love it. I want to take a closer look, but right now I need to be inside you." His fingers thread through my hair now. His voice is darker, creating a tendril of desire.

James captures my lips with his and plunges his tongue into my mouth. There's a bite to his kiss, a bit of aggression that makes me melt inside. My hands move frantically over his chest. It doesn't take long for me to undo the rest of his buttons and remove his shirt, then I'm unbuckling his belt and pulling down his zipper. Suit pants and boxers fall near my dress, then my hand wraps around his erection. His kiss deepens as my fingers move over his cock. He's ridiculously hard and my need only intensifies for him.

My fingers glide softly over the crown of his head. James knows I love to feel how swollen and thick he gets. It's fucking sexy to know his dick stands tall and hard because of my touch. There's something about making him feel good that rocks me. I want to take him in my mouth and send him past the clouds and make him go out of his mind.

I purr into his mouth and feel my heartbeat quicken. Needy fingers thread my loose curls as James angles his kiss deeper over mine. His need increases and within seconds, he scoops me up into his arms and takes a few steps to the makeshift bed he had made up in front of the fire.

James cradles me gently over the flannel blankets then shifts his body before mine. He's careful not to touch my tattoo. My legs spread wide for him and I raise my arms above my head. My large breasts lift, and my rosy pink nipples harden from the way he's looking at me. I want him to devour me.

Grabbing my knees, James glides his palms over my smooth inner thighs to the crease near my hips. My hips undulate in a sensual flow. I'm not shy in the least and want him to look. His thumbs pull back my pussy lips as he slowly opens me. I watch as his teeth bite into his bottom lip and his eyes lower to slits. Between the pressure building inside of me and the heat of the moment, I don't know how he's able to hold off. I want to jump on top of him and ride him into next week with him pulling my hair to the finish line.

Not wanting to wait another minute, I reach for him.

Cupping his palm to his mouth, James spits in his hand then rubs it over the tip of his shaft. My lips part and my knees fall wider at the simple act that makes my pulse skyrocket. He strokes himself a few times, then leans over and positions himself at my entrance.

Looking into my eyes, James places the tip between my swollen folds then closes the distance with his mouth and slides in until he can't get any deeper, kissing me at the same time.

Neither of us are in control tonight.

Tonight, we're one.

Tonight, we allow the passion and love we have for each other to take the reins.

Our groans echo around the crackling fire. We both hold still, feeling the click between us lock in place. Even our kiss is clutched still.

I feel it.

James feels it.

Trembling above me, James separates his lips from mine and looks down at me. He laces his fingers with my left hand and presses his palm to mine.

"You're it for me, sweetheart. I hope you know that."

The happiness in my eyes matches the contentment on my

lips. "You just put a huge rock on my finger. I better be."

"We're going to have a great life together."

"We already do."

I'm a firm believer in you get what you give. Even after the scandalous life I've lived, I have no qualms about my past, and he doesn't either. Finding a partner who accepts their flaws and sins and lets them loose is what causes the relationship to flourish. In the end, we're all after the same thing—we want someone to want us the way we are. James and I love each other just the way we are.

I lock my ankles around his back and beam up at him. The sexy grin that tugs at the corner of his lips sends my heart into overdrive.

Pulling his hips back slightly, James's kiss is demanding as he surges back inside me. Warmth explodes through my blood and I sigh. My skin is tingling from my neck to the tips of my toes in sheer pleasure. We break apart and both moan in unison, holding on to each other for a second longer so we can catch our breaths. My trembling limbs are tangled with James's, and the hammering against my chest beats into his. The masculine scent that oozes off him drives a dark need through me. We're lost to each other for the better, and there's no place else I'd rather be but here with him wrapped in my arms.

My lips suction around the skin just below his beard and I tug it into my mouth. James's cock twitches inside my pussy in satisfaction. He hits just the right angle and I spasm around him. My tongue twirls over his pulse before my teeth gently scrape down his throat.

James's sexy groan gets louder the harder I pull on his neck. I find it incredibly attractive. "Leave a mark. I want you to," he says, his voice strangled with ecstasy.

Chills dance over my arms at the thought. I kind of want to leave a mark on his cock with my mouth, but that will have to wait.

There's no more talking now. Not from the grunt that just

reverberated from his chest into mine. My thighs tighten around his waist as I thread my fingers through his soft hair. James's hips rear back, and I lift mine for him to plunge back in deeper. I gasp as he slams into my pussy. We both moan this time. I tug on his hair and lift one leg higher up his back. He reaches down to grab my ass cheeks so his drive is richer for us. His fingers dig into my skin, causing a delicate heat to border the place he's gripping me.

"Oh, James," I say breathlessly. The feel of my clit being slapped while he's pummeling into me carries me to a higher level. "I'm close, baby."

My legs fall open and James takes that as his cue to pick up his pace. This is a man who knows what he wants and how to give to get it. This kind of passion brewing between us is a once-in-a-lifetime type of passion that I'll hold onto forever.

Chapter 25

Heart racing, my skin is damp from how hard my pulse is thumping. I'm on the verge of orgasming, but I want James to come with me at the same time. My back bows and my nipples press into his chest. A slow purr slips from my lips.

James dives toward my lips but teases me by hovering just centimeters away. "Ready to fly with me?"

My eyes shift back and forth between his. Be still my heart. "Always."

"Then kiss me."

I do without hesitation.

With my left hand still joined with his, the need is closer and my breathing is growing deeper. James pumps his hips into mine and my body shudders in response. I moan into his mouth and feel the orgasm crawl up my legs. We're so close to the edge I can hardly take it. James shifts his legs so one knee is higher, allowing him to drive in deeper, then he places his large palm halfway over my throat as he cups my jaw. His lovemaking is raw, his kiss is unforgiving. James makes love to my mouth the way he does to my body, giving me everything he has to offer so I know I'm his in every conceivable way.

My mind is solely focused on the way my pussy feels suctioned around his cock, the way he's applying pressure to my clit. It's so incredible that it makes me wild for him. Our chests rise and fall into the other's, we're both struggling to hold on. With another three plunges, our kiss becomes a desperate pant. Euphoria layers over us until we're flying together into the most beautiful sunset.

Fingers squeezed together, his hips undulate nice and slow with a good, hard drive. Our hands stay joined the entire time as James spills into me. He hums under his breath. I love making my man feel good.

"James." I pant. "How do you manage to make love better every time?"

He chuckles, and when he does, semen slips from my tender pussy. I let out a long sigh.

His nose grazes mine. "Takes two, sweetheart. You make me want to beat the last time just based on the way you fall apart in my arms."

My eyes are heavy as I stare up at him when the idea I had earlier pops into my head. "It's my turn, lover," I say.

How to make a man fall to his knees? Give him the best blowie of his life.

I manage to roll him onto his back and pull him out of me. There's a soft pop between us, and then his cum is dripping out of me onto the blanket.

"What are you doing, Aubrey?" he asks, peering at me on propped elbows.

"I'm going to make you fall apart now."

His head falls back between his shoulders and he lets out a guttural moan as I lick myself off him so I only taste him. The veins spinning toward his neck are jutting in strain.

I palm his heavy balls and run my fingers through our combined release dripping down his sack, then I move up toward his shaft to grasp his thickness. James likes a tight fist and that's exactly what I give him. I hollow out my cheeks and pull him as hard and as deep as I can to the back of my throat. His knees come up, but I quickly shove them down. One time he almost put me in a headlock with his damn thighs while I was sucking him off.

My tongue smooths over each rigid crease and the thick fold around the tip of his cock, then traces a straining vein as I lick him clean. I don't prefer to taste myself, but I find it highly erotic when I do it for James.

I drag my teeth gently up his shaft and wrap my tongue around the width. He thrusts into the warmth of my mouth like he can't hold on any longer and releases a deep moan.

"That fucking mouth of yours," he says through gritted teeth, which only encourages me to suck him harder.

Eyes closed, he's drowning in pleasure. I suddenly feel deprived of him. There's an urge clinging to me to climb up his beautiful body and ride him. I attempt to rub my thighs together to apply any ounce of pressure I can to my aching clit. My growing desire makes me work his cock like it's my job.

"Aubrey, sweetheart, give me that pussy."

Ignoring James, I focus on the tip and slurp the crown loudly knowing he likes to hear me suck. James rewards me with a groan deep in his lungs. He threads his fingers through my hair and gives me a good tug until my mouth pops off him and he's dripping down my chin.

"Climb over here and give me that pussy, now."

Shaking my head, I know I only have so much time left before he overpowers me. I begin sucking the tip like I'm sucking down a thick, frozen milkshake, working his cock with my tongue to pull him to the top.

I glance up and see his head thrown back. James is a sight to see at this angle with his hands fisting the blankets beneath him. I taste his pleasure and know he's close. I drink him deeper and feel his erection twitch in my hand.

"Oh, fuck ... Aubrey ... stop it ... oh, oh, oh."

He's about to come any second. I open my mouth and lower myself, taking all of him in like I'm going to drink him dry. I swallow, creating a tighter space. Just as he's about to reach his pinnacle of bliss, James changes it up before I can stop him and turns, placing my body parallel to his.

I let out a soft sigh as he latches onto my pussy with his mouth, and I feel myself leak on his face. Unfazed, James rubs his beard on my sensitive skin while holding my hips firmly in his hands like he's on a mission. He slaps my ass then places his lips on my pussy like he's sucking the juice of a peach. I whimper, digging my nails into his leg trying to fight my orgasm. My toes curl in ecstasy as his tongue vibrates over my clit.

"You're so fucking hot from his angle," he says more to himself.

My inner thighs are shaking and I'm on the verge of release. My hips move on their own while I drink him down faster, greedier, to the point that I know he's going to combust any second.

And that's exactly what he does.

James pulls up his knee and drives his heel into the floor. A sexy-as-hell growl erupts from his lungs as he comes, shooting into my mouth with zero shame. I close my eyes and focus on the way he's torturing me. My hips rear back while his lips seal a tight suction. He holds me in place and that only makes my skin tingle more when stars explode inside of me. I climax into his mouth as pleasure takes over both of us.

My body rolls to the side and my knee pulls up, flopping open. Opening my eyes, I'm staring up at the rustic wood beam ceiling in a hazy daze trying to catch my breath.

"You're so pink right now," James says. "It's raw." His finger reaches out to softly touch the inside of my folds. "Does this hurt?"

"No. It feels like a feather is touching me." I swallow, my mouth parched.

"What about now?" he asks, with two fingers deep in my pussy. I clench around him and shake my head, unable to form words.

I'm too weak to move but James has other plans. He plays with my sex, tracing the lines and inside my folds with his finger. I love that he's so comfortable with my body.

I watch his eyes study the act like he's lost to what he's doing. His gaze travels lower when the evidence of his pleasure mixed with mine slides down my ass. James sits up and maneuvers himself that so his cheek is resting on my thigh and he kisses my tender clit. This man needs no lessons in how to please a woman.

"James, I can't. I need a second."

"I'll be gentle. Just lay there and let me play with you."

Who am I to argue with that?

There's no rush to James's kiss. He takes his time, lapping my sex with soft, gentle caresses. I hardly move when the orgasm appears like a burst of energy blowing into me. My legs attempt to scissor his body, little sighs push past my lips. He keeps the slow and steady pace the entire time while holding my legs in place so I have to take what he's giving me. Having to remain still while a torment of heat and emotion tears through me always proves to be the biggest challenge of the day.

Chapter 26

I gaze longingly out the French doors. Little flurries of snow fall before my eyes roll shut and another intense orgasm blows through me. A sexy, long moan pushes past my lips. The sound of James sipping down my pleasure causes a tremble in my bones. I lift my hips to his face, angling them so the orgasm hits harder.

Rising to his knees, James presses kisses up my belly, over my nipples, then to my mouth. He grins above me, his smile grows larger.

"Hey, beautiful," James says, then sits to the side and pulls me with him so we're leaning back on the couch in front of the fire.

A tender kiss is pressed to the top of my head. I'm nestled in the security of his arms, feeling the intimacy between us go from two heartbeats to one.

I lift my left hand and stare in awe at my engagement ring. Round diamonds bonded together make the band that holds the flawless stone at the center. I flutter my fingers through the air, watching the amber flames from the fire dance over the teardrop diamond. It's gorgeous. James picked out a stunning ring.

"Thank you for not giving up on me," I say, grateful. "I was scared I lost my chance to be your wife."

"I had no plans of giving up." James pauses, then says, "We're good together, Aubrey."

"We are, aren't we."

Picking up my head, I gaze at him with loving eyes. My palm skims up his stomach toward his chest. He grips four fingers in his hand and holds them over his heart. We stay like this, relaxing in front of the fire while the snow falls heavier outside. One thing I love about this cabin is that there are no curtains or blinds in our second-story room, just floor-to-ceiling glass windows that give way to a snowy morning or a dark forest at night. We're sitting on ten acres of private land in the mountains and surrounded by wildlife.

"I can stay like this forever," I say, my words thick with contentment.

"Same, sweetheart."

A little more time passes before we stand. I'm dying to tell Natalie about the engagement and decide to FaceTime her to witness her reaction.

"Where are the suitcases?"

James glances at me, contemplating while he uncorks the champagne. My lips twitch. He rarely strays from cognac.

"Wait. Did you know I would say yes and that's why you have bubbly here? So we could celebrate getting engaged?"

"Today is your day, and I wanted to celebrate with you the best way I could. Did I hope you'd say yes when I proposed? Hell yeah. The way I see it, the engagement is just a bonus."

A chuckle rolls off my lips. It takes effort to prove one truly loves someone more than just words. Don't tell me you love me. Show me you love me. And he does. Every second of the day he shows me. I'm so lucky to call him my fiancé.

"Check the closet." He nods with his chin.

Stepping into the walk-in closet, I see our black luggage in the corner and go to retrieve them. I grab both in case James wants to put pants on, only to frown when they're in my hands. I glance down. One of the suitcases feels awfully light. I shake my head. Typical James. He usually under packs, then has to buy clothes. I hope he at least packed a pair of flannel sweats to wear. He looks mighty fine in them.

With two flutes between his fingers, James comes to stand

near me. I place his down and turn around, holding my bag.

"That's mine," he says.

I pause.

"The heavy one? I assumed it was mine and that Natalie just packed everything under the kitchen sink for me."

"Look closer."

My gaze roams over the luggage. I cup my mouth and stifle a laugh behind my palm. There's a keychain that says "My Daddy is #1" hanging from the bottom where the two zippers meet. I got it for James when we were in Barcelona at a little hole-in-the-wall after one of the natives kept referring to him as Papá, thinking he was my father. I thought it was hysterical that he loved it and put it on his suitcase.

I glance over my shoulder at James, shaking my head. "Why do you put up with me again?"

His eyes glitter with amusement. "I could count all the ways I love thee, but I fear it would take centuries to complete."

"You're a riot, James."

I reach for the other suitcase and kneel on the floor to unzip it, then throw the top back. A whoosh of air blows past my lips as the contents appear in front of me.

One content, actually.

Shaking my head, I reach for the yellow Post-it note stuck in the center with Natalie's handwriting.

You're welcome.

I giggle while tapping the back of the sticky part with my index finger. "She's such an asshole. Why am I not surprised?"

I stand up and hand James the note. He squints, then his nostrils flare and I watch as an amused look moves across his face.

"I can't believe she did that."

"Did she know you were going to propose?"

"No." He huffs out a laugh still looking at the note. He drops his arm and raises his eyes to mine. "I didn't trust her not to tell you. She did say that if you didn't come back with a ring on your finger to consider my brownstone torched. She had a crazed look in her eyes. I wouldn't put it past her. Women are mental."

I raise a brow. "And yet you just put a ring on one of them."

The corners of James's lips curl into the cutest, most heart-melting smile I've ever seen on a man. He drags an arm around my neck and leans over to give me a bear hug.

"The best one," he says, and a cheesy smile lights up my face.

"I need a shirt to wear," I say, pulling back.

James looks up and down the length of my naked body. "I think you look fine just the way you are."

"I can't call Natalie without a shirt on." I hold up my left hand. "And I want to tell her we're engaged." I faux pout.

James fluffs my hair. I realize he hasn't stopped smiling at me since I said yes. I wish I would've said yes sooner.

I wish ... I decide right then and there to let go of my past decisions. I got the man. Why harp on the past when I can focus on the future?

James hands me one of his shirts. "Technically, you can since she didn't pack you any clothes."

"How about I take it off the moment I hang up with her?"

"Deal."

Once my breasts are covered and James has a pair of shorts on, he tends to my tattoo with soap and water, then applies lotion. There's a little tightness and some burning, but he assures me it won't last more than a couple of days. He refills our flutes with champagne while I fix up our makeshift bed in front of the fire. It's toasty and picture-perfect to cozy up next to my fiancé for the rest of the night.

My fiancé.

"James." He places the bottle back in the ice bin then looks at me. "You're my fiancé." James studies me with a peculiar look in his eyes, and a blush fills my cheeks. I don't know why I say it, it's not like he obviously doesn't know. I guess I'm just giddy as hell that I blurt it out.

"And you're mine."

"We're getting married," I state the obvious like a fool. James seems more amused than anything.

"And I can't fucking wait," he says.

Be still my heart.

James walks over and takes a seat next to me, then hands me a glass. He places the blanket over us and I pull up my knees and lean into his side. He wraps an arm around my shoulders. I can hear the bubbles fizzing as we tilt them toward each other to celebrate.

"To us."

Simple. I love it.

"To us," I repeat.

James and I toast, then we take sips.

"I can't believe we're getting married," I say excitedly.

"I think you're in shock."

I chuckle and James smiles. "I think you're right." James gives me a knowing look. "So, when are we getting married?"

This time he laughs. "That's up to you and the kind of wedding we're going to have."

My eyes light up at the thought of our wedding. The gowns I get to try on ... My lips curve into a smile. It's going to be so much fun dress shopping with Natalie.

I pucker my lips and think about a date. I say the first one off the top of my head. "I say we get married February 25th."

James's brows shoot up and he seems a bit overwhelmed now. "That soon?"

My brows furrow. I feel a pang in my heart over his response. "Now it's too soon?"

"No, it's whenever you want, sweetheart," he rushes to say. "I just didn't expect it, that's all. You said no every time. Want to elope tomorrow in Vegas? We can do that. It's whatever you want, whenever you want. Just tell me where to be. All I'm asking is to see you in a wedding dress."

The tension in my neck loosens. He's right. My eyes soften and I smile up at James. He returns the gesture and kisses my forehead.

"I'm really happy," I tell him softly, but it sounds like I'm talking to myself.

"I am too."

My cheek presses into his chest. Drawing in a breath, the burning fire blends seductively with the subtle scent of James's cologne. I exhale. The bergamot and lavender create a cozy softness around my heart. I'm right where I'm supposed to be.

"You smell like cognac and Cubans," I tell him.

James studies me with a deep fondness in his eyes that moves me to snuggle closer to him. I gave my heart to a man thirty-plus years my senior, and it was the best decision I ever made. We went through a devastating heartbreak and nearly lost each other forever. We almost didn't make it here. Our love tested my friendship with Natalie. Through it all, I still wouldn't change a thing if it would mean changing this moment right now.

Age is just a number, and love truly does conquer all.

"I guess becoming a ritzy prostitute has its benefits after all."

Chapter 27

I hold the phone in front of my face waiting for Natalie to answer.

"What time is it in Italy?" I ask James.

"I think we're about six hours behind. So, it's probably early in the morning."

I glance at the time and my shoulders drop. "Natalie isn't a morning person. Damn. I really wanted—"

She picks up.

"Aubrey," she says excitedly, drawing out my name like she's loving life.

Before I can say anything, I flash my left hand in excitement with a huge, cheesy ass grin on my face. I wiggle my fingers and she squints her eyes. Her jaw slowly drops as she leans in to get a better look. Natalie's sitting against a headboard with a sheet covering her chest, her hair a wild mess, and there's black coal liner smudged under her eyes. Looks like someone had a fun night.

She pops up when she realizes what she's looking at and screams her excitement. "Ohmigod! Fucking finally, Ram Jam!"

Laughter spills from my lips. "I know, right?"

Natalie tries to get a closer look and I hold my fingers still. I can see the ring glistening on the screen, but the camera doesn't do it justice.

"Wait until you see it in person. It's stunning."

"A teardrop stone? Oh, Daddy did good," she says, staring at the rock.

"Who are you calling *Zaddy*?"

My brows furrow at the unexpected voice in the background

and I bust out laughing, covering my mouth. "Who the hell is that? And did he just say zaddy? Does he know what that means?"

I'm dying inside. A zaddy is a hot-as-sin older man with swag and sex appeal. James to a T.

She rolls her eyes playfully and she's blushing hard. Natalie never blushes. "Yeah, that's the lemon guy. His accent fucked up that word."

"I'm the lemon guy?" I hear.

"Who's the lemon guy?" James asks, chiming in.

James leans in to view the screen and waves to Natalie the same time the lemon guy leans in too. I see the space between his eyes crease. Natalie and I watch as they both stare at each other trying to figure out who's who. It's quite comical. We're all quiet for a moment until Natalie speaks.

"Luca. He's the flavor of the week," Natalie says, her lips twitching. "Lemon."

"I hope you're using protection, Natalie," James says, his voice a little firm. Spoken like a true, concerned father. If they weren't so open with each other, I'd think this is weird, but it's not.

"Who is that?" Luca asks.

Luca has a full beard and what looks like hazel eyes, which surprises me. Natalie hates beards, says they're unsanitary. She once told me she'd rather lick the subway floor than kiss a man with a beard. Guess she changed her mind.

"Hey, Dad," Natalie says.

I bite back a laugh. She's fighting the laughter herself. I can only imagine how odd this looks. I'm FaceTiming my best friend with her shirtless dad next to me. We've all clearly had sex judging by our lack of clothes and the relaxed flush on our cheeks. Natalie's got a rat's nest on her head while my mane is just everywhere. I'm going to have to call her later when she's alone to get the details on her date and what happened.

"That's your father?" the lemon guy asks, perplexed.

"Yeah, and my best friend."

A pregnant pause, Luca turns to look at Natalie. He's confused as he looks at her flawless skin like he's trying to figure out what one plus one is.

"They're together?" he asks, and she nods. "Engaged?" She nods again. This time Luca has a longer pause, then says, "We don't do that sort of thing in my country."

Natalie gives him a bland stare. "You just got done telling me your inbreeder cousins got married in the hills of Italy."

"What is an inbreeder?" he asks, and I laugh. It sounds much funnier coming from him.

"Country folk who fuck their cousins," Natalie says, dead serious too. Luca almost looks insulted, but something tells me he's actually not.

"We are not cousin fuckers, Natalia." I love that he calls her name in his native tongue. It sounds sexy coming from him.

"To a New Yorker, you are. Cousins who marry are inbreeders."

Luca gives her a serious look. "That's because New Yorkers are crazy. They're not normal people."

"Oh, and you've been to New York?"

"Many times, actually."

"For what?"

"Natalie, did you know anything about this man before you got into bed with him?" James asks.

She ignores James and continues with Luca. They talk like they've been married for twenty years, and honestly, I'm loving every second of it. Not many guys can go toe-to-toe with Natalie.

"You told me you're one hundred percent Italian."

He sits up a little taller and his eyes lower. "I am."

"That's not possible, unless you're keeping it in the family."

A boisterous laugh expels from James. "Don't torture the man, Natalie."

"Poor lemon guy doesn't know what he got himself into,"

I add as James stands up and gestures that he's going to use the restroom. I nod and watch my fiancé walk away, taking in the powerful muscles in his shoulders that paint a path to a sexy pair of dimples right above his butt.

"Oh, I know exactly what I got myself into," Luca says, and I turn back as he tilts his head and looks at the screen with a proud smirk on his face. "I've gotten myself into her a lot already."

I gasp and Natalie looks at Luca like she's actually bashful for the first time in her life. He drags an arm around her waist and pulls her to him. A sweet smile curls her lips. She doesn't even fight him. She's rarely the type to ever blush from a man, and she totally did with Luca. I feel a little spark in my chest for them. Natalie's got her hands full with this one. I hope she goes on another date with him.

"Shut the fuck up, Luca," she says, but is completely playful, and he sees that.

"That mouth." He shakes his head. "My mother does not like women who curse."

"Since I don't plan to ever meet your mother, I don't really give a shit."

"We're getting married," Luca states. I'm pretty sure they're in their own world right now.

Red heat flames Natalie's cheeks. I'm dying over this.

"The fuck we are. I just met you ten minutes ago."

"And nine minutes ago is when I realized you are to be my wife."

Natalie turns to look at me with a straight face. "I'm gonna stick an ice pick in his fucking eye."

I'm trying to hold back my laughter, but it's impossible. Seeing Natalie clearly smitten over this guy is what makes this moment so memorable. A loud giggle erupts from me when I think about what she'd said over the phone in the early evening. She had told me she thought it was dangerous to drink with him. Now I see why.

"Make sure to fuck James every day when he wakes up. Happy wife, happy life," Natalie says with a cheesy grin.

"I will be sure to remember that too," Luca chimes in, extremely proud. It's hard for me not to get a rise out of these two. "Why do you call your father by his name?"

Natalie grinds her teeth together and exhales through her nose. That look makes me think back to when I used to nanny the little twin monsters and they'd ask for water for the hundredth time after they were tucked in for the night. Twenty minutes later they peed the bed.

"I can't call him daddy when he's marrying my best friend," she states.

Without looking, she spreads her fingers and palms his face, then shoves him down to the bed while holding the phone. He goes down in one swift motion. Natalie is entirely too happy with herself, until Luca snakes a surprise arm around her and tugs her down too. She goes down and the phone flops to the bed. All I see are white sheets now. Natalie giggles like she's being tickled as Luca says, "Say goodnight, Natalia."

"Goodnight, Natalia," she repeats purposely. Natalie giggles. The smile in her words doesn't go unnoticed.

"Talk to you later," I say.

"Goodnight, James and bestie!"

"That's stepmama to you."

We hang up and I place the phone on the floor.

James steps out of the bathroom. "Should I be worried?"

"Nope. Trust me when I say she can handle this. She's going to take lemon guy to school."

He's contemplative. "Did she really just meet the guy only ten minutes ago?"

"Aw ... baby."

James runs a hand through his hair. We both saw the flirtatious way Luca and Natalie were with each other. I know he felt how comfortable they were the way I did, but he's still her father.

"I just want to make sure she's okay. She's in another country."

I turn to look at him. I want to add that she didn't meet him ten minutes ago, but earlier in the day on the beach, but I realize it wouldn't help the situation.

"I bet she brings him to the wedding," I say, hoping to smooth his feathers.

"You're that sure she's okay?"

I nod. "Yes."

James tugs me until I'm sitting between his legs with my back pressed against his chest. His arms are around my stomach and his cheek is pressed to the side of mine.

"You girls are my world. If anything happens to either of you, I don't know what I'd do with myself. If you're confident she's okay, then I trust you."

I lace my fingers with his, then fold our arms under my chest and cuddle up into his shoulder. "I am."

We're quiet, watching the fire together and feeling at home. Neither one of us speaks for a bit, and I think it's because both of us are recounting the night. A soft smile stays on my face. I feel like I'm floating on cloud nine. This is what love is and why people want to marry, I realize. I get it now. I'm not naïve to think it'll always be diamonds and cognac, but there isn't one other person in the world who I'd want to spend quiet nights with, in the middle of nowhere, just watching a fire as time passes by.

"I'm going to love you more than anyone, James."

Epilogue - James

I'm one lucky son of a bitch.

My hands are crossed in front of me and my tux feels like I'm wearing an extra layer of skin. There's a harp playing an Ed Sheeran song gently in the background, but it does nothing to lower my blood pressure, let alone soothe me. All I can hear is my heart pounding against my chest and feel the nervous bounce in my heels as I wait for Aubrey to walk down the aisle. If she doesn't hurry up, I'm going to start sweating any second.

I shoot a fleeting glance at my daughter, who's wearing a massive smile and dreamy eyes. There isn't a day that goes by that I'm not grateful for Natalie's blessing. Those two years I was separated from the love of my life were hell on earth for me. Countless times I found myself looking for her everywhere I went, trying to catch a glimpse of her. I wanted to go to her and tell her to drop the shenanigans and be with me, but I respected my daughter too much for that. Natalie was devasted for months, and I had to work to correct what I messed up. I wasn't going to come between them again, despite how utterly alone and broken I was inside.

The world works in mysterious ways, though, and the day Natalie demanded I meet her at a specific time in Chelsea Park, I didn't question it. I fucking jumped.

In my gut, I knew what this meant and that it was my only chance.

Now she's watching and waiting for her best friend, my wife-to-be, to make her grand entrance. I follow her teary gaze and take in the room of guests. We opted for a small, intimate wedding of no more than fifty people in the heart of Manhattan. Tomorrow we leave for Aspen, again, because Aubrey insisted, and then we're off to Greece for a couple of weeks.

The music flows into a different song and the lighting in the private room lessens to cast a soft glow. Aubrey had told me when the lights change is when she'd be walking out. She had gone on and on about some special rose gold bulbs she needed to have that would set the lush, romantic mood and reflect her dress. I had no idea there was such a thing, but it didn't matter to me. I'd shrugged my shoulders and told her she could have whatever she wanted. I wasn't kidding either. This is our one and only wedding, and I want it to be perfect for her. I wasn't going to give her a reason to divorce me.

But now I understand why she needed these lights.

My lips part and I freeze while chills run down my tepid arms.

She's here.

Aubrey steps into the room and I feel like my heart is actually going to stop. She's unbelievably breathtaking. I've never seen anything so magnificent in my life. Our guests turn to watch her walk down the aisle, the photographers are snapping pictures, I can even hear Natalie sniffling, but all we see are each other.

There's a tawny hue to her skin that makes her look kissed by the sun. She didn't want a veil, so her dark hair is in some messy, curly braid thing that is pulled to the side with little wispy strands that dangle around her beautiful face. The braid hangs past her breasts that my eyes can't help but stop on. I'm definitely more of an ass man now that she's got a little extra cushion back there, but her boobs are just as spectacular. There are ornate pearl and diamond embellishments embedded along the top of her bodice and plunge down the center. They look almost amber from where

I'm standing. The elegant pale ivory corset that cups her breasts makes me drag my teeth over my lip in sheer desire. She said there were layers of tulle that start at her waist, but she forgot to mention the ruffles that look like three-dimensional feathers and butterfly wings floating down the sides toward the train.

"Fuck," I mumble under my breath. She's just incredible.

I'm in awe and overcome with emotion seeing her like this. If I shed a tear, Natalie would never let me live it down, but man, am I fucking close to it. Every day I imagined what Aubrey would look like walking down the aisle, but my imagination didn't do her justice. Not even close. She's the light of my life, my other half, my best friend, my lover, and the reason I feel like I'm going to have a heart attack from how fast my heart is racing.

She's everything I could ever want and imagine and more.

I can't tear my gaze away from her. Aubrey is fierce on the heart and devastatingly gorgeous on the eyes. And she's all mine, forever.

But then ... then she flashes a smile with a look in her eyes only meant for me, and I can hardly hold back another second.

Aubrey makes it a little more than halfway before I'm walking down the steps and striding toward her on autopilot. She doesn't have time to process what's going on and I really don't either as I take her face and kiss the fuck out of her. I didn't plan this, and while our guests definitely didn't expect this, they roll with it just like we do, clapping and hollering their excitement around us.

I had to have her.

I pull back and gaze into her eyes, feeling like my heart is going to explode. "I'm sorry. I couldn't wait." I give her another small kiss.

A slow smile spreads across her face and reaches her eyes. "I wouldn't want it any other way."

Goddamn, I love this woman.

Taking her hand, we walk together until we reach the altar.

She's blushing and I love that she is. My palm is damp from nerves and there's a slight tremble in my fingers, but she doesn't acknowledge it. Today means a lot to me—it's one of the most important days, next to when Natalie was born—and she knows that.

I guide her up the steps and Natalie bends to fluff out her dress then takes the bouquet. The harp music descends so we can begin the ceremony, another romantic touch Aubrey wanted.

I move to stand in front of her, grinning like a fool because I'm so damn happy. Her eyes are glossy, and I can tell she's fighting back her emotions just as much as I am. Unable to fight the urge and how ecstatic I am, I reach in to steal one more quick kiss.

"James." Aubrey giggles under her breath and her cheeks deepen in color.

Natalie nudges her and checks if her lipstick is smudged. She wipes a small spot away. Aubrey turns back to look at me, and I mouth an apology.

She shakes it off and looks deep into my eyes, unfazed. It's another reason why I fell in love with her. She gets me, I get her, and we both make it work. We don't fault each other for who we are.

Aubrey blinks, giving me a smile where she's biting her lip in anticipation, letting me know she feels the same way I do. A sensual curve slides into place and it's all I need to see to know she's ready to be my wife.

Turning, I look at the officiant. "I'm not getting any younger. Make her my wife before she has the chance to leave me for someone her own age."

***

"Salute," Reece says.

"Salute," I respond, and we clink our glasses together, throwing back a shot. Shots are for millennials, but on the rare occasion, I'll have one.

"I can't believe you locked her down."

I glance at him and nod in agreement, then wave two fingers at the bartender for fresh drinks. I'm not trying to get drunk on my wedding night, so I'm going back to what I'm used to and know best—cognac. Aubrey and I both agreed on a couple of drinks, but that's it. We want our wedding night to be a moment we both remember vividly.

"Tell me about it. I'm still questioning what it is she sees in me," I say.

"Never would've thought the girl you had me fuck in front of you would be your wife one day."

A loud cackle flies out of me. I turn to Reece while laughing hysterically and pat him on the back a couple of times. A grin lights up my face thinking back to that night and how he has the balls to bring it up now. I had to trick Valentina into seeing me at that time. She was fighting fate, even then.

Typical Reece, though. I'm not angry. I got the girl in the end. I know who she's under at night and who she's on top of in the morning. That's all that matters.

"You fuck." I laugh again. "I knew you were going to say something like that tonight."

He shrugs unapologetically and smirks. "I couldn't resist."

I take a sip of my poison then turn to glance around the reception room trying to find my wife. "It was a fucking hot night, wasn't it?"

"It gets my dick hard just thinking about it."

I nod in agreement and lift my glass to his. I watch as Aubrey and Natalie are deep in conversation. I frown, wondering why they look so intense.

"All jokes aside," Reece says, dropping the humor from his face, "I'm happy for you, man. You guys kind of give me inspiration. You know I love to live the bachelor life, but now I'm thinking maybe I need to slow down and enjoy the good life."

I tilt my head and give him a knowing look. "The good life it is, Reece. Take my word for it. Get yourself a woman who knows you and loves you more for it."

Sipping my drink, my brows crease when I see Aubrey reach for Natalie's arm only for Natalie to yank it back and whip it behind her back.

"Mind if I have one dance with your wife?"

I snap my eyes back to Reece. He's got a good poker face, but I know he's dying inside holding the laughs in. "Don't even fucking try it."

"But I didn't bring a date."

Eyeing him, I raise my hand and point my pinky at him. "Not my problem." I finish off the cognac then place the sniffer on the bar counter. "I'll be back in a bit. I need to see what my wife is up to."

"I'll be here scoping out the room, hoping to find my own cradle to rob."

I shake my head. Reece is such a douchebag. I laugh because he's a good guy at heart and I know he's not serious. He has wedding fever right now. The phase won't last long. Come next week, I'll get a call from him saying he was acting like a pussy on my wedding night and that the bachelor life is for him. I bet he'll say the bartender drugged him or something equally as dumb.

I stride to where Natalie and Aubrey are standing, still deep in conversation. Just as I reach the little corner they're in, Natalie lifts her hand to Aubrey and I catch a sparkling reflection under the chandeliers. It happens again, and harsh frown lines fill the space between my brows.

"What the hell is that?" I blurt out as I stare at a fucking diamond ring on my daughter's left hand.

She snatches her hand away and places it behind her back. Natalie's eyes are round and wide, like blue marbles ready to pop out of her head.

"Are you engaged and didn't tell me?" I say, slightly accusing.

I'd only gotten a quick look at it, but I'd say it's close to the size of Aubrey's, and she's wearing seven carats. I wait, hoping for a solid response, but Natalie watches me with apologetic eyes knowing she's been caught red-handed.

Something dawns on me. "How come I didn't notice the ring before?"

"She had it turned around," Aubrey says, and my eyes shift to her. "I didn't see it either. All you see is a thin gold band. When she was dancing with Luca, I spotted it. She'd unconsciously turned it around with her thumb to the right side up."

"Is he wearing one?" I ask.

Aubrey frowns. "I don't know. I didn't look." She looks at Natalie, her frown deepening. "You were with me all last week prepping for the wedding, going to the final dress fitting, looking at the flowers. You weren't wearing it then. I would've noticed."

I glance back at Natalie, who's looking guilty as sin. "I took it off," she says, her voice quiet.

My chest is feeling a little tighter at the thought of my only daughter not only getting married but keeping it a secret too. My mind is running a thousand miles an hour. I'm not upset. She can marry anyone she wants and I'd support her, but I'm shocked as hell.

"Did he force you?" I ask, my voice low. "Are you in some sort of trouble?"

Natalie shakes her head. "It's not like that. I'm not engaged." She drops her arm, still hiding the ring.

Aubrey waves her fingers at Natalie. "Cat's out of the bag now. Let me see the ring and tell me what you did."

I snake an arm around Aubrey's waist and pull her to me. I want to see it too. If Luca bought her a fake stone, then I'm putting a fucking stop to whatever bullshit this is until I get to the bottom of it. She deserves the real thing.

I look down and lean in as the engagement ring appears before us.

Fuck.

I'm stunned to the bone.

The clarity is blinding. There's no way that's fake. Aubrey shifts Natalie's hand and the stone glistens under the low lights. Now I'm wondering what the fuck this guy does for a living to afford a huge yellow sapphire diamond. That's easily one hundred grand sitting on her finger. Maybe more depending on where it's from.

"It's not what you think. It's complicated," Natalie says, her words stilted.

"What do you mean it's not what we think? You're wearing a canary engagement ring. He didn't get this out of a Cracker Jack box," Aubrey states. "I didn't know you and the lemon guy were serious. Why didn't you tell me?"

"We're not ... I'm not ... We ... He's not." Natalie stammers. I look at her, hearing the nerves in her voice waiting for an explanation. It's unlike her to trip over words.

"Why yellow?" I find myself asking. "It's nice, don't get me wrong, but what happened to a classic diamond?"

She pauses then says dryly, "It's the color of lemons."

This time I laugh. "Is that why it's oval cut?"

"Yup," Natalie says. "Shape of the stupid fruit."

"Aubrey giggles and lets go of Natalie's hand. "You like him and you can't admit it. Typical of you. Kind of like the way you didn't like that naked musician from back in the day."

She chuckles and it causes Natalie to release a little of the tension, but she shakes her head and gives Aubrey this look in her eyes that makes me think it's a girl code look. Now I'm confused.

Women. I'll never understand their language.

From the corner of my eye, I see Luca striding over to us. I watch as he approaches. He's carrying two drinks, and thankfully only has eyes for my daughter. I try to get a view of his left hand, but it's blocked by the glass he's carrying. He doesn't strike me as a criminal or give me a bad vibe. My instincts are usually on the money, but I'm also human and I make mistakes. He doesn't scream wealth either, but then again, the one percenters aren't always flashy.

I clear my throat. Aubrey notices Luca approaching, and the smile slips from her face.

"Like I said, it's not what you think," I hear Natalie say like she's almost heartbroken. "He's ... he's not my type. That's all. I'm having a little fun, but he's not my type. It'll end soon."

I can't tell who she's trying to convince, Aubrey or herself.

"Hey, Luca," Aubrey says, her voice tight.

Her eyes wide as blood drains from my daughter's face. Natalie freezes. I shoot a glance at her apparent fiancé, who's acting completely blasé. Luca heard what Natalie had said. There's no way he didn't being as close as he is, but he's acting like he didn't. For a split moment, I feel bad for him. No man wants to hear the woman he's with say something like that.

Natalie turns to greet Luca, but she's looking at him completely different than she was to us two seconds ago. I squint my eyes and shoot a brief look at Aubrey to see if she noticed it too, then turn back at Natalie. Gone is the torn look, having been replaced by someone who is happy and carefree. It's like she blinked, and a new person appeared before us.

Luca hands Natalie a glass. She takes it and leans in to give him a kiss on the cheek, then steps closer to him. They're staring at each other as if they've been in love forever. It's almost alarming and now I'm more confused than ever. I have no idea what the hell is happening. I open my mouth to ask a question when Luca puts his hand out.

"Congratulations, Mr. Riviera," he says, dipping his head

respectively toward me and my bride. I place my hand in his when he delivers his next set of words like a man proud. "I'm Luca Enzo Alessio Bianchi Francesco the third, Natalia's husband. It is nice to finally meet you."

I still.

His greeting is a shock to my heart.

"Husband?" I repeat, my voice raised.

I aim a pointed look at my dear daughter. Natalie pleads with her eyes, but I don't know what she's asking for. To not push? Demand answers? Ask what the fuck is going on?

I realize I'm gripping Luca's hand harder than I intended to and pull away. Aubrey instantly laces her fingers through mine and brings me back to where I am. Her thumb strokes over the top of my hand. I glance over and meet her sympathetic gaze. She smiles softly. I feel like Aubrey is giving me some sort of look to just shut up for now. But I can't.

Dumbfounded, I say again, "Husband? As in husband and wife?"

"That is correct. Did she not share the wonderful news that we married last month on my vineyard?"

I look at Natalie, but she gives nothing away. "No, she did not," I say still looking at her. I feel my blood pressure rising by the second.

"We have been on our honeymoon for the last three weeks. It must have slipped her mind," he says, cheekily.

Before I can say anything, Aubrey jumps in. "I was going to suggest that we should all have brunch tomorrow. Seems like we have a lot to catch up on."

Luca's smile is genuine. I wish it wasn't.

"We would love that, right dear?" Luca says.

Dear? What is she? Eighty years old?

"Great. It's settled for now. I'm going to need a stiff drink to process this news then I want to enjoy the rest of the evening with my wife."

Maybe it's the heightened emotion that comes with weddings, but I can't bring myself to be angry with Natalie at the moment. I just want her happy, and if marrying some lemon guy from Italy with a mouth full of names does that, then who the fuck am I to tell her no? I just married her best friend.

Though, her poker face is better than mine. I know something is up.

Letting go of Aubrey, I step forward and give my daughter a hug. "We're going to talk about this," I say near her ear, only for her to hear. She nods and I give her a kiss on the cheek.

"Congratulations," Aubrey says excitedly, but I can hear the tightness in her voice. I think she's hurt learning her best friend got married and didn't tell her. I offer my good wishes as well and tell myself I'm going to shelf this fucking bombshell Natalie dropped on me until tomorrow.

Lacing my fingers through Aubrey's, I steal her away and walk her toward the dance floor. She wraps her arms around my shoulders as I pull her close to my chest.

"Look at me," she says, and I do.

Except I can't get this news out of my head. "How does my only daughter get married and not tell me?"

Aubrey doesn't respond to my question. I know she's trying to make sure I keep my cool, but it still upsets me that I wasn't given the option to walk Natalie down the aisle let alone know about the union at all. It makes me wonder if this is payback for secretly dating Aubrey.

"Baby. I'm sure she has a valid explanation. Natalie isn't going to do something so drastic without thinking it through."

"Aren't you at all concerned?"

"Of course I'm concerned. She's my best friend. I won't deny that I'm not hurt I found out this way, but I also don't want to let it ruin the night."

I shake my head, baffled. "She went from engaged to married in three point five seconds, then says he's not her type? What does that even mean? How is he not her type when she married the guy? I don't understand how she couldn't even mention he proposed. Do you think she ever planned to tell us?"

The words rush out of me before I can stop them. I take a deep breath and exhale. Aubrey places one finger over my lips to silence me.

"No more talk about this. I feel the same way as you, but we'll discuss it over brunch tomorrow. Now dance with your wife."

She's right. I snap my lips shut and bring her in closer. Gavin DeGraw's "More Than Anyone" begins playing through the speakers. A slow smile spreads across my face and I hold her closer to me. She had the DJ replay our first dance song again. We're swaying together to the ballad. Everything fades away and I fall into her beautiful brown eyes. Aubrey starts lip-synching the song's lyrics, saying she's going to love me more than anyone, something we always tell each other.

I can't wait until I have her naked in my arms tonight and we make love as husband and wife. My heart beats so fucking hard for this woman and the way she makes me feel inside.

"Want to know a secret?" I ask. She nods excitedly. "I can't wait to wake up to my wife tomorrow."

The thought makes me embarrassingly giddy, but I don't give a shit. I got the girl and she's going to be mine forever.

Aubrey cups the back of my head and pulls my mouth to hers, placing a gentle kiss on me. Her lips feel like pillows.

"Want to know a secret?" she asks, and I nod. "Valentina is dying to get a taste of her new husband."

My head falls back, and I let out a full belly laugh.

I'm going to cherish the fuck out of her.

THE END

Acknowledgments

To the readers who fell in love with Hush Hush, Say Yes was written solely for you. Thank you for reading my books and asking for more. You're what motivated me to revisit the Hush world, and I'm so happy I did. Being with James and Aubrey (and Natalie) is a blast. Because of you, one day Natalie will get her book.

Jill Mac, Nadine Winningham, and Amber Hodge, thank you all for coming together to help me publish this story during the hardest time of my career. Your help and encouragement mean everything to me. I couldn't have done it without you.

To my family, thank you for being there during the dark time, pushing me to continue writing.

Continue reading for the bonus novella: *The Proposition*

THE
PROPOSITION

Chapter 1

I gaze down at the black cursive font in the center of the drink menu. Nostalgia fills me when I get to the bottom and read *Manhattan*. A smile plays at the corners of my lips when I think of that fun-filled night with my best friend.

Back in college, Natalie and I had a themed party for our twenty-first birthdays since there was only a month that separated us. We went with The Roaring Twenties and had to dress, drink, and eat the part. Luckily anything goes in New York City, and people didn't bat an eye when they saw us dolled up. I wore a black sequins and silver-fringed dress with a rope of pearls that reached my stocking-covered knees. We changed our names for the night and even adopted an accent. I was Betty, she was Mary—sisters visiting the Big Apple for the first time all the way from Texas. Our daddy was in the oil business. A stranger overheard us talking at the swanky bar and suggested we order a Manhattan since it was our first night in town. He insisted the timeless cocktail was just what we needed to experience the concrete jungle. I never had one again after that night.

A waiter appears at the edge of our table to take our order. I peer up at him, ready to request a Manhattan for old time's sake, when James orders two cognacs then tells him to keep them coming.

Confused, I shift my gaze to him. "Are we celebrating something?" I ask playfully.

"I wouldn't say celebrating. It's more so a proposal."

"A proposal? To whom?" I pull my brows together.

"To you," he states. James pauses. "I wasn't sure how to broach this topic, but it's something I thought you might be open to." He's not blinking his baby blues. "We should wait for the drinks to get here," he suggests.

I bob my head in understanding as my stomach backflips. Waiting for drinks means he's unsure about something and needs a buffer to take the edge off. I lower the menu, fold it closed, and place it on the dinner table. Appetizers can wait. I don't tell him I was going to order a Manhattan. His pressing tone causes a flicker of apprehension to trickle down my spine. Whatever he wants to say feels serious.

"Is everything okay?" I say under my breath.

"More than okay."

I sit back, stumped. My eyes bounce from table to table as I contemplate what kind of proposal he has for me. A match strikes, and my gaze snaps to a tealight candle being lit at the table next to us. A thought flashes through my mind. The other night I tried to take a bath, but the water was ice cold. I walked downstairs to talk to James as it warmed when I overheard him say my name to someone on the phone. Normally I wouldn't think twice, but it was how he said it that caused me to stop and listen.

"I can't ask Aubrey to do that," he'd said.

Can't ask me to do what?

He'd paused and laughed. "You take her first if she does."

I didn't want James to think I was eavesdropping. I pretended to not have heard and strolled into his home office, after which he hung up quickly.

This *proposal* could be about that. Or maybe worse.

After all, we met while he was married.

The waiter strides up to our table holding a black tray with two drinks. He places them down then quietly turns away.

"If this proposal has anything to do with you leaving me or something stupid like sleeping in our own rooms, need I remind you that you took a vow and made a promise to be mine forever. That includes sleeping in my bed every night. Even when hospice is called when you're old and decrepit, you're still going to be in my bed. Does this have to do with my smothering you at night?"

My lips pout playfully. His eyes soften.

"I know you get extra hot," I continue. "But I want to be next to you always. I'll try to stay on my side of the bed, but you're so warm and cuddly. We can lower the air conditioning. Also, Natalie would kill you if you tried to leave me. She's partial to me as her stepmother. She would disown you if you left me."

Under the low-lit room, the glow of his smile spreads across his handsome face. A year into marriage, and he still manages to fluster me with a simple look. James lets out a genuine laugh, and I shy under his gaze.

"Is that what you think I want?" he asks.

I lift a brow. "When was the last time you had a *proposal* for me? I'm not a colleague at your law firm, James. Look at the circumstances we met under."

James reaches across the small, round table and turns his palms up. Instinctively, I place my hand in his, and he gives me a loving squeeze. I was a high-end escort working at Sanctuary Cove, a private members-only club in Manhattan when I—using Valentina as my alias—was matched with James for a blind date. He was plagued by his dark desires, and I was there so he could explore them freely. Despite the rules, I fell for him. Our attraction was instant. The chemistry sparking between us couldn't be denied.

I catch the black ink peeking out on the inside of his wrist and smile sweetly. James has an intricate design that spirals up his arm and leads to a tattoo he got once we were married to show his devotion to me and us. I've traced over the design many times with my tongue.

Like his other arm, there is a map of moments in time inked

with the very finest tip of a needle. Only, the tattoo doesn't appear like a map. There are drawings with places we've visited, like a skyline of snow-capped mountains for Aspen when we stayed in his cabin. Another is of tall, dense pine trees with a psychedelic background dotted with stars for when we saw the Northern Lights together, something I'd always wanted to do. There is also one of a woman—me—with the long maxi dress he loved so much to mark our first encounter in Bryant Park. He used an infinity symbol to mark our marriage and the date when I finally said yes to his proposal.

These are designs only we are meant to know and understand. On the anniversary of my grammy's passing, he revealed angel wings in her honor. That one made me bawl my eyes out. They are all connected by a long green vine of various flowers from the islands we've visited, like the frangipani flowers—the first tattoo he started with.

"Neither one of us are going anywhere. We're stuck with each other until our last days. Let's just get that out of the way now." His eyelids lower into a sultry stare. "You and I, we're different than other people. We're not spending our evenings playing scrabble and drinking tea. You're not just my wife; you're also my mistress."

I laugh. He's not wrong. We are different. And I love that about us. The smile causes the lines around his eyes to crease. The mini white candle between us flickers. I love the way the shadows of light cross his face. His thumbs rub the tops of my hands.

"I want to take you somewhere for New Year's Eve."

I perk up. "Where do you want to go?"

"Belize."

Excitement courses through me. We haven't been there yet. I'm so over the cold and miss the sun on my skin.

"Of course I'd love to." I pause to frown. "Is that the proposal?"

James looks over my shoulder, and that answers my question. His gaze is far away, like he's trying to gather his thoughts. He exhales a breath, and I brace myself, knowing more is coming.

"I want my wife to come with me to Belize, but I want Valentina to join us for one night." Then he shocks me. "I'm open to bartering to have Val there."

My jaw drops and my brows shoot up. I'm puzzled. He's open to bartering? Am I missing something? James hasn't propositioned Valentina like this since the days when we first met. Whatever he wants, he's desperate for it.

Suddenly the memories come rushing back. The dates he paid me to go on with him, the late nights we sipped cognac, our forbidden affair that almost ruined multiple relationships, the heated words we exchanged, the once-in-a-lifetime kind of love we shared, and all the ugly lies we told. They all flip together like a complicated kaleidoscope.

James can have Valentina. He knows that. What more does he want? Dread fills my stomach. I try to sit back and take my hands with me, but James has a firm grip and doesn't allow me to move. Every time I try to pull away, he pulls me back.

"Tell me what you're thinking," he says, low and only for me to hear.

"That I'm not enough for you."

The strangled words slip out before I can stop myself. Emotions consume me, and my eyes fill with tears. James tightens his grip. My hands feel cold in his warm ones. I swallow thickly, trying to take the tears with me. I thought the honeymoon phase would last longer, but maybe I was wrong.

"You think you're not enough for me?" Color begins to drain from his cheeks.

My lips form a thin flat line. Our hands separate this time when the waiter appears and asks if we're ready to order. James can't tear his gaze away from mine and tells our server to give us another moment.

"Sweetheart," James begins before a chuckle falls from his

lips.

His jolly expression only causes me to heat in annoyance. The love I have for this man is nothing to laugh at. He owns my heart in ways I can't explain. I want to be more than enough and everything he's ever wanted. My eyes lower, and so does his voice.

"Of all the ways I saw this conversation going, this wasn't one of them. When have I given you the impression that you're not enough for me?"

"When have you ever requested Valentina like this?" I rebut.

James reaches for his drink and ushers for me to take mine. I swallow a huge gulp and feel the bitter burn go down my throat. Valentina doesn't come out to play often. She's more so reserved for special occasions, like after a fundraiser I hosted seven months ago for children in need. The night started with Aubrey and ended with Valentina. My body comes alive like a sweet symphony. I'd needed the confidence Valentina possesses in the beginning, and James took her in the end, satiating both our cravings. He consumed my entire being to reward the embodied goddess I'd become that night.

I know I'm panicking, but I can't help it. The way he eyes me over the rim of his crystal glass has me squirming in my seat.

"You're more than enough for me," he says as he places his drink down. "You're everything I could have ever dreamed of. I'm the luckiest guy in the world. You're it for me, Aubrey. I've never known love like ours."

"You promise? You swear?"

"Yes. I can't believe you're asking me this." Disbelief is written all over his face.

"Then do you just want to order me around sexually? Be your little pet?"

"That's exactly what I want. For what I have in mind, I'd prefer you be Val. But we can compromise."

I can't say I don't like the idea. James exercises the beast inside him when I'm Valentina. He's more aggressive with his kisses, his touch is firmer. He can command my body with so few words and easily overpower me when I'm being rebellious. We're a good balance. Giving James power over my body and mind is what I love the most when I'm her. I never know what he's going to do, because when I'm Val, nothing is off-limits. I trust him. When we experiment under his control and guidance, I'm desired and wanted, a deeply sexy woman who pleases her man. Sex is how I connect. He pushes my body when I don't think I can go any further. When James takes what he needs from me, I win too.

I have another sip. My mind is running a mile a minute with theories. "Why don't you just say what you want, and then we can discuss?"

His mouth twitches. "I want to watch Reece fuck you again. I prefer he fuck Val."

I sputter on my drink. The bitterness of the liquor burns the inside of my nostrils, and I almost choke when it doesn't go down the right way. I reach for the cloth napkin and dab my mouth. I cough like I'm breathing fire.

"You want to share me?"

Reece is a curve ball I hadn't seen coming.

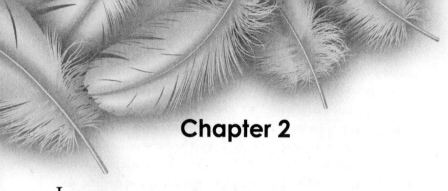

Chapter 2

I say it louder than I mean to and flinch when I notice the aghast look on the woman seated at a table near us. She must've heard me.

"Yes, I do." James smirks, unbothered by the looks. He says it so matter of factly that I don't know what to think. My first thought is that I'm not satisfying him completely. My second is how long has he been considering this?

James wants to share me.

With Reece.

Again.

And I think back to that phone call. It must have been Reece he was talking to.

"You take her first..."

Lust throbs between my legs at the memory from years ago.

The waiter returns at the worst possible time to review specials on the menu. I study my husband, listening to the server but not hearing what he's saying. I'm not opposed to the idea of bringing Reece back for a cameo. I assumed after we married that we weren't inviting anyone into our bed. What would this do to our marriage? I'm attracted to Reece, but in the heat of the moment, could James handle seeing my lust for another man? His best friend? This isn't some guy we'll never see again. Reece also happens to be a major donor for my charity.

If this is what James desires, his initial hesitation and the need for alcohol confuse me. My overthinking mind is having a field day. He has to know I'd give this to him in the end, right?

"Reece is okay with this?" I ask once the waiter leaves.

"Reece is the one who suggested the reunion," he says. "There's an adults-only resort on the island that's clothing optional. Each suite has its own private hot springs pool. Volcanoes and waterfalls surround the land. We can even hike if you want. Reece will be there for a few days, but he'll only be with us one night. Otherwise, it's you and me."

"Hiking? I'm not the type to hike. I don't even own sneakers. The only thing I want biting me is you. Not the damn mosquitos."

He tries not to laugh and shrugs. He knows I'm not the type to do any sort of exercise unless it's on his dick.

"I'm just giving you options."

I have another sip of my drink and just decide to down the whole thing in one shot. James is always whisking me away any chance he gets. I love that he wants me to be with him when he gets wanderlust. With each trip, we try to do something new and adventurous that we normally wouldn't do. He's not into hiking either, but if I wanted to, he would also. I place the glass on the table and lick my lips in anticipation. James hasn't taken his eyes off me since he's stated what he wants. He stares at me. I feel like he's trying to read my thoughts before I answer.

"If it's not something you want to do again, you can say so and everything will be the same. Nothing will change. I'm still taking you to Belize regardless."

"It wouldn't make you mad to see your wife have sex with another guy?"

"Valentina isn't my wife." James leans into the table. "My wife is off-limits. To everyone."

The corners of my mouth curve at his correction. Deep down I know that if I didn't want to take part in a threesome, James would drop the subject and never bring it up again. But why not? We've done it before. And I like pleasing my husband. Pleasing my husband pleases me. I want to give him what he wants and be the woman who fulfills his every desire. Even if that means seeing me get rammed by his best friend. But I also don't want to put our relationship in jeopardy.

I tilt my head to the side. Normally James has rules for Valentina. "What are the rules?"

"He can't call you Aubrey, and you can't orgasm with him."

He says it so quick that I let out a laugh. "No wonder you want Valentina for this."

His eyes grow heavy with love. "Your orgasms are mine," he says.

Leaning in, I whisper, "*You're* mine and only mine. Forever."

"Having Reece with us is nothing more than a little fun." He leans in and lowers his voice. "I want to see his mouth on your pussy and watch his tongue taste what I taste. I want Reece to devour you so I can be the one to take you over the edge."

I swallow, pretending not to feel the tingle of lust run down my spine. James knows all my buttons. He's the best lover—and husband—I could have asked for. But two guys? A pulse of sin strums through my blood.

"You really want this? Enough that you're willing to barter with me?" I ask, looking straight in his eyes.

"Yes."

"So you'll go to the top of the Empire State building with me for a night of debauchery?"

He chuckles, and damn, how it makes my belly flutter. I can feel the heat rising to my cheeks. His eyes twinkle with mirth. James is terrified of heights.

"If that's what you want."

I'd never do that to him, so I'll have to come up with another idea.

"Reece is a sloppy kisser," I tell him. "Maybe you could enforce a rule that there's a two-drink maximum. I don't want to feel like a dog is licking my mouth again. Unless that's how he always kisses," I say, my face scrunching up.

James barks out a laugh.

The waiter deposits a set of new drinks to the table then leaves.

"I have one last request if you agree to this," James says.

"I can't wait to hear this."

"Don't tell Natalie."

My jaw drops for the second time tonight. "You know we share everything."

"Try to refrain this time. At least don't let me hear that you told her. I don't love my daughter knowing the details of our sex life, to be honest."

"Fair enough."

To the outside world, maybe it is a little strange we talk about those things, but Natalie already knew about her dad's sexual escapades when she discovered he was a member of Sanctuary Cove, the high-end escort service she and I worked at together. Only, James doesn't know his daughter used to be a prostitute also.

"So what do you say?" he asks.

**

While James is in the shower, I head downstairs to my favorite room in our home to clear my mind so I can give him an answer.

After we left the restaurant, we didn't continue talking about the proposition. James said he didn't want to pressure me into making a hasty decision only to regret it later, which I appreciate. But to say that he caught me off guard is an understatement. I was shocked. Taken aback. Having sex with Reece is the last thing I ever thought James would ask me to do.

I think back to that one night James and Reece shared me. Even now, the same white-hot heat rushes through my blood recalling how I reached for James while his friend was deep inside me. I squeeze my thighs at the memory of their tongues caressing my pussy together, how they pushed my knees open and brought me to the edge of the world. I shouldn't be turned on by any other man but my husband. But in this moment, I am. Guilt prickles the inside of my chest. The combination of the two of them devouring my body was lethal. I was vulnerable under them, exposed in ways I'd never been, and I loved every second of it. I haven't thought about that night in a while, and now that I am, a part of me wants that again. Being Valentina showed me how to confidently own my power and sexuality. Only, I hadn't known it at the time the way I do now.

Slowly climbing up the stairs toward me is my grammy's cat—my constant companion after she passed away. I reach down for Lucy, snuggling the elderly kitty against my cheek. Her purring makes me smile. I want to give James every part of me, but I'm conflicted. If I agree, will James think I want his friend? Because I don't. I'm satisfied never sharing Valentina again. But marriage isn't about what only I want. Marriage is compromise and understanding your partner's needs. The love I have for my husband is more than I could ever put into words. James is my heartbeat. He deserves the world, and I want to give it to him. Valentina is who brought us together. If James wants to replicate that evening with my alter ego, I don't want to deny him, or us, that experience. I like becoming Valentina. She unlocked my sexual prowess, allowed me to come into my skin and be comfortable with who I am. I get to exercise a certain freeness when I'm her.

Once I officially quit escorting, I had made so much money I didn't know what to do with it other than go on shopping sprees with Natalie. And boy did we ever. Finally money wasn't an obstacle for me. We were in our early twenties living our best lives shopping on Fifth Avenue in Manhattan then charting off to Rodeo Drive in Beverly Hills to do more damage. That summer in LA was one for the books.

As odd as it may sound, I'm grateful for the time I spent working at Sanctuary Cove. I don't have any regrets. When I ran into Madame Christine a couple of years later and told her the name for my nonprofit was inspired by her establishment, I'd never seen her smile so big. She lit up like a star. I wouldn't have Sanctuary if it wasn't for her.

I hold the furball close and round the corner to the custom room James had renovated for me when I moved into his brownstone. I need to clear my mind of these intrusive thoughts so I can make a conscientious decision. Lucy helps me feel close to Grammy.

My hand palms the green glass knob, and I step inside my oasis. Miss Dior perfume lingers subtly in the air. The soft floral, feminine scent brings a smile to my face. James purchased the largest bottle he could find. It's a stylish accent piece sitting on the counter near my vanity. He even bought the silk headscarf Natalie Portman wears in the advertisement. I draped it over the bottle. Something about it always reminded me of Grammy.

The room is illuminated by the extra-large, black ostrich feather chandelier hanging by a brass metal base on the ceiling. It's girly yet exudes opulence and glamour. After I expressed how much I loved ostrich feathers, James had it shipped from Europe. Then he hired an interior designer, and we built a closet around it. It's a beauty room even Carrie Bradshaw would envy. As a billionaire, he spares no expense, and it shows. James loves to spoil me. Most little girls dream of a closet fit for a princess, with purses, gorgeous designer gowns, and high heels stacked from floor to ceiling in every color. James gave me the queen's version of my princess dreams. Chanel purses, Christian Louboutin skyscraper high heels, and glittering couture dresses.

I peer down at Lucy's aging eyes and kiss her nose with mine. "You know all of my secrets by now," I say quietly, more to Grammy than her cat. "I wish you could've met James. He's incredible. You would've loved him. He treats me exceptionally well. He's all you and my parents would've wanted for me."

Lucy nestles deeper into the crook of my arm and hums.

"I'm sure you can see my dilemma. I could use some advice."

The last time I was in here was right before a fundraiser I hosted that raised over two million dollars. I'd been anxious. We were raising money for the largest children's coalition in the five boroughs. Not every child is as lucky as I to have had a grammy like mine to raise me after my parents died. Many are placed in the system and in need of basic essentials that the city can't afford to pay. Grammy inspired me to be generous and give love unconditionally.

So when I need to channel my inner diva to help raise money, this is where I go. I put on my That Girl playlist, give myself a pep talk, massage shimmery lotion into every inch of my body, then dress to impress. And *voila*, Valentina appears. Valentina didn't just give James the freedom to explore his darker side. She gave me the confidence to accomplish my ambitions. She reminds me to be strong and walk with a crown on my head.

I sweep my gaze around the lavish Old Hollywood–style room. It's mostly black and white with touches of antique gold. Drapes are held open by three ropes of pearls. There's a velvet chair pushed in at my vanity table. The corners of my mouth curve at the words written in the bottom right corner. James snuck in and wrote *I <3 U* in fire hydrant red lipstick before he took me out for Valentine's Day. I never erased the love note.

A *meow* catches my attention. Lucy paws at my face softly, and I smile. I swear can feel my Grammy's presence. I miss her so much.

"I never thought I'd be coming to you for sex advice, Grammy," I mumble to myself. My gaze falls on the rose gold necklace Grammy gifted me that I put on display. "The decision to accept the proposition doesn't change my feelings for James. The issue lies with me. James asked me to become Valentina, but it feels wrong having sex with another man even if my husband wants to watch. I feel like I'm cheating. I love James unconditionally, but this—"

I stop myself.

There should never be a "but" following unconditionally.

I know James loves me without restriction, or he wouldn't have accepted my history as a sex worker.

I open the pocket doors to the stylish windows that display my favorite garments, among them the maxi dress I wore the first time I met James in Bryant Park. I'll never forget his compliments and the way he had me glowing from the inside. Beside it is my wedding dress and a corset made of powder milk tulle, cream pearls, and Swarovski crystals. I tug the next door open. The rod is lined with tweed, crocodile skin, studded jackets, and bustiers. There's clothing for every mood and season.

Then, I turn to the island that stores my jewelry and lingerie and eye the exquisite diamond-encrusted head chain displayed along with the two-inch wide matching choker. The pads of my fingers graze the clear stones, and I contemplate how the Aubrey in me needed Valentina's heat and pressure to help my brilliance shine through. Carefully, I lift the dainty piece off the mannequin, positioning the small branches full of diamond leaves over my hair. Then, I wrap the choker around me. Electricity tingles down my spine as I look at my reflection in the mirror with the crown on my head.

I'm not a materialistic person, though one may assume it by this room. Valentina transformed Aubrey from a broke college kid to a powerhouse of a woman who owns and manages multiple nonprofit organizations for homeless families in Manhattan. I'm a woman and a wife with the ability to bring powerful men to their knees. If it weren't for Valentina, my life would be vastly different.

Reaching for the same lipstick James used, I paint my lips. Valentina is openminded and liberated. She loves sex. The world is her oyster. Valentina pushes Aubrey's limits. She raises the stakes.

Yet I have this nagging feeling in my stomach. The last *ménage à trois* with James and Reece was different because James and I weren't married. Bringing a third person into the bedroom is a risk to my marriage, regardless of whether I'm Valentina or not.

I placing the lipstick back into the makeup caddy. Deep down, Valentina wants to play.

And she expects payment for her services.

Chapter 3

I skim the intimate room crowded with white-collar men just getting off work. There's a low chatter in the air and a chilly breeze from the front door that wafts through the room every time someone walks in. James sent a text about a half hour ago that he was leaving the office and was on his way to join me and his daughter for happy hour.

I reach for a fried dill pickle and pop it into my mouth. Natalie couldn't have visited at a better time. She only trusts New York doctors and came to the city for Botox and physical exams she has done yearly. She flies back to Italy tomorrow night. I always rearrange my schedule to accommodate her.

My dilemma with becoming Valentina has been consuming my mind. I thought spending time in my beauty room with Lucy would help sort my messy thoughts, but what I really need is my best friend to talk to about this whole thing. Knowing Natalie, she'll probably tell me to go for it. She's been there through every major situation in my life.

"We need a girls' trip so we can really catch up. I miss hanging with you. Somewhere hot, where all we have to wear is a bathing suit."

Her eyes brighten as she sits taller against the high-back barstool. "I completely agree. Where should we go?"

I think for a moment. "What about Greece?"

Natalie shakes her head. "Too close to Italy. I want to make it hard for Luca to get to me. What about Brazil?"

"Ooo," I say in agreement. "You want to go across the ocean.

I see what you're doing. The food is supposed to be outstanding."

"The men too," she adds, waggling her manicured brows. "Let's go there."

Shaking my head, I can't help but laugh. Natalie is a maneater. If I didn't know better, I'd swear that she and her husband are having marital problems. They're not. Natalie would've told me. She's secretly attracted to her husband chasing her. Natalie loves playing hard to get, and Luca likes the hunt.

The waiter deposits two Manhattans on the bar where we're sitting. I thank him, and before he dashes away, I order a cognac for James. Natalie and I reminisce about playing Betty and Mary all those years ago on my first visit to New York City.

"I forgot how good these are," she says. "And dangerous too."

I giggle and eat another fried pickle, savoring the saltiness. We ordered vegan appetizers so Natalie can munch too. "I could eat the whole basket."

"We should order pickleback shots," Natalie suggests.

My nose scrunches. "My palate cannot handle pickle juice and bourbon together," I tell her. "My gag reflex would activate. That's disgusting."

"You said you were craving pickles," she states casually with a shrug. "Don't knock it 'til you try it."

A stranger in a rumpled shirt stumbles past us and accidentally elbows me. My boobs are tender, and the slightest touch hurts. I wince in pain and grab my breast over my black mesh blouse, not caring that I'm sitting in a bar and people can see. My last shred of modesty danced away when I gave Madame Christine an orgasm at my audition for Sanctuary Cove. And any dignity? That vanished with the client with the *Silence of the Lambs* fetish.

"What's wrong?" she asks, her gaze where my hand is.

"My boobs are aching, and his meaty elbow didn't help. My period must be around the corner. Speaking of boobs, how did your appointment go?"

"Not as I hoped. My gynecologist tried shoving some plastic, bendy ring inside me as a form of birth control. I told him I'm vegan and to get it away from me," Natalie says across from me.

I almost choke as I laugh. "What does being a vegan and birth control have to do with each other?"

"I consider my body a temple. Plastic is terrible for you. I'm not allowing that thing to marinate inside me. Also, it doesn't seem very reliable. It's like a hula-hoop I'm supposed to bend in half and shove inside. My doctor wants me to finger myself every month to make sure it stays in place." She pauses as she brings the pickle midway to her mouth and says, "Then he tells me it could fall out or get stuck inside. Why the hell would anyone use that?"

"Those methods are equivalent to pull out and pray in my opinion. You're just asking to get knocked up," I say then eat another pickle. "You look so insulted."

"I am," Natalie exclaims, eyes wide. "After I refused, he suggested I rub some topical cream on the back of my thighs."

I frown.

"I looked up the medicine and found out he was trying to give me menopause cream."

"And this is the doctor you fly around the world to see?" I say, questioning her seriously.

She scoffs with an eye roll, and I chuckle at her annoyance. "I didn't even see him. My regular doctor was called into the hospital for an emergency delivery, so I had to see the nurse practitioner instead." Natalie takes a long pull on her drink. "I can't stand kids. If I got pregnant, I think I'd cry. Then I'd sue. Sorry, but I won't be making you a grandma in this lifetime."

"Fine by me because I don't intend to make you a big sister."

We both laugh. I respect that. Her body, her choice. Natalie is extremely careful and never has sex without a condom on top of her contraceptive. She never even wanted to date a man with a kid. Too much baggage, she said.

"I refuse to have sex with Luca until I get on a new birth control. A condom is not enough for me. He's old-school Italian and would love nothing more than for me to be barefoot and in the kitchen. What do you use?" she asks.

A huff of annoyance rolls out of me. "I'm actually in between pills. My old ones got pulled from the shelf because of some lawsuit, and these new ones are the worst. My body is still adjusting. Probably why the elbow jab hurt."

Natalie takes a bite of a stuffed mushroom. "I've been meaning to tell you that I won't be visiting for the holidays," she says. "This is probably the last time we'll see each other until next year. Luca wants to go to Sicily. He's building a house there. More like a castle. He's probably going to lock me away in a tower to keep me from jet setting around the world. I told him I want no part of going to Sicily, but he's forcing me to go."

I highly doubt he, or anyone, can force Natalie to do anything she doesn't want.

"You act like you hate him," I say.

"I do!"

"You're such a liar," I say, smiling. She forgets that I can read her like a book.

Natalie lets out a fake sigh and reaches for another mushroom. "I hate him, but I love his dick. I don't know what that says about me."

"Sounds like you're dickmatized."

Her eyes glisten with truth. "I am. God, I hate it. I wish I wasn't, but he's just so good at sex. Of all the guys I've slept with, none of them compare to him. He makes it his mission for me to crave him. I swear, Italian men are only good for three things— food, fucking, and fighting."

"Your three favorite Fs," I say. "At least he knows how to cook."

"Luca hates that I'm vegan. I refuse to try a meatball, and it infuriates him because he spends hours cooking them. I told him he's lucky the only meat I eat is his." We share a laugh. "He isn't wrong."

"I bet he's a really good cook," I say.

Her expression makes me chuckle. This is what I miss most about Natalie living in another country—how much we laugh when we're together. Nothing is off limits. Just how best friends should be.

"There's a whole ocean between us, and that man still has the ability to get under my skin with just a thought."

"That man, meaning your husband?"

"Shhh," she says, using her hand to brush the comment away. "I don't give him the satisfaction of calling him my husband. The only time I say that horrible word is when he's giving me orgasms. He makes me say it or else he doesn't let me finish. He literally pulled out and walked away right in the middle of fucking me. I almost killed him for that. Have you ever had a man work you up so good you'll basically crawl to him for his dick? That's Luca. And he knows it. Anyway, enough about my love life. Tell me something new."

I place my glass on the bar top and stare at the round base. It's been two days since James dropped the bomb that he wants a threesome with Reece.

"What aren't you telling me?" she asks, her eyes narrowing my way.

I don't like lying to my husband or breaking his trust. He'll never know if I tell her. I shoot a quick glance over my shoulder to make sure James isn't behind me. "What I'm about to tell you must stay between us. You can't tell James I told you."

"I knew it. What are you keeping from me?"

"Do you remember when I was working at Sanctuary Cove and your dad tricked me by having his friend Reece set up a date with me?"

Natalie nods and waves her hand to hurry me up with the

gossip. I trust her with my life and know that what we discuss will stay between us.

"The other night, he told me he wants to share Valentina with Reece again."

Natalie's jaw drops and her blue eyes light up. She stares in shock at first then does a happy dance in her seat. I relay the entire conversation I had with James, not leaving out a single detail. Once I'm done, the pressing weight on my chest is lighter, despite the antsy butterflies in my stomach.

"He wants a redo," she says, her voice airy from surprise.

"James has rules." I lean in and meet Natalie halfway. "I can't orgasm unless it's with him, and Reece can't call me Aubrey," I whisper.

Her face twists up, and I let out a laugh.

Natalie pulls back. "Make it a competition. Who can make you come harder, or bet's off."

"James would win any day. He's not going to let another man bring me more pleasure than him."

She chuckles and then pauses, seeming disturbed. "Sometimes I forget we're talking about my dad."

I laugh. "Me too."

"You lucky bitch. Two guys get to nail you. When and where?" she asks.

"One night in Belize. He wants to take me there for New Year's Eve, so we won't be here for the holidays either."

"Are you excited? I already know you said yes." Natalie sets her glass down. "Didn't you? You said yes, right?"

My lips flatten and I shake my head. "I'm torn. A part of me feels wrong for wanting it, but at the same time, I'm not sure if I really do? I like when I get to be Valentina, but we haven't shared her since we got married, and we didn't intend to. He changed his mind."

"It's okay if people change their minds," she says gently. "You still love him just the same, don't you?"

"Don't ask me a dumb question like that. Of course I do." Maybe even more that he was comfortable enough to ask this of me.

"Then what's holding you back?" she asks.

I hesitate. "That fact that I want to have sex with a man who is not my husband?"

"Why? This is exactly what he wants." She leans in close and eyes me. "He wants you hot for his friend so he can remind you who you belong to."

"He'd be watching us," I tell her.

"That's so hot," she says with a smirk.

"It is. I think that's what I'm most eager for. But Reece sucks at kissing. He's like a dog slobbering on my mouth, but he gives good dick rides." I swirl the tiny black straw around the ice in my cocktail. "Do you think I should be concerned about anything? Like maybe the spark died down and James is trying to bring it back? Maybe he's bored with our sex life?"

She shakes her head, vehemently disagreeing. "Not at all. As much as I love my mom, I've never seen him with her the way he is with you. You walk on water in his eyes. Consider what he wants as role play. Some guys get off on watching their wife get railed by another dude. Luca would never allow it, but different strokes for different folks." She pauses, her brows furrowing. "I think Luca would kill the other guy. Maybe that'll finally get me divorced."

"Why can't you just walk away?"

"We made a deal. Italians take that shit serious. I'm not Italian, but we understand loyalty the same. I gave my word. I don't like to go back on it. Plus, it's not that bad."

I gasp in mock horror. "Did you just admit to enjoying your marriage?"

"Don't try and change the subject," she counters. "I think I know the issue," she says. "Aubrey doesn't want this. Val does."

Taking a sip, I swallow the bitter cool drink, musing over her words. "I hadn't thought of it like that."

"It's easy to mix up emotions and identity when you're juggling more than one. Lines get crossed."

"James told me there's room for me to negotiate, given the proposition."

Her eyes light up with mischief. "What would you ask for? You should take advantage of that."

"I'm not sure," I say, but it's a lie.

I already know what I'm going to ask James. If I'm agreeing to be Valentina, then he can do something big for me in return, like visit Natalie in Italy where she lives with Luca. This would go a long way for patching up the relationship between Luca and James. They haven't been around each other since our wedding when we found out Natalie and Luca got married. James is a bit old-fashioned. He's still bothered Luca didn't ask for permission to marry his daughter. It's why we haven't visited them in Italy.

Everyone deserves a second chance. I should remind James of that. After all, Natalie gave us one.

From the corner of my eye, I see James enter the building. A massive smile splits across my face as he strides up over to us. My husband is the most handsome man on the planet.

"Hey, baby," I say and reach for his lips with mine. The faintest hint of his peppery cologne fills my senses.

James greets Natalie with a kiss on her cheek then says he needs to go wash his hands. He walks away just as the same stranger from earlier who bumped into me stumbles over. He's holding a drink in his hand that's about to spill over the edge. His clothes are as disheveled as his hair and there's a foul odor radiating off him. He stops in front of us.

"I haven't seen you in a while," the drunk stranger says. He's only looking at Natalie.

"Do I know you?" Natalie says.

The stranger rears back, insulted. "You don't remember me?"

Natalie shakes her head.

"You're Natalia." He pauses then lifts his arm with the glass. The ice sloshes around as he says, "Yeah. Yeah, you're Natalia."

Natalia. My heart sinks. That's a dead giveaway. This guy must be a former John of hers.

James still doesn't know that Natalie also worked for Madame Christine at Sanctuary Cove, and we plan to keep it that way. If this guy spills the beans, James is going to be devastated. Some secrets are not meant to see light. No parent wants to hear his daughter sold her body for money, even if it was her choice. Luca doesn't allow her to work there anymore, but it doesn't mean her past is erased.

"You got me kicked out of Bliss. I'm not allowed back there," he states like he's just remembering, his tone turning to anger. "And I still had to pay for you. That bitch wouldn't give me my money back." The line between his brows deepen. He steps closer. "You owe me."

"I don't owe you a single penny," Natalie says. "I didn't take your money. You got yourself kicked out for being too intoxicated. You couldn't keep your hands to yourself and got reported by multiple women. Not my fault you're a fucking creep."

Fury ignites in his eyes. Leave it to my Natalie to say what she really feels. A shade of red colors his cheeks. I sit up taller and look for James, bracing for whatever comes our way. This stranger is making me uneasy.

"You cunt bag slut bitch—"

Natalie waves her hand back and forth, unimpressed. "At least be a bit more creative if you're going to insult me."

The former client's eyes fill with rage. He begins mouthing off obscenities, this time loud enough to turn a few heads our way.

James reappears, catching a few of the harsh words. His eyes narrow at the stranger, and then he inserts himself next to Natalie.

"Don't talk to a woman like that. Get the fuck out of here. Leave, and there won't be a scene."

"Yeah? What are you going to do about it?" the man slurs, eyeing James up and down. "You want to take it outside?"

I cringe. I'm embarrassed for this guy. James is a lover not a fighter, but he'll do whatever it takes to protect his daughter.

"At the rate you're going, you're going to be banned here too," Natalie adds, and it's like fuel to the fire.

"You fucked me over, bitch," the drunk yells. "You cost me three thousand dollars. I want my money back."

"Sounds like you did it to yourself," James says. He reaches into his back pocket and removes the billfold to reveal a stack of one-hundred-dollar bills. "I've got eighteen hundred on me. Take it and don't ever fucking bother her again. Consider your bar tab paid in full too."

He scoffs but swipes it anyway. "What are you? Her dad?"

James ignores him. "Don't come back here either."

"Skank," he mutters under his breath.

"So is your mom," Natalie says, but I don't think he heard her because he stumbles away.

James looks at his daughter as he sits on the barstool. I hand him his drink, and he thanks me. I pat the top of his spread thigh.

He takes a long pull and says, "Don't tell me you dated that guy."

Natalie shakes her head. "God, no. I met him on a dating app. He catfished me," she says, the lie smoothly rolling off her lips. "Thanks for that. I'll pay you back." Natalie's phone dings, and she picks it up. She scans the screen then rises from her seat. "Duty calls," she says then slides it into her purse.

"Where are you going? I just got here," James says.

"Business. My husband is calling. You know how that goes. Have fun in the sun. Just don't come back pregnant. The heat makes people do crazy things."

I almost choke on my Manhattan. She said so much without saying anything at all.

"Can we meet for lunch tomorrow? I'll take you to the airport after," James suggests.

Natalie fixes her pencil skirt and gives James a kiss on her cheek. "I'd love that," she says then gives me a hug. "I'll call you later."

Once she's out of the restaurant, James turns my way. He gives me a glare like he already knows the truth, even though we both know I'm going to lie.

"I only told her that we're going to Belize."

I bring the drink to my lips. His unblinking stare sends a flutter of heat to my cheeks. I try not to grin, but I'm a terrible liar when I'm put under the spotlight.

"I didn't ask," he says nonchalantly.

My heart is pumping fast. The corners of his blue eyes crease. Then he smiles, and I melt inside. I know he's screwing with me.

"Don't pretend like Reece doesn't know about our sex life. You tell your best friend, I tell mine. This is what happens when you marry your daughter's best friend."

It's rare that James blushes, but when he does, it's the cutest thing in the world.

Chapter 4

You know what they say.

The higher the hair, the closer to God.

The humidity in Belize is something I'm not used to. Since I got off the private plane a few days ago, my hair has been a massive frizz ball. I'm not even attempting to style with anything other than a messy ponytail. James says all the flyaways are cute, that I look young and innocent, but I think he's just being nice. I'm coated in a damp sheen of sweat. When James said clothing is optional, I see why now. Every type of fabric sticks to me. It's pointless to wear anything other than a bathing suit and a flowy coverup. But I'm not going to complain. I wanted out of the cold, and I got it.

"Sweetheart, I'm not sure ziplining is for me," James says wearily, eyeing the steep drop. The trees below us shift and sway with the breeze. We're two hundred feet in the air, and the people look like ants crawling below us. "I'm a big guy. Can it hold me?" He looks up at the instructor. "What's the weight limit on one of these things?"

"Babe, you're going to be fine. Didn't you see the line of people who went before you? Everyone lived." He's not impressed and doesn't say anything. I nudge him with my elbow. "Just remember that at the end of the ride, there's a hot spring waiting for us." We're visiting all the springs so James can say that he's fucked me in different bodies of water. Two days here, and we've visited seven springs. Granted, they're all within walking distance and the same body of water, but still.

"A waterfall too if you take a small walk through the rainforest," the instructor adds.

"Oh, we're definitely doing that," I say.

"What if it snaps and I plummet to my death?" James asks, referring to the steel cable.

I chuckle. He's so dramatic. But I guess most attorneys are.

"We have a mesh netting you can't see beneath the trees. You won't die," the instructor responds dryly.

James nods then gives the ropes a tug and says, "I'm ready." He looks over his shoulder to me. "Give me a kiss."

I smack one right on his mouth and pull away with a pop. "I love you. You got this." I give him two thumbs-up then take a step back as he gets into position.

James white-knuckles the rope with both hands. He bends his knees, lightly bouncing, like he's preparing to jump. His safety belt is snug around his hips and circles each thigh. The tension makes his butt look bigger, rounder. My bottom lip rolls between my teeth as my gaze travels. James is in great shape for a man pushing sixty. I can't help myself and rear back to smack his ass.

"Aubrey."

James stills. It's all he says. It's basically a demand to stop, and I'll never do that.

I chuckle. "You got this, big daddy."

James shakes his head. I can't see his face, but I can tell he's grinning.

He exhales a loud breath and then begins to count down. His chest lifts, and in the next blink, he's springing from the ground and gliding on the rope wire at breakneck speed. A huge grin spreads across my face. His knees are pulled back so all I can see are his feet sticking out and his salt and pepper hair blowing in the wind. He dips through the foliage and disappears. I giggle to myself, proud that he's doing something that scares him. James isn't the type to back down, but his fear of heights is real. I wasn't going to push him if he didn't want to do it, but I'm glad he did.

The instructor motions me forward. I step into the harness, and he secures it. He gives it a few good tugs then looks at his watch. Dipping his head, he gives me the go. I grip the same places James did then jump off, feeling my heart drop. I hold my breath as happiness whips through me. My cheeks hurt from smiling so hard. I dip beneath the branches of the trees and feel the energy around me. All of a sudden, the floral scent of exotic flowers fills my senses. I'm surrounded by black orchids as I swing into the grotto. The aqua water shimmers in the shadows along the cave wall. My toes slip into the spring before I'm quickly splashing to a stop. The instructor unbuckles the harness, and James is swimming toward me. I reach for him and notice how the color of his tattoos gleams from the tunnel of light above us.

"Was it as bad as you thought?" I ask.

He shakes his head, and I light up inside. It's all James says before pressing his lips to mine. He was nervous, but he didn't let that stop him. My legs automatically wrap around his waist. He twirls me around as we slip underwater, our kiss still intact. He's been doing this since we got to the island, kissing me underwater any chance he gets. It's adorable.

A few minutes later, after we leave the grotto, we're walking through the rainforest, me in my bikini and James in boardshorts. We're holding hands, and neither one of us are speaking. This is just one thing I love about being with James. We don't have to talk when we're together. The quiet is peaceful, comfortable. The only sound is rushing water in the distance and rainbow toucans perched on branches chirping at each other. White flowers surround us. Guava and mango trees are ripe for the picking. The wildlife is unlike anything I've ever seen before. There are monkeys literally hanging around in the trees. We're told jaguars are known to hang high on the branches too, but I haven't seen one. Massive, color-changing iguanas run in front of us. The giant-looking lizards attack, so we pretend to not notice them.

"If you don't want to go through with tomorrow, we don't have to," James says quietly.

He's talking about Reece, whose plane is due to arrive early tomorrow morning. We haven't discussed the proposal since the night he asked.

I look at James. "Are you having a change of heart?"

His brows furrow. "No? Maybe? I've really enjoyed our time here. I'm not sure I want to share you. I'm wondering if it was a mistake."

"You know, I was surprised you even suggested it. I remember when you told me about the conversation you had with Reece at our wedding about sharing me and that it would never happen again. What made you change your mind? I'm not against it, but for a split second, I thought you were bored with me and wanted to spice things up."

James stops walking. He turns toward me and looks down. "That's what I was afraid of," he tells me. "I almost didn't ask because I didn't want to give you a reason to question our relationship or my love."

He places his hands on my hips and steps closer. His pensive gaze hits me right in the chest. I lift my arms and drape them over his shoulders. There's a storm forming in his blue eyes. Shame is written all over his handsome face, and that's the last thing I want for James. I want to ease his mind, not cause him distress.

"I'm never bored with you, Aubrey," he says. "You're more than enough for me. I'm the luckiest guy in the world. Sometimes the happiness terrifies me. I never want it to end. Every day is an adventure with you, even if all we do is go to work and come home. I love waking up next to you. You're the best part of my day."

"I'm glad you asked me. I appreciate it more than you know."

"You do? But I made you second-guess us."

Shaking my head, I say, "I know how you feel about me.

You don't miss a chance to show me or tell me. When the topic is bringing another person into our marriage, even if for one fun night, questions are bound to arise. That comes with the territory. I knew who you were before we married. Just like you knew about me."

"If having Reece here is going to change our dynamic, I don't want him coming."

My heart softens, knowing where his feelings lie. "I want Reece to join us."

His brows shoot up, and the storm fades in his eyes. "I didn't think it was possible to love you any more than I already do."

"Which is why I'm okay with becoming Valentina for the night."

James growls in the back of his throat as his mouth captures mine. He doesn't hold back and kisses me deeply, his tongue pushing past the seam of my lips. His cock swells against my thigh, and my body heats up. I shift so his straining erection is nudged up against my pussy. I circle my hips and let out a little moan when he rubs past my clit. His hands slide down to cup my ass cheeks, his fingers kneading me aggressively. James gives me a good squeeze and pushes his erection against my center. He does it again, and I moan into his mouth. His nails dig into my skin. I love when he does that. Wetness seeps from my pussy, and my nipples harden against his bare chest. I know he feels it because the tiny bikini I'm wearing is thin and has no padding. I hook one leg around his hip and grind against him, only to break the kiss to look up.

"I knew I felt eyes on me."

James follows my gaze and sees a monkey looking down on us. I giggle. Better than seeing a jaguar.

"I need you," he says, dropping his forehead to my shoulder. He peppers little sensual kisses on my neck, moving over my jaw and toward my mouth.

"What if someone sees us?" I ask, threading my fingers through his hair.

"Let them."

I blink at my husband, liking this adventurous side of him.

"Take me," I whisper. "I'm yours, always. Only ever yours."

James looks at me, his fingers finding the string tied at my hip. His eyes are as blue as the water surrounding us. The need in his gaze doesn't go unnoticed and draws me closer to him. James unties one side of my bathing suit as I tug his boardshorts down his thighs, my eyes never leaving his. My bottoms slip away. His hips rear back, and his erection springs free, pointing straight at me. James hoists me up and presses my back against the wall of an old Ceiba tree for leverage. I wrap my arms around his shoulders. Thank goodness the wood is smooth like bamboo and not covered with prickly bark. Palming his thick length, James coats his tip with my wetness and circles my clit.

"Always ready for me," he says, his voice low and husky.

My hips angle toward his, silently asking for more. "Don't tease me."

James drags his cock down the center of my pussy and thrusts in without a second thought. My back bows from being filled. A groan vibrates in my throat from the initial force it takes for him to get through, the bite of pain from being stretched.

"Yes," I whisper.

He shifts his feet and hold me under my thighs with both hands. His mouth finds mine, and I whimper. James matches my hunger and uses the base of his cock to circle against my clit, knowing how much I love that. It's a craving he understands. His fingers dig into my skin. His chest presses into mine, and my thighs squeeze his waist. James slowly withdraws so I experience every inch of his delicious cock. He breaks the kiss and glances down. I follow his gaze, panting. We watch his swollen length disappear inside me.

I don't know how it's possible, but sex with him gets better and better each time.

"I'm addicted to you," I say.

He peers into my eyes. "You know I love you more than life itself, right, Aubrey? All I ever want is to see you happy. This thing with Reece means nothing. If doing it makes you feel any less loved, I'll cancel it. You're my world. Everything I do is for you."

"I've never questioned your love before, and I'm not going to start now," I say, my voice breathless. "But I do have one request."

He nips at my lips. "Name your price, sweetheart."

I chuckle, thinking back to when he first said those words to me. He remembers too or else he wouldn't have said that.

"I want you both to fuck me at the same time."

James thrusts in and holds it there. The veins in his neck jut out. I've never been taken by two men at once, and the thought arouses me.

"Fuck," he groans, his fingertips digging into my hips. He's going to leave bruises with how hard he's gripping me. I guess he likes the idea too. "You mean ..." He trails off.

I nod, answering his question. "I want you in the back and Reece in the front."

"Fuck, yes."

Our mouths collide in a heated kiss once more. My imagination begins to run wild with the fantasy I never thought would happen.

James and I have had anal sex a few times. He's a well-endowed man, and the initial breach feels like fire ripping through me. It's not something I typically like, and it takes a lot of foreplay to get me there. Once we do get there, the orgasm hits ten times harder for the both of us. It's unlike anything I've ever felt.

"James," I say in warning.

"I know, baby. I know. Touch yourself."

I do as he says and rub my aching clit. James bites my bottom lip. My pussy throbs, and wetness coats my inner thighs. I slide my triangle top to the side to expose my breast, offering him my rosy nipple.

"Reece isn't allowed to come inside your beautiful pussy. Only ever me."

Before I can even nod, James suctions his mouth around my breast. He tugs almost to the point of pain then flicks his tongue over the bud, his beard grazing my heated skin. He's not gentle. I hold the back of his head to my chest. Threading my fingers through his hair, I fist the strands as my toes curl, meeting him thrust for thrust. James flattens his tongue and laps my nipple with speed. The beginning of an orgasm forms at the base of my spine. Heart pounding, my breathing deepens.

"Baby, I can't hold it any longer."

"I don't want you to hold back. Come on my cock," James says.

The orgasm takes over, and I'm coming in a rush of ecstasy. Chills dance down my arms, despite the humidity. My pussy pulses around his cock. He pistons his hips over and over until every bit of my pleasure is wrung from me. No longer can I hold myself up. My legs dangle at his sides like wet noodles.

"What about coming in my mouth? Do you want me to swallow his cum?"

Saying it out loud makes my tender clit throb. My heart races in anticipation. James grumbles in the back of his throat, and it vibrates against my chest.

"Yes," he hisses.

"Do you want Valentina to swallow both of your cum ... at the same time."

"Fuck," he grits between his teeth. "Fuck," he says again. "Yes."

James slams into me so hard the slap echoes around us. I draw in a breath of air. His cock jerks inside me, and then there's the tell-tale moan that he's orgasming. He unloads, and the sounds coming out of him cause a lazy smile to spread across my face. Making my man feel good pleases me. James doesn't stop until he's released every ounce of his orgasm. Warmth seeps from my pussy, and I hear a dollop fall to the ground.

I have a feeling tomorrow is going to be the ride of a lifetime.

Chapter 5

I forgot how much I love a full glam makeup routine. Feeling extra pretty and seductive, I bronze my cheeks and brush them with a light coating of mauve blush. All I have left is to line my lips red. Men love red lipstick. I lean forward and adjust my false lashes then use the pad of my pinky to swipe away the eye shadow dust above my cheek. I went with a smokey Cleopatra eye, wanting to embody the goddess of disguise. Valentina is a sexual illusion. Full of dark desire and craving. But she comes with a price, and her fee is how I live out my fantasies too. The thought of two men owning my body for the night so they can do whatever they want wets my panties. I'm turned on just thinking about them manhandling me. Demanding I do what they please.

My palms are starting to sweat. Reaching for the travel-size perfume, I spritz Miss Dior all over my body, making sure to add a light squirt between my thighs. I place the bottle down when my cell phone rings. I see Natalie's name and swipe to answer her FaceTime call. She smiles and sits down on a high-back chair that resembles a chaise lounge.

"*Hi Valentina*," Natalie says, her deep voice resembling a man's. "Wow. You look gorgeous."

I smile. "Thanks. I feel gorgeous." The tension in my shoulders loosens. "I'm so glad you called. I could use the distraction."

"Perfect timing. Where's James?"

"He's down at the hotel bar with Reece."

"Good. So we can talk before they get there. Are you excited?"

"I can't tell what I am. Maybe anxious. I'm nervous to see

Reece. I mean, I see him occasionally, but never for a rendezvous. This is different. Then I wonder if things will be different the next time we see each other. Like awkward."

"Has it been weird between the three of you since that night?" she asks.

I tilt my head to the side, musing over her question. I think back to all the instances I was with both James and Reece and how everything seemed completely normal.

"No, actually, it hasn't."

"Everything will stay the same. There's no reason for it to change. Since you're already pretending to work for Madame Christine again, take a shot of vodka before you get started like you did back then. I'll take one with you."

I eye the liquor bottle on the private bar in our bungalow room. "Good idea."

"You're going to have so much fun. I want the details immediately. I can't believe James is into sharing." She nods with her chin. "Show me your outfit."

Standing up, I untie my silk belt on the long satin robe I'm wearing and show her my two-piece, deep-purple lingerie outfit.

"They're going to eat you alive."

I beam a huge smile at her.

"I may buy something like that just to fuck with Luca. What heels are you going to wear?"

Picking up the designer heals from the white shelf they sit on, I hold them in front of the camera. Natalie leans in. The pointed stiletto is wrapped in black satin, and the back of the heel is covered in crystals and gemstones. One can't go wrong with Badgley Mischka pumps.

"Love them. Leave them on until the night is over. What are the rules?"

"Reece can't orgasm inside of me."

She shrugs like it's a reasonable rule. "What about your

mouth?" she asks.

I chuckle but then pause. Blinking, I say, "He didn't say no to that. I told James I'd swallow them both."

Natalie yells in excitement, her eyes wide and large. "You sick biddy. I love it. Can he touch you anywhere?" she asks. "Kiss you?"

I nod. "Not much is off-limits," I say.

"No wonder James was a member of Sanctuary Cove."

I chuckle under my breath and pour a shot. "I guess the apple doesn't fall far from the tree."

"Yeah, but my Natalia days are over for good."

"Do you miss it?"

"No. Despite all the shit talking I do about Luca, he keeps me grounded. He'd kill me with his bare hands if I ever tried anything like that. Could be fun, though."

I gasp dramatically. "Who are you, and what have you done with Natalie?"

"Did I hear you say my name, wife?"

I watch as a real smile spreads across Natalie's face at the sound of Luca's voice. Her entire face lights up. I wonder if she's even aware of it. Natalie giggles this time.

"No. I wasn't talking about you," she lies. "Get out of my room."

"No," Luca counters.

"Wait. You have your own room?" I ask, my brows bunching together.

"Oh, yeah. I need my space," she says but doesn't look at me as she does. Natalie's eyes are trained on Luca's. They're twinkling. It's so cute seeing her in love, even though she'll never admit she is. "It was part of our arranged-marriage agreement."

"What did you do?" Luca asks.

"Nothing." But she says it too quickly.

"Then why would I need to strangle you?" Luca says, his voice growing closer.

"If I wanted to bring another man into the bedroom, you'd strangle me for asking."

Silence permeates in the background. Natalie's smile grows bigger, and her blue eyes stand out. Luca starts speaking in Italian. Then says, "That is because no one touches what is mine. And, my love, there is no other man who can satisfy you the way I can," Luca says confidently in broken English.

"Is that a challenge?"

"Natalia" is all Luca says. He says her name like it's a warning, and it does the trick because she changes the subject.

I chuckle quietly to myself. Luca is from Italy. Natalie is Natalia there. Her past is part of her present.

"What?" she says innocently, knowing she's far from innocent. "Have a shot with Aubrey and me," she tells Luca. "We're celebrating." Natalie stands to walk with the phone. She places it on a counter like I did and then sets up her shot glasses.

"If I have a shot, then you have to kiss me."

She gives him a droll stare then drops her eyes to look at the phone. She exhales a dramatic sigh. "The things I do for you," she says, as if it's a hardship.

I smile, grateful Natalie is a ride-or-die best friend. "You've done worse for yourself."

She raises a brow and the corner of her lip at the same time. "True."

"Is there a bar in your room?" I ask, curious, looking at her background. I just realized she didn't leave her room to get alcohol.

"A bar for both coffee and cocktails. I even have a mini fridge so I never have to leave my room."

I bob my head, impressed. Natalie hands Luca a shot glass in the shape of a skull.

"I give her a castle, and she acts like a prisoner."

Natalie puckers her lips at Luca in response.

Luca shakes his head. He isn't playing around. "No. I want to kiss my wife. Give me your tongue."

Her eyes light up with delight. "That's going to require two shots," she tells him. "You didn't stipulate that the first time."

"Negotiating? That is fine, my love, but you better be prepared to handle me after."

Natalie turns back to the camera and smirks. Luca peers around to the phone and waves at the screen. I smile, greeting him.

"What is the celebration for?" Luca asks me.

Realizing she can't tell Luca about my party-of-three secret, Natalie gives me a fleeting look before she says, "Aubrey is going to a nude couple's spa for swingers." She lifts her shot glass. "Liquid courage."

My eyes widen in shock. Natalie is so serious that Luca stills. Of all the lies she could have come up with, she goes with that. His perplexed stare makes it a struggle not to laugh.

He peers cautiously at me. "Your husband is okay with this?"

I catch the aversion in his tone, but it doesn't bother me. "It was his idea."

Luca pulls back and stands tall. "I do not understand Americans," he says. "All you need is one good lover."

"Speak for yourself," Natalie tells him.

"I speak for you too," Luca says quickly. His eyes lower. He speaks Italian, and Natalie raises her glass.

"Ready?" she says.

Natalie counts down, and we all three take a shot together. I grimace from the awful taste. It's been so long since I've drunk straight vodka that I've grown to dislike the liquor. I'm partial to cognac now because of James. But vodka was part of my ritual in becoming Valentina. I swallow thickly, and a cringe follows. The hair on my arms rises.

"*Salute*," Luca says then turns toward Natalie. "Come see me when you are done so I can claim my prize." He puts the glass down, swoops in to give Natalie a quick kiss, and then walks away.

I catch the faint sound of the door clicking shut. "You love to get under his skin, don't you?"

Her eyes twinkle with trouble. "It's my favorite part of the day."

I chuckle, but my heart races in anticipation. It's almost showtime. I'm a little anxious since I didn't think I'd be doing anything like this ever again, but there's a part of me that's excited to explore James's fantasy together.

Knowing James wants to see another man's hands on my body has me eager for this night to begin. He's possessive, and I know deep down it makes him hard with envy. I'm going to lay it on thick and be a seductive temptress that'll make him crave me. My thighs rub together just thinking about it.

"Twenty minutes before they'll be here. I want to freshen up and get dressed. I'll text you when it's over. I'm already starting to sweat," I say.

"Normally I'd say spit or swallow, but something tells me that tonight you're going to only swallow."

I giggle. "Now it really is just like the old days."

"If I don't hear from you the moment Reece leaves, I'm going to turn into the stepdaughter from hell for you."

Chapter 6

The doorknob to the suite jiggles. I turn sharply toward the sound, and my heart begins to slam against my chest.

James pushes the door open and walks in with a radiance surrounding him. I'd left the sliding glass doors open to watch the sunset, and I'm glad I did. The yellow-amber glow from the late-afternoon sun slipping past the horizon illuminates James's entire being. He's carrying a drink in one hand as he holds the door for Reece to walk through with his other. Reece also has a drink. The guys are mid-conversation when they notice me.

I'm sitting on one of the lounge chairs in the living room, sipping on sparkling water as the vodka streams through my veins. I'd purposely turned the blinds to half-mast so slivers of long shadows crossed my body. My freshly shaven legs are crossed at the knee and exposed to the tops of my thighs. The satin robe splits down the center and drapes down the sides of the chair, making my legs appear extra-long in my five-inch pumps.

James brings the glass to his mouth and takes a sip, a fire burning in his gaze as he swallows. The tattoo across his chest plays peak-a-boo from the buttons left undone. Our eyes meet, and my body hums to life. I'm eager for his hands to be on me.

Standing next to him is Reece, his mischievous grin filled with interest. He's attractive, but he's no match for James. Blond men have never really been my type. Still, Reece works the salt and sandy hair well.

I can't believe I'm going to have sex with him tonight.

The guys look like they just walked in from a casual business meeting, wearing dress pants and button-down dress shirts cuffed to their elbows. James dons his favorite comfort shoes—velvet Gucci loafers—while Reece wears a common business shoe. Very bougee of James, but I low-key love how confident he is in his skin. He's a suave silver fox. And he's all mine.

Stepping forward, James groans under his breath as I stand. "Unbelievable," he whispers. He rakes a satisfied stare down the length of my body, obviously pleased with what he sees. His baby blues are twinkling in approval. "Is that new?"

A seductive smile curls the corners of my mouth. "I got it for the trip. I brought a few new things."

"Never thought I'd see the day the three of us would share a bed again," Reece says as a way of greeting and kisses my cheek. He pulls back to peer down at me. "You look radiant as ever." His gaze immediately drops to my chest.

The lacy robe falls off my shoulder, showing the tops of my breasts. I'm wearing a bra, but I purposely bought it two sizes too small so it'd give me great cleavage.

"You and me both," I say.

My eyes shift to James, who's watching us with interest.

"How was your pregame date?" It's not like they don't see each other often at work and needed time to catch up.

James kisses my cheek. "It was ... interesting."

"A few drinks helped ease the conversation," Reece adds.

Seems like we're all starting with a buzz, a necessary evil for a night like this. I don't plan to get sloshed, but tipsy enough to let more of my inhibitions down. Back when I was actively playing Valentina, it was easy to get the show going. I was in charge, and there was a time limit. While tonight I get to play her again, I'm not sure how it's going to start. It's a little awkward now that I'm married. Do I make the first move? Should I just get on my knees and start by sucking them off?

We make small talk for a couple of minutes, until there's a

knock on the door. James answers it, and a man walks in rolling a cart that contains three peach-colored drinks. Reece tips the gentleman before he leaves.

James hands me a glass then raises his in the air. "A night to remember."

Our glasses clink, and I swallow the sweet tequila mixture all too easily. Drinks like these are dangerous, so I pace myself.

Reece and James have been friends for over twenty years. They met at the law firm they both work at. Sharing women is nothing new to them. While they don't hook up or kiss, they're comfortable being naked around each other.

"How do you want to start this thing?" I ask, taking my last sip.

Reece and James both share a look, like they already have an idea in mind.

"There's been a change in the plans. Instead of having Valentina taking care of us, we're going to take care of her," James says.

Surprised, I shoot a glance at Reece to gauge his reaction then back to James for clarification. "What do you mean?"

"I want you to feel good. Seeing you drown in pleasure gets me hard. You can orgasm as many times as you want. You can kiss him, fuck him, suck him, as long as my mouth is on you at the same time."

Heat rises to my cheeks. My nipples harden, and I can sense them poking through my robe. James notices, and his gaze drops.

"What do you think about that?" Reece says.

I stare at him, stunned and nearly speechless.

This is a fantasy come to life. Two men want to devour my body and be at their mercy. Why the hell would I say no to that?

"You want this, don't you?" James asks.

Bobbing my head, I finally find my words. "I'm definitely not going to reject the offer." I pause. "Yes, I do. I want it."

Excitement glitters in his eyes. "Come here, sweetheart."

I stand and reach for the bow at my waist and walk toward James. He's seated on the edge of the armrest with his knees spread wide, hands resting on his thick thighs. His fingers replace mine, and he unties my bow, looking up as he slides the robe off my shoulders. The robe falls in a soft heap around my feet. James hisses in approval, and Reece make a similar sound. I'm standing tall in only lingerie, the pumps, and thigh-high elastic stockings. James's palms skim up the outside of my thighs. When he reaches my butt, his brows pinch, and he peaks around to my backside to see the thong I'm wearing. His nails trail my pebbled skin. James leans in and kisses my stomach. My fingers thread his hair, and I stare down at him.

"Are you already wet?" he asks, his voice low.

"Yes," I admit.

"Before I even touched you?"

"Yes."

A low growl comes from him that sends chills down my arms.

"You want us to both fuck you tonight?" James asks.

A blush crawls up my chest. My heart is pounding in my ears. It's now or never. "Yes."

"This is how that night years ago should have gone."

I swallow hard. James reaches between my thighs to cup my pussy, only to pull back in surprise when he touches my bare skin.

"Easy access," I say then spread my stance so he can see the splice in my panties. "Thought you might like it."

"Fuck," he groans. "Get on the bed and spread your legs. Show Reece what you're wearing."

I nearly sprint to the king-size bed in the other room. They follow quickly. Only, I don't open my legs to show Reece.

"I want both of you naked," I tell them before they come any closer. "Strip."

They remove their clothes in a matter of seconds. I wanted

to sneak a look at Reece's cock, but James has my full attention as he walks toward me. Once their clothes are on the floor, I slowly spread my knees open.

"Fuck, that's hot," Reece says.

My cheeks burn from how exposed I am. James kneels on the bed and slips behind me. He lifts me to sit on his lap, shifting me so his hard cock isn't pressing into my back. He palms my knees and spreads them for his friend.

"Tell me if she tastes like you remember."

My heart is racing. This is really happening.

Reece eyes my pussy like a starved man. He wastes no time and dives between my thighs. His lips suction around my clit like a vacuum, and he sucks. On instinct, I try to close my legs, but James holds them open. Reece swipes up the center of my pussy with a flat tongue then spears my entrance. I gasp and yell out, my hips nearly coming off the bed.

"Fuck, I forgot how good she tastes," Reece says, lapping quickly.

"I want you to eat her pussy until she's creaming into your mouth."

My clit throbs at his words. I dig my fingers into the tops of James's legs. Reece has an unusually long tongue. He drags it up the length of my pussy, twirling the tip around my clit then back down to the bottom, where he delves inside surprisingly deep. My inner thighs quiver. My heels dig into the bed, and my breathing grows shallow. A heat of desire shoots up my spine. Reece picks up the speed. I inhale a large gulp of air to catch my breath, yelling out. My legs are restless. He suctions his mouth around my clit and begins sucking so good that another moan rolls off my lips. James palms the back of Reece's head and holds his friend's face to my pussy. Wetness seeps from me at the sight. I can't believe this is happening.

"Like I said, we're taking care of you tonight," James says in my ear.

Chapter 7

James pulls down the top of my bra. He caresses my breasts until my nipples are hard. I turn toward his face and search for his lips. He kisses me hard and deep, his tongue stroking powerfully against mine. Reece gently bites down on my clit, and I moan in the back of my throat. He inserts a finger into my pussy then another. I tighten, sighing. I need more. My orgasm is right there, and I want to free fall into it.

"I could lick her pussy all night," Reece says, running the tip of his nose between my folds. "You're a lucky man, James. She tastes so fucking sweet My cock is like a rock from eating her out."

"I feast on her every morning," James says. "It's a great way to start the day."

"I need more," I say before I can stop myself. "I want to come."

James taps the side of my hip, signaling for me to lift. "Reece, guide my cock into her pussy."

My eyes fly open. I almost choke on my saliva as Reece palms James's erection. He grips his width, swipes the pad of his thumb over the milky fluid dripping at the tip, then gives him a good stroke. White-hot desire consumes me at the sight. Reece rubs the cream into James's skin, and fuck, is that such a turn on. I've never seen another man touch my husband intimately.

James places his hands under my thighs to help lift my hips. Reece angles James's length toward my entrance. I hold my breath. The crown slides in, and my clit begins to throb. I exhale a long sigh. He places his hands on my waist and guides me down until every inch of my husband's cock fills me. James resumes kneading my breasts, but Reece can't tear his eyes away. James stretches me open, and it's a sight to see.

"Now, eat her out," James orders.

My eyes widen at his words. Why did that sound so hot?

James rocks into me just as Reece leans down and takes my clit into his mouth again.

"Oh, oh, oh," I moan out, my thighs quivering. I begin squirming on James, my pussy growing wetter. "Oh, my goodness. This feels incredible."

"Good. That's what we want to hear," James says.

Reece laps circles around my clit like a fucking pro, tapping and flicking at just the right pace. James rolls his hips into mine, thrusting in and out. I can't help but wonder if Reece is licking James's cock when he pulls out.

"Oh, damn. This is all too much." My nails dig into James's thighs as I try to fight the orgasm begging to be freed. "It feels so good," I nearly whine. "Don't stop."

My hips move on their own accord, rolling over James's swollen cock. He continues to kiss my neck, nipping and pulling my skin into his mouth. The sensations are reaching a point of no return. My breathing deepens, and I begin moaning out loud, unable to control myself.

"You're soaking wet. You must like what Reece is doing," James says. "Tell me you like it."

"I love it. He has a wicked tongue and sucks my pussy so good," I whisper, channeling Valentina. I roll my hips up his erection until only the tip is left in me. "A perfect match for the way your cock fucks me," I say then sink down.

We moan in unison. James's thrusts quicken and become harder as Reece pulls my tender clit into his mouth. James thrusts, his balls hitting Reece's chin. I cry out, whimpering from the intense pleasure about to consume me.

"Do you like seeing your friend lick my pussy?"

"Makes me hard," James says.

I want to come, and I need to. I won't be able to hold on much longer. My mind is hazy from both men taking control of my body.

"Make her come with your mouth, Reece," James says then palms the back of Reece's head and presses him against me. The sight soaks me. "I want to feel her come on my cock."

Reece's tongue speeds up. He flattens it then flicks my clit, alternating until I'm panting.

"Take it," James grits behind. He thrusts deeper, and I gasp. "Take it," he repeats just as Reece's teeth bite into me.

All I can see are Reece's broad shoulders and his messy curls, his head bobbing. James smothers Reece with my pussy. Both men are taking me, devouring me, and it makes me soar into the sky. Knowing that my husband wants his friend to make me orgasm makes all the difference. Valentina can enjoy herself, which means Aubrey can too.

The pressure builds, and it feels oh so good. My pussy pulses, and I exhale a sigh that turns into a long moan. Every nerve ending comes alive. Stars explode behind my eyes, and I come hard. I can't stop the orgasm from taking over. James's cock combined with Reece's tongue is a gift. I roll my hips into both men and take what they give me.

"Don't stop. Don't stop. Don't stop," I pant.

"That's it. Come for us," James says. "I want you to soak my cock before Reece gets the chance to fuck you."

His words get to me. Is it wrong that I'm looking forward to having sex with Reece? Neither one of the guys let up until my breathing slows and the tension in my body leaves.

James's cock twitches. His stomach dips against my back before he's following in my bliss. One of his knees comes up as his orgasm spurts inside me. Reece has James's balls gripped in his palm. I search for his other hand, but it's lower, near his butt. His wrists flex. My eyes narrow. I wonder if he's pressing his thumb against James's asshole. Warm fluid seeps out, and I know it's his cum. I love when that happens because it tells me how good he feels too.

James slows down and releases his hold on Reece and me. His breathing matches mine. I can feel his heart pounding against my back. My head falls to the side, and he kisses the exposed side of my neck.

"Don't move," Reece instructs.

With wild eyes, Reece leans forward and licks clean the creamy white cum. His tongue tickles my sensitive skin as he licks away. I watch in utter fascination, unable to tear my gaze away. My clit throbs, and my nipples harden to points again.

"Reece swings both ways," James says low in my ear. "He'd suck my cock if I let him."

Huh. I didn't know that.

Reece throws a thumbs-up. He lifts his face, and there's a glaze all over his mouth and chin.

"He's ready for you. Make him see stars the way you do me."

I listen like a good girl and move off James. His cock leaves my pussy with a plop. Reece lays back on the bed, his head close to the edge. He motions for me to come to him, and I do. James gets out of bed and picks up his drink. He takes a long swallow like he's parched and watches me crawl to his friend.

"Ride me," Reece says.

"Your wish is my command."

Reece grips his erection and holds it steady as I throw a leg over his hips. He positions the tip at my entrance. Inhaling a deep breath, I look to James. He's watching closely, his gaze trained on my pussy as I sink down on his friend's cock. Goose bumps cover my arms. Reece lets out a long, sexy groan.

"Fuck," he groans. "God, you feel so damn good. I can feel James's cum still inside you. James, take her top off. I want to see her tits bounce."

The way he uses me for his own good fills me with satisfaction. I like being the source of someone's euphoria. James places his drink down and walks back to the bed. He reaches around to unclasp my bra then gives me a deep kiss. James pulls it off so Reece can palm my breasts, pushing them together and rubbing my nipples. It sends a zing through my blood straight to my clit. I love nipple play.

"What a view," Reece says.

We break the kiss then look down. James's cock is standing tall between us where his friend lays his head on the bed. He widens his stance and begins stroking his cock, watching me while I ride his friend. Reece groans, and something about it causes me to bounce harder.

"That's what I like. Fuck me, ride me. Take my cock," Reece says through gritted teeth. I nearly whimper. "Make James come with your mouth but don't swallow. Let it fall out."

James cups my jaw and lifts my chin to meet his gaze. He said if I was having sex with Reece, then his mouth had to be on me.

But then the rules changed.

Leaning forward, I place my palms on Reece's chest and take James's semihard cock into my mouth. My tongue wraps around his length, and I hollow my cheeks to suck him hard. I know what James likes, so it won't take me long to make him orgasm.

"Hold still. We'll do the work," Reece says, and I nod. I'm not going to argue with that.

James pumps into my mouth while Reece drives into my pussy. My breasts are swaying and bouncing. Reece fingers my nipples, tugging and teasing so good it shoots right to my pussy.

"Fuck. I'm closer than I thought," James says.

I glow in satisfaction.

"Good, because I can't hold on much longer. I'm gonna flip her over and fuck her from behind after you come."

I groan in the back of my throat, and James chuckles. I love doggy style, and he knows it.

Minutes later, James announces that he's coming. He holds the back of my head to the center of his hips and unloads with a loud groan. The warm, salty liquid hits the back of my throat. I don't stop until I take every bit of James's cum. Creamy white fluid slips out from the corners of my mouth and dribbles down my chin. Normally I would swallow, but Reece made a special request and asked me to spit. It's so thick and gooey as it plops onto Reece.

James releases a sated sigh. He cups my jaw lovingly then steps back. My tongue pushes against the fluid, and the rest of his orgasm spills from my swollen lips. Reece reaches up to rub the cream into my chest and over my neck. His eyes are glossy, heavy, and he has James's orgasm all over his neck and chin. The sight of him covered in my husband's cum sends me close to the edge. His tries to lick away what he can reach. He doesn't see the dollops on his neck, so I lean down and clean him up with my tongue until there's none left. I pull on Reece's neck, and he hums in approval. His body clutches to mine, his arms and legs holding me tightly. Our limbs tangle each other's as we search for the same blissful state. Reece's fingers thread my hair, and he becomes ravenous. His hips jerk into mine, and he rubs against my clit. It's the best of both worlds. I cry out, desperately wanting to come again.

"Use my cock and fuck yourself with it. Ride me hard."

Reece guides my mouth back to his. The kiss is filled with seduction. Reece drags his tongue across the roof of my mouth. I moan against his lips. A hand paddles my ass cheek so hard that it causes my pussy to squeeze Reece's cock. For a brief moment, I wonder if it was James who spanked me.

My fingers thread Reece's curls. I tug his hair and fist the small strands. His mouth never leaves mine, and I become an animal, pumping my hips against his, trying to fuck him back. I use Reece like I'm told I can. Without abandon. We don't stop kissing until an orgasm rips through me. Shuddering in ecstasy, I let go and come on a cock that isn't my husband's.

My movements slow, and Reece notices. He lifts my hips to pull out then turns me over. Arching my hips back, I spread my knees and press the side of my face to the bed. I barely have the strength to hold myself up after the orgasms and being fucked so hard.

Valentina doesn't take a lunch break on the job.

Reece spreads me open with one hand on my ass cheek then glides his rock-hard cock back into my pussy. I close my eyes and sigh from being filled. He grips my hips, fingers digging roughly into bones. His thighs pound against mine as the bed shifts under us.

"Can I cum on her?" Reece asks James, panting the words.

My gaze lifts to James. Our eyes meet. Not everyone likes to be shot with cum. Some people consider it degrading, but I don't. James knows I find it erotic.

"She's all yours," James says, his voice guttural.

A little smile of appreciation splays across my face. James notices.

Reece guides my hips up higher so I'm arching at a deeper angle. My knees slip on the comforter, spreading me wider. He rubs one butt cheek with the palm of his hand then slides along the length of my spine to grab the back of my neck. He clutches tight and slams into me with force.

"Do you want to cum on me too?"

Reece groans at the question directed toward James. His cock hits deep, and I gasp at the spark of pain it caused. He's going to tear me in two if he keeps going at this rate.

"You did say you would swallow our cum at the same time," James says, reminding me of my earlier words.

He reaches for his cock, and I wave him over.

Reece surges into me. He holds himself still and doesn't move. His thighs are pressed against mine when his cock jerk inside me.

I can sense he's close to finishing.

"Fuck. Hurry up," Reece tells James.

James walks over and reaches under to rub my clit. He's fast like a vibrator and knows exactly how to get me off quickly. Little moans push through my lips as an orgasm forms. My hips rock back into Reece, chasing the gratification. I'm aching. My nipples graze the sheets, sending spikes of need through me. From the corner of my eye, he's already hard.

"Oh, I'm right there. Don't stop, don't stop, don't stop," I say, my words breathless.

Fisting the blanket, I cry out in ecstasy, orgasming again before falling into a heap on the bed. My eyes roll close in a blissful haze. Heart racing, I'm trying to catch my breath. James gently rolls me over. My knees flop open, and my legs spread. I exhale a long sigh, the cool blanket feeling divine against my heated skin.

Pushing up, I sit on my knees, my sticky breasts hanging out. There's a mess of our fluids on the bed.

"I won't be able to fit both of you in my mouth at the same time, but I can suck the tips if you want me to."

They both move forward. I've never done this before, but I'm going to try.

I take James into my mouth first, giving him one good lick, and then Reece squeezes in. I do the same for him. It's not easy. They're both well-endowed men. There's a lot of slurping and spit dripping onto my thighs, and I can't get my mouth to close around them.

James takes my mouth for himself. I suck him off so good that within seconds, he pulls out and tips my head back. My eyes lift to his.

"Open your mouth, Valentina," he orders.

Chills cover my arms. I like when he tells me what to do.

I stick my tongue out just as James orgasms. He squeezes his cock, twisting his wrist with a moan. He paints me with his cum then draws over my breasts until he's wrung every bit of pleasure from himself. I run my tongue over my bottom lip and swallow. Reece grunts and groans. He guides the back of my head toward his straining erection, and I suck him the same way I sucked James. It doesn't take Reece long. He pulls out, and I open my mouth just like I did for James. His orgasm is hot. Thick streams of cum streak across my chest, mixing with James's.

"Rub it on you," Reece says, his voice low. "Rub both on your pussy. Stick our cum inside of you."

My eyes widen with excitement. The thought arouses me.

Lying on my back, my knees spread, I do as instructed. Holding my pussy lips open with two fingers, I put on a show by using their orgasms as lubricant and touch myself. A wet, sticky sound echoes in the room before I slip two fingers inside. Sticking their cum inside me is filthy, but damn if it doesn't turn me on. My fingers softly caress the walls of my tender pussy, sliding in and out. A little purr vibrates in the back of my throat as I curl my fingers and stroke. Two pair of eyes can't look away.

Just when I thought we were done, Reece takes my wrist and pulls my hand away. He eyes my fingers that are coated in all three of us then brings them to his mouth. My eyes lower. His tongue delves between my digits until they're clean. He releases my hand then leans down and gently laps at my tender clit. He's not wild, but soft. Like he's saying thank you. I gasp, unprepared for the little shocks to reverberate through me. My hips push subtly into his face. Reece uses his thumb to tease the little space between my clit and my entrance. A sigh of bliss rolls off my lips.

James hovers above me, eyes sated, and presses a soft kiss to my mouth. His tongue tangles with mine as Reece quickly carries me over the edge one more time.

"You were incredible, sweetheart."

Chapter 8

I'm sitting on James's lap, naked in the private hot spring tub facing Reece.

It's like a mini jacuzzi without the jets and just what I needed to recover from the pounding my pussy took. The orgasms were mind blowing and intense, more than I thought possible. Just thinking about Reece's mouth wrapped around my clit while James's cock was inside me makes me ache to be touched again.

The night isn't over. I secretly needed a break and was glad James suggested one. We've been soaking in the warm water for over thirty minutes now.

"I didn't know you liked men," I say to Reece, intrigued from earlier.

He shrugs one shoulder casually. "I don't broadcast that I'm bisexual. If it happens, it happens. I enjoy having sex with both men and women. The experience is completely different."

Under the water, James cups my pussy and tugs me to him. He presses the tip of his finger against my opening. My legs spread on their own accord, and his cock bounces lightly against my back from the gravity of the water.

"Do you think you'll ever settle down and get married?" I ask.

"No," he says quickly, shaking his head. "Unless I can be in an open relationship, the answer is no. Never."

James's laugh vibrates against my back. "Reece is going to be a bachelor his whole life." He's teasing my entrance with his fingers, stroking over my swollen lips.

Reece's boyish grin is contagious. He runs his fingers through his damp hair, the curls tight at the ends. "I'm okay with that. I like my freedom," he says. "Most people aren't comfortable in their own presence. I welcome the solitude. Peace and silence are a wonderful thing."

I raise my champagne glass. "Good for you for knowing what you want. Half the world still doesn't know, and their time is running out."

James slides a finger into my pussy, and I nearly choke in the middle of swallowing my champagne. I hook my legs around his calves.

"You guys aren't playing without me, are you?" Reece says, swimming toward us.

My nipples pucker in anticipation. James holds out my breast as an offering to Reece. I inhale a small breath, a new wave of desire falling over me.

"Your tits are bigger than I remember," Reece says, stopping in front of me.

He smushes them together then leans down and takes one into his mouth, twirling his tongue around the pink part in a way that, if I were standing, would make my knees shake. He pulls back with a pop, the tip of his tongue lingering on the tip of my nipple.

James takes one of Reece's wrists and pulls it underwater. A moan pushes its way from me as both their fingers slide into my pussy.

"Fuck," I mumble inwardly. The thought is just as hot as the real thing. They rub the walls of my pussy, manipulating me wider. "That feels incredible," I whisper.

James takes my glass and places it on the ledge. He slips his hand underwater again. This time he goes slow. "I propose an idea."

A thrill of excitement moves through me. Valentina never

turns down an offer. "What is it?"

"What if we both fucked you tonight." He pauses. "And I don't mean one in the back and one in the front."

My brows draw together at what he's implying. "You mean ..."

"Fuck your pussy. Together. Both of our cocks at the same time."

"Yes," Reece groans out. "Hell, yes."

His request renders me speechless. James doesn't exactly have a pencil dick, and neither does Reece. If they were smaller I'd consider it, but I don't think both could fit inside me. Some days I walk bowlegged because of James and his cock. Now he wants to stuff two inside me?

"I don't think you guys will fit," I say, dead serious. "I'm not sure I even want to test it out. I'm afraid I'll rip from hole to hole."

"We'll fit. I've done it before. It's just a muscle. It stretches. If a woman can birth a ten-pound baby, you can fit two cocks," Reece states.

I can't control the laugh that flies out of me. I giggle so hard that tears form in the corners of my eyes. I mean, I guess he's not wrong and that it is possible.

"What do you say, sweetheart? You want us to both fuck you?"

Yes is my first thought.

James presses on my clit, and I suck in a deep breath of air into my lungs. I'm not opposed to it, but the idea of it does leave me with apprehension from the mechanics of it.

"How ... and where ... What positions? Not in the water, right?"

"Instead of telling you, why don't we show you?" James suggests.

Something about that makes me come alive with burning need. My hips rear back into James's lap. Their joined fingers bring me to the edge, and euphoria takes over. I've had so many orgasms already, I've lost count.

We get out of the water and dry off. Reece and James talk about how they want to make this work, where we'll be and what we'll need. Listening, I grab the bottle of lube I packed.

"We can do it standing where we both hold her body up, or we can do it in bed sort of like missionary."

"I think the bed would be easier. That way I won't feel like I'm going to slip," I say.

I also think with both dicks inside me while standing makes it easier to rip, which is what I'm secretly afraid of.

"We won't drop you," James says quickly.

I smile at him. "I know, but it just seems like so much more work."

"Bed it is," Reece says. "Aubrey, get on top of James. Chest to chest. You guys do your thing, and then I'll join. Don't come, Aubrey."

Reece is speaking when it dawns on me he hasn't seen James and me have sex before. James has watched me with Reece, but not the other way around. Need drips down my inner thigh at the thought of being watched with my husband. Taking one last sip of the mixed drink James gave me earlier, I place the glass down on the counter and then climb onto the bed.

"I imagine I won't be able to have much more sex after this, so make it worth it," I tell them.

James is on his back in a matter of seconds. I straddle his hips and take his cock in one long thrust.

Ah, feels like home.

We moan in unison, my eyes closing shut. Our bodies click together too perfectly, and my heart rejoices. I stay upright as he slowly fucks me, showing me who ultimately owns my body and soul. James doesn't just get Valentina. He gets both of us.

"Her pussy is soft and warm. Now is the time to join in," James suggests to Reece then looks at me. "Come here and kiss me."

Chapter 9

Leaning down, I close the distance with my lips.

James's tongue expertly strokes mine, his hands roaming my body. I forget all about Reece and begin making love to my husband. I'm aching to orgasm again, but I hold it in. Reece comes up behind me and grips my hips. He pushes me back and forth into James, helping me take his cock.

"Her pussy is dripping around your cock," Reece says, his voice raw.

His words make me wet. A part of me stays wet, knowing another pair of eyes is watching us have sex.

"A little pressure, but trust the process. You're going to come harder than you ever have." He pauses then says, "Keep fucking her, James, and don't stop. Slow and small thrusts. Don't pull all the way out."

James does exactly what Reece instructs. He keeps his hands on every inch of my body he can touch. The physical touch is necessary to take my mind off the fact that I'm about to be stretched open. I'm a little apprehensive, but I'm willing to try anything at least once.

The tip of Reece's cock presses into my opening, and the crown miraculously slips inside with ease. A breath gets lodged in my throat, and James notices. He deepens the kiss. I'm not in pain, but I realize how much I need the distraction. Reece is careful. He's not ramming into me. He surges forward again, and the sensation of being filled is suddenly electrifying. It's all I can feel, all I can think about. My pussy is pulsating, my kiss hungry. I melt into James and allow myself to fall into the pleasure both men are giving me. Reece slides in until his thighs press against the backs of mine. The pressure pushing against my clit is otherworldly. I'm throbbing. It takes every ounce of strength not to orgasm. I'm about to lose my damn mind.

"That's it," Reece says through gritted teeth. "Fuck. I'm all the way in."

I break away from the kiss, gasping for air. Reece grips both of my hips and slowly begins pumping.

"You okay?" James's eyes are wild. His breathing is labored, and there's a sheen of perspiration coating his chest.

"More than okay," I answer honestly. "I just don't know how to move."

"Just lie here, and we'll take care of the rest. Let us fuck you."

I swallow thickly. It hits me that they can feel each other's cock. "What does it feel like for you guys?"

"Un-fucking-believable," James admits, his words a whisper.

"I wish you could see what you look like from here," Reece says, his voice low and deep. "You and James."

Reece is sitting on his knees, not lying on my back. He has a view of everything. He grips the back of my hips and leans in like he's going to give me a deep-tissue massage. He runs his hands up the sides of my body. His fingers slip under over my ribs seductively slow. He cups my breasts. My forehead presses into James's chest as Reece teases my nipples with his palms. My hips try to lift on their own accord, but I don't get anywhere.

I'm trapped between them.

A sigh escapes me. My toes curl as my body unwinds. I'm at their mercy, knowing they can do whatever they want to me and I have to take it. Hands are in my hair, they're on my back, grabbing at my breasts, pulling at my ass cheeks. I don't know who is doing what, and I don't care. I have two men loving on my body in the best way possible. They're pumping and surging, moaning deep in their throats as they unleash on me. Wild abandon fills the air. Reece leans down and nips at my back. His tongue licks along my neck. My hips arch, asking for more. Reece answers my silent request.

"Go harder. Fuck me harder," I say breathlessly. "Don't hold back."

James locks me to him and thrusts deep and hard just how I like it. He holds me by the ass cheeks and spreads me open, lifting me for Reece. This angle causes a burst of lust to spear through my clit. A loud and long moan exhales from my lips. Being so turned on makes it easy to fit them both.

Reece reaches around to tug and pinches my nipples. His teeth bite into my tender skin as he thrusts into me from behind. The sensations are so overwhelming that I find myself moving my hips. We find a rhythm that has us breathing heavy and close to the edge.

"Oh, hell. I need to come. Oh, oh, oh," I chant, unable to control myself. "I won't be able to hold on much longer."

"Come whenever you want," James says.

Biting my lip, I say, "I want us to come together. We came this far. Why stop now?"

I hold my breath. James originally said Reece wasn't allowed to orgasm in me, but the thought of them spilling inside me makes me weak.

"You want Reece to come inside your pussy?" He thrusts in all the way, making sure I'm filled.

"I want you both to come inside me at the same time. Fill me with your cum. Show me how good I make you feel. Give me everything you got."

James digs his fingers into the back of my thighs. "If that's what you want, then we'll give it to you."

"Fuck," Reece whispers. His hands grip my hips as he drives into my pussy.

"Reece?" I call out.

"Hmmm?"

"How does my husband's cock feel sliding against yours?"

James's eyes narrow, and a little smirk curls the corners of his mouth.

Each time one pulls out, the tip drags down the other's length.

"Better than any wet dream I've had of him. I'm going to explode inside you."

I can't help the airy chuckle that leaves my throat. "What about you? You can tell me you like it," I say to James. "I'm turned on by the image of your cocks rubbing together."

"My cock is hard, isn't it? Fuck yeah, I like it," James says then tangles his tongue with mine.

I can't think straight. I'm making sounds and noises I've never made before. Reece takes me hard. James takes me deep. Both men are giving me the ride of my life, and all I have to do is just lie here. "I'm about to come. I can't hold on any longer," I say, feeling my orgasm climb rapidly. They plow into me, thrusting back and forth without shame when an orgasm rips through my entire being. It hits me like a wave and sends me over the edge. The pressure and friction consume me. I cry out and shake from head to toe as stars burst behind my eyes. Our limbs tighten around each other's. The sinful bliss tearing through me is so intense that I'm crying from it. They're relentless as they pound into my body.

"Oh, fuck, that's tight," Reece grits.

The feeling of being dominated by both men sends me over the edge, and I fall into the same wave of euphoria. James growls as his cock pulsates inside me. My toes curl, and I fist whatever I can grab. This is by far one of most intense orgasms I've ever had in my life.

"Fuck, that felt incredible," Reece pants.

"Never better. Never fucking better," James says, his voice hoarse. "God, that was good."

I fall in a heap on top of his chest. My hair falls around me. He's panting. His heartbeat thumps wildly against the side of my face, and his fingertips dance across my back. Reece carefully removes his cock, and the delicious pressure is immediately gone.

The mattress dips as he sits back on his knees. James gently brushes the hair away from my face. He doesn't say anything. He doesn't need to. The love in his blue eyes speaks more than words could ever say.

"I don't think there's any more cum left in me," Reece says in jest.

"Are you sore?" James slips his cock out then sets me on the bed.

I lie down, roll over onto my back, and release a sated sigh. I'm suddenly exhausted. Now I really do need a moment. My pussy is swollen, tingly in the best way.

"I am, but it's a good sore. I'm going to need a bath to recover."

Reece nudges my knee to the side then slides between my legs. He pulls back my pussy lips and stares down. His gaze darkens. Cum is dripping from me, and he's eyeing it.

"You don't have to," I say.

"I want to. Let me thank you and clean you up. I'll go easy."

"We're giving you a break before the next round," James says.

Reece leans in ever so softly and laps my pussy with his tongue. He lets out a moan as if he's enjoying the taste. He does an exceptional job cleaning up the cum from the three of us. He's so gentle. My body is still simmering from the last one that it doesn't take long for me to shatter again. I mew like a kitten, coming undone.

I've decided that Reece's tongue is the best thing about him. These are the types of sloppy kisses I could get behind.

Eventually we fall asleep in a tangle of limbs as the sun is rising. We spend most of the next day in a blissful haze, lounging in the private hot spring together. James never lets me leave the sanctuary of his arms. In the silence is where we find intimacy. Peace.

There's a stillness in him that settles my soul. My heart beats fast, knowing I made the right decision to be with both men. I nuzzle my face in the curve of his neck. My eyes grow heavy. James smooths out my feathers the way Valentina unruffles his. I needed yesterday just as much as James did, only I wasn't aware the way he was.

Valentina is more than a fantasy. She's the glue that binds us together.

Chapter 10

Glancing down at my ringing cell phone, I swipe to the side and finally answer Natalie's call.

"I swear, if you'd hit the fuck you button on me one more time, I was going to fly to New York and shake some sense into you. How could you leave me hanging like that? You call before the romp and then disappear? I waited for you! What happened to the old ram jam? Don't tell me marriage changed you. You know, you deserve to have your best friend card revoked for this."

I giggle, despite the nausea roiling through my stomach. She's basically reading me the bestie riot act. "I'm sorry, girl. But I've had food poisoning since we got back. I think it was the oysters we ate before we boarded the plane. I've been sick ever since. I've been dry heaving for days."

We've been home for a solid week now, and I'm just finally coming back to myself. I've dodged all of Natalie's calls, even though I was dying to tell her about my hot night with both men. When the night was over, I sent her a few text messages saying how sore I was and I'd get back to her the next day because I needed rest.

The guys wore me out. It wasn't that I didn't want to share what happened, but between sleeping and feeling like my stomach was eating itself. I couldn't get out of bed. James called out of work one day to take care of me, worried about the low-grade fever I developed. He waited on me hand and foot, even held my hair back when I threw up. Today was the first day I felt well enough to show my face at Sanctuary. I made it through a half day and then decided to leave so I can climb back into bed. I'm in the town car headed home to the flat in Brooklyn James and I live in. Thank goodness I have an incredible team of women who help keep the business afloat when I get knocked down.

"I talked to James, but he doesn't sound sick," Natalie says.

"He felt a little queasy, but nothing like what I've been going through."

"Man, I thought the dicks took you out. I was about to put out an Amber Alert."

I fight the giggle again and shoot a fleeting glance toward the rearview mirror to see if the driver is listening. I pray Natalie's voice doesn't carry over the phone. I never put her on speaker in public for this reason. She can't be trusted.

"Well, they kind of did," I admit. Reflecting on that night causes my panties to dampen. If our driver heard anything, he doesn't show it. "I'll tell you when I get home. Promise."

"I know you will because we aren't hanging up until I've heard every last detail."

"You're insufferable sometimes," I say. "Rode hard and put up wet is the CliffsNotes version."

She gasps. I plan to tell Natalie everything. She has no choice but to listen to me about this one.

"Maybe you're pregnant," she suggests in a passing way. "I don't think food poisoning lasts this long."

I'm going to be sick.

"That's not funny," I say.

"Pregnancy is always a possibility. I won't take the chance. With my luck, Luca will have super sperm and I'll end up with triplets from one egg that just won't give up. I always make Luca wear a condom even though I'm on birth control. He fucks me like he hates me for it. Makes the sex so much better."

My heart starts to beat faster, my chest tightening. Could there be a possibility? I guess there's always one super sperm that makes it through and that's how women end up pregnant. But that won't happen to me.

I decide to shift the topic. I'm not pregnant. Symptoms don't even happen that fast.

Right?

Exhaling a suddenly tight breath, I say, "I made your dad go hiking. He couldn't catch his breath. I wish you could have seen him. I think climbing a mountain helped with his fear of heights. James didn't realize how far he'd reached until he looked down. He was so impressed with himself."

"He hiked? Never thought I'd see the day. I'm sort of surprised you did."

"I dreaded it at first, but then we were surrounded by the most insane view of the forest. I was so glad I did it. The hike led to a private plunge pool that was basically a hot spring. Afterward we went on a chocolate tour. I smuggled some back for you."

"Thanks, bestie!" she says excitedly.

"Our room had its own garden attached." I pause. "It was one of the best vacations we've ever taken. On New Year's Eve, James surprised me with a helicopter ride over the entire island. If I could marry your dad again, I'd do it in Belize. I'm trying to convince him to buy a vacation home there."

"Was Reece there for that too?"

"No. I mean, he was there, but not with us. He had his own room. I have no idea what he did with his time."

"Where's Daddy now?" Natalie asks, her voice sugary sweet.

I snort. "You're such a brat." The car comes to a rolling stop. I unbuckle my seat belt and thank our driver, exit the car, then walk up the stairs to the red brick building.

"He's bringing me home soup and saltine crackers. It's all I've been able to handle," I tell her.

"I say take a test, just to make sure you're not preggo."

I insert the key into the bolt and turn it. "I just got a new pill, remember? I basically doubled up."

"It doesn't work like that. Most doctors suggest using protection for at least three weeks so the pill has time to be effective."

Panic runs through me. "Don't say that."

But she keeps pushing. "These are considered your childbearing years. I'd be extra careful if I were you."

"You're the worst friend."

"It's not like you have to worry about who the baby daddy is." She pauses. She's quiet then says, "You used a condom with Reece, right?"

"I'm on birth control. Reece is clean. James made sure."

"Sperm doesn't care," she says as a matter of fact. "That's why I double bag. If it gets through the second layer, then it deserves a fighting chance."

Shaking my head at her logic, I throw my keys on the foyer table and drop my purse next to them. My shoulders sag as moments of the trip flash through my mind. I don't want to tell her that Reece didn't wear a condom.

I continue. "I got really sick one night and threw up. I thought it was because I drank too much alcohol, but now I wonder if it's because I drank sink water from the bathroom after we got back from dancing and that's why I vomited. Then the night with Reece." I pause. "I have cognac with James often."

"The baby is already doomed," Natalie says in a serious tone, probably to mess with me.

But I'm not laughing. My nerves coil until it's almost hard to breathe. "Stop fucking with me, or I won't tell you about my raunchy night. Do you think it's possible I could be?"

I can't even bring myself to say the word.

Natalie sobers marginally. "Stranger things have happened, like my bestie marrying my dad. If you're worried, just take a test. I don't think symptoms happen that fast, but then again, I know nothing about kids and I like it that way. I'm telling you right now that I'm not changing diapers."

My head lulls back with a loud groan. I don't want kids. James and I already had this conversation and have taken the proper measures to make sure it wouldn't happen.

Fuck. Fuck. Fuck. Why did the birth control I've been on for years stop being manufactured? Pregnancy never crossed my mind. I really thought it was the seafood and that my stomach is weaker than James's.

"If I could reach through the phone and punch you, I would," I say, though my voice doesn't match my words. I sound like I'm moping.

"Are you going to bring this up to James or just take a test?"

I pull in my bottom lip and bite down hard, running my teeth back and forth over it. "I don't know. Maybe I give it a couple of more days?" I put Natalie on speaker so I can slip into something comfier. I pull out a pair of cashmere pajamas and run my palm over the baggy pants. "I'm going to ask your dad to get a vasectomy."

Natalie bursts out laughing. "I wish I could be a fly on the wall for that conversation."

"Do you think he'll say no?"

She's quiet for a moment, like she's actually giving the question some thought. "I'm sure he won't like the idea of being neutered, but I bet he'd do it for you."

Natalie has a way with words that always brings a lightness to the gravity of the moment. While most people probably wouldn't like it, I do. Sarcasm blends well with stressful moments. At least for me it always has. Walking into the kitchen, I begin making a cup of peppermint tea. It's been soothing on my stomach lately.

"I might even have my tubes burned too," I tell her as I put the kettle on the stove. "That way nothing gets through."

"Very extreme. I like it. Now that you're home, tell me everything and don't leave a single thing out."

"Isn't it like two in the morning there?"

Natalie hesitates. Lowering her voice, she says, "I can't sleep when Luca isn't home."

A smile spreads across my face. I laugh and goad her for actually caring about her husband.

"Sometimes I like him," she admits.

I begin replaying the eventful night. Just like in the past, I start at the beginning and don't leave a single detail out. She asks questions, and I answer them. More than two hours go by when I've finished confessing my night. Luca strolls into their house, and she has to hang up. Perfect timing. I need to run down to the pharmacy before James gets home. I want to pick up a few tests since sometimes they can be wrong.

"We need to plan our girls trip," she says.

"Let's do it next week," I suggest, and she agrees.

We say our goodbyes. After placing my teacup into the sink, I slip my feet into a pair of boots and pull on my winter coat. With my wallet in my hand, I march down the stairs and walk a few blocks to the pharmacy.

On the tampon aisle is where I find an assortment of tests. Funny how I've never noticed them before. My eyes scan the shelves. I blink rapidly at the words that are jumbled before me.

I'm suddenly overwhelmed. There are so many brands with various detection dates that I don't know which to pick. My first instinct is to call my husband, but I decide against it. He's at work, and I don't want to worry him. He doesn't even know what I'm doing.

Using the self-checkout, I purchase seven tests and walk home.

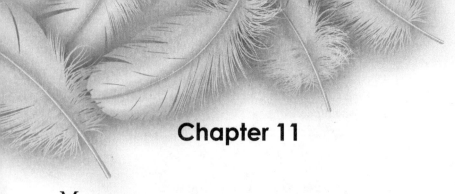

Chapter 11

My stomach churns at the sounds of the bolt.

The door slides open, and I hear James's keys drop onto the table. He closes it, and I flinch.

"Aubrey?"

"Hey," I say, my voice sounding small.

"Why are all the lights off?"

My heart pounds in my ears. I've been curled up on the couch in the dark since I got back, replaying how this moment would go. How I would tell James why I could be sick. I might not even be pregnant, but I can't stop the intrusive thoughts from running through my mind. I almost wish Natalie hadn't joked about it. I'd rather be oblivious than feel the torrent of emotions consuming me right now. We weren't supposed to have kids.

Could it be possible? And if so, what is the possibility that Reece could be the father? My gaze falls to the brown bag on the coffee table. The opening is crumpled from fisting it so tight on my walk back.

I took a test the second I got home, but I refused to read the results. I stuffed the stick back into the bag and left it there. I decided I would read them when James got home.

"Sweetheart? What's going on?" He flips on the chandelier overhead. His eyes search for me as the room fills with light. "Are you okay?"

Tears well in my eyes. I nod, struggling to find the words. I wish I could keep it together better. "I'm okay," I say, my voice shaking.

James's forehead wrinkles, his brows pulling tight as he rushes toward me. I reach for him, needing his security. In an instant he's holding me. I climb into his lap and nestle my face in his neck. His lavender and spicy scent envelopes me, and I breathe it in, finding comfort.

"What happened? Are you hurt? Is Natalie okay?"

"Everyone's fine," I say, my voice squeaky.

"Then what is it? You're worrying me."

Looking down, I can't meet his gaze.

"You can tell me anything," he says, his voice full of concern. "I brought home your favorite soup. The bakery had fresh bread. I got you a loaf."

His words cause a sudden rush of emotion, and tears spill down my cheeks. A bun in the oven. I start crying at his thoughtfulness. James leans back and takes me with him. I pull my knees up, and he wraps his arms around them.

"Did you read a book that made you cry again? That Nicholas guy?"

This causes a sad laugh to escape me. That Nicholas guy never gives a happy ending to any of his books. "No." Silent tears fall down my cheeks. My mind is running with ways to tell him what's going on. After a few moments, the words fall from my lips. "I think I might be pregnant."

"Really?" Two seconds later, he rumbles with laughter. "Is that why you're crying?"

I nod, still unable to meet his gaze. "Yes," I say, but it comes out like a squeak.

"That's nothing to cry over."

His response startles me. "But we didn't want kids."

James is quiet.

My voice is low. "I was worried you'd be mad."

He studies me, his eyes shifting back and forth between mine. Confusion sets in. "Why would I be mad? It takes two to make a baby. Whatever happens, happens. We'll figure it out together."

"I bought some pregnancy tests."

"And?"

"And I took a test then shoved it back in the bag. I was too scared to look at the results. I was going to wait until you got here so we could do it together."

"Are you late? Did you miss your period?"

I shrug. "I spoke to Natalie earlier and told her how I'd been feeling all week. At first she was joking about being pregnant, but then she brought up how I switched birth control and that it isn't effective at first. I only started taking the new one right before we left for Belize." I lower my gaze. "I didn't know that was possible."

My chest hurts from how hard my heart is racing. It's one thing to get pregnant.

It's another thing entirely to get pregnant by your husband's best friend.

The silence is deafening, and it's starting to get to me. James is quiet for too long, and I know it's because he's thinking the same thing I am.

James stands and steps away from the couch. My stomach drops. I'm sick. Instinct has me reaching for him, but I fight to keep my hands to myself. He runs a hand through his silver hair and looks up at our wedding photo above the fake fireplace he had installed for me.

"I never should have brought Reece into this."

My shoulders sink. I hope he doesn't think this is his fault.

"The test you took is going to be invalid. You'll need to take another one. The results are only good for the first couple of minutes."

"Oh. I didn't know that."

"I only remember from when Natalie was conceived. Do you have another? Sometimes two come in a box," he says.

My heart is thumping in my throat. Damn tears are rising to

my eyes again. "I bought seven in total. I got overwhelmed. I didn't know what to buy."

James turns around, walks over to where I'm sitting, and bends down. He presses a kiss to my forehead and then says, "Let me get changed, and then we'll take the test together."

I fall back into the couch, trying not to count how many seconds pass before he comes back to me. It's only a few minutes when I hear him walking down the stairs.

My husband is so fucking fine.

Despite the fact that it's twenty-seven degrees outside, James only has on a pair of navy-blue sweatpants. His toned chest is bare, and one arm is completely covered in tattoos now. He's been itching to fill the other one up. The sweats sit low on his hips. I love when he wears them like this, how the V dips into the waistband and the smoothness of his waist shows. My gaze automatically drifts to where his cock lies. His balls push his cock forward as he walks. I scan the wide outline, knowing exactly where the tip is. I'm a total pecker checker when it comes to him.

"Don't look at me like that," he says.

I straighten and sit on my knees. My knuckles hurt from gripping the hem of my hoodie in my fist. I flex my fingers. A blush crawls up my chest and heats my cheeks. "I can't help it."

James waves me over, and I follow like a lost kitten into the kitchen. He reaches into a cabinet and then hands me a red Solo cup.

"Go pee in this cup. We'll be able to take more than one test this way. Maybe save two for the morning."

I turn to walk away but James grabs my elbow and spins me around. He cups the side of my face and plants a kiss on my lips that steals my breath. He pulls back but doesn't move and presses his forehead to mine.

"Wipe your tears. I love you."

James lets me go.

I walk back into the living room and swipe the brown bag from the table then make my way to the guest bathroom, hoping for the best but expecting the worst.

Chapter 12

My heart is racing in fear of my future.

I stare at the empty red cup in my hand then look at my reflection in the bathroom mirror.

Could I be pregnant? And if I am, would I keep the baby? Would James want to? Would he want an abortion? Would I even be able to be a mom? Can I be a mom? Do I want to be? The thoughts don't stop coming.

I don't have a maternal bone in my body. The only thing I've parented is a cat when my grammy died. How could I take care of a whole, helpless person? At least the cat is self-sufficient. For the most part, anyway.

My eyes skitter around the large bathroom, wondering where Lucy is. I need to snuggle her and mush my face into her neck. She's old, and once she passes away, I won't have anything left of my grammy's. Tears fill my eyes. I wish she was here to help me sort out my thoughts. She'd have the right advice and walk me through the fog of shock I'm currently suspended in. Closing my eyes, I imagine her face and hear her comforting voice tell me it's going to be okay. She always found a way to make her life work for her and taught me to do the same. I pull on her strength and courage and exhale the anxieties. I have an amazing husband who would move mountains for me. That thought alone nips away the worries floundering around in my heart. I wish Grammy could have met James. She'd love him as much as I do.

My nerves are through the roof, but I manage to get the urine sample and walk back into the kitchen.

"You know, this is all your fault," I say as I place the plastic cup on the counter.

James turns his head to the side. He takes one look at my pout, and laughter fills his face. "Yeah? How's that?"

"If you didn't suggest Reece join us, at least I'd know the baby is yours."

His eyes flirt with mine. "That's the least of my concerns. It's not his."

I frown. "How can you be so sure it's not Reece's?"

"Six days is too soon for symptoms to show. You got sick right after we left. That was only two days later."

I stare, unblinking. "How can you be so sure?"

"It doesn't happen that quick. Google it on your phone," he suggests confidently.

I reach into my back pocket for my cell phone and begin typing. It says from the time of conception that it's possible to have symptoms seven to fourteen days, but that it could take a couple of weeks to feel anything. I repeat what I read to James, who is ripping open a pink box. I count back days in my head. Then common sense kicks in.

"So then I would've been pregnant before I even got to Belize?"

James nods. "Most likely."

"Which means my baby got drunk when I got drunk? It went ziplining? It ate seafood?"

My voice rises with each decision I'd made. A dramatic gasp gets caught in my throat. At least I didn't take a Percocet like Natalie suggested I do.

"Is that a grin on your face? I'm panicking on the inside. How are you so calm about this?"

His blue eyes hold experience, and that gives me the reassurance I didn't know I was looking for. James huffs out a laugh, and it makes me smile until he says something that makes my eyes pop out of my head.

"I like the idea of you pregnant with my baby."

"What?" I screech. My throat is starting to close. "Where is this coming from? Since when?"

I must've missed the memo, because this is not what we agreed upon.

James dips a test into the urine then caps it and places it on a stack of paper towels. He does this with three more tests. My emotions are all over the place, and there are too many thoughts running through my mind to make sense of any of them. James looks my way, reaches for my hands, then closes the distance to hug me. I wonder if he sensed it. Resting my head on his chest, I close my eyes and listen to the steady rhythm of his heartbeat as he rubs my back.

"Since tonight, I guess. I pictured you waddling around eating everything in sight. I sort of liked it."

"So you want another kid?"

"Not exactly," James says, his voice low.

My shoulders sag with relief. "What if it comes back positive?"

"Then we make a doctor's appointment to do blood work." He pauses then says, "You should make one anyway, just to be sure. These tests aren't always accurate."

He's right. Blood work would be the deciding factor. I'm getting all worked up, and it might show that I'm not pregnant after all.

I'm feeling frazzled and overwhelmed, stupid for not being more careful with the possibility of pregnancy. James and I never use condoms. I've never missed a dose in all the years I've been taking birth control. If I was ever sick and needed antibiotics, I made sure we didn't have sex. We took measures to reduce the risk of pregnancy. I've taken the pill for so long that I thought it'd be hard to get pregnant if I wanted to.

James kisses the top of my head. I nuzzle closer into the curve of his shoulder and study the colorful ink that lines my husband's arm. I gently trace the outline of one of his tattoos with the pad of my finger.

James pushes my hair over my shoulder then twirls it with his fingers. "I was thinking of getting one for my two favorite girls, actually."

I tip my head up to meets his gaze. James doesn't say anything. He stares into my eyes with nothing but absolute love, which chokes me up. He brushes his knuckles over my cheek then cups my jaw, running his thumb along my bottom lip. He leans down and gives me a soft kiss. I swallow back the lump in my throat and question how I ever got so lucky in love.

My voice is low as I say, "I don't want to look at them."

I'm scared of being pregnant. But I'm also curious. It's a strange set of emotions and feelings to pass through while stuck in limbo. I don't want it, but do I? I wish I could shake my thoughts away.

"Want me to look first?" James asks.

I give him a look that only takes a second for him to understand. James flips it over, and my eyes immediately scan the results. I gasp as he turns over the second then the third one. He lines them up and places them side by side.

Tears blur my vision. "What the hell does that mean?" I whisper, covering my mouth with my hand. Looking to James for an answer. "Why are they all different?"

Goose bumps pebble my arms. My ears are ringing. Bile rises to the back of my throat.

I'm going to be sick.

Two of the three tests are positive.

My heart plummets.

Turning around, I lean against the counter and slide down the cabinets. James grabs my shoulders before I can reach the floor. He pulls me into his embrace and holds me against his beating heart. His presence surrounds me. The security of his arms brings me comfort, and I lean into them. James kisses the top of my head.

"Sweetheart."

Embarrassment colors my cheeks.

"Look at me," he says.

"I can't."

"Aubrey Riveria, look at me right now."

I sniffle, trying to hold back the tears. I love when he uses his last name to address me.

"I won't say it again."

I give in and tip my head back to meet his gaze. Sadness colors his blue eyes. He lifts me up, places my butt on the counter, and steps between my thighs. My arms drape over his broad shoulders. His hands rest on the outside of my legs.

"I'm sorry."

"Why are you apologizing?" he asks, confused.

"Because this is my fault. I should have known to wait for the new birth control to activate or whatever. Then this wouldn't have happened."

"No birth control is foolproof."

"What if that false one is broken, and what if I really am pregnant?" Panic begins to smother me. "What if—"

He cuts me off. "Shh. No more what-ifs for the rest of the night. This is not an end-all to our world. It'll be okay. We'll figure it out. Tomorrow morning, you'll take the other tests and call your doctor. Until then, we're not going to stress about it."

"But I don't understand how you can be so calm—"

James silences me with his mouth and kisses me. It's a deep, powerful, and unruffled kind of kiss that forces me to slow down and feel him. I get lost in the sensation of my husband and lean in, hugging him as tight as I can, needing to fill the sanctuary of his arms. The little hairs of his beard tickle my lips. His palms skim up and down the outside of my legs, warming my body to his. I kiss him back with just as much vigor, and he lets out a little moan. James eats it up. My body comes back to life, and the desire I have for the man in front of me sets a fire in my veins.

James breaks away. Frowning, I blink rapidly, wondering why he stopped hugging me.

His eyes bore into mine with an intensity that sears into me. I know then that whatever happens, we'll get through it together.

Chapter 13

"I think you're right. After all of this, James must get a vasectomy."

I laugh so hard coffee burns the lining of my nose. I cover my face and reach for a napkin. My eyes water. Hearing Natalie talk about James as if he's not her father cracks me up.

I pull the phone down and yell, "James, Natalie said you need to get your nuts snipped."

She laughs on the other end. James lowers the newspaper and looks over it at me for a long moment then raises it.

"He has no comment," I tell Natalie.

"He thinks I'm kidding, but I'm being for real. This is too much. I have sympathy stress for you. I don't understand how those tests can be all over the place. You're basically fifty percent pregnant."

Tell me about it. My teeth sink into the muffin James brought back on his walk this morning to get our coffees and the paper. I didn't ask for it, but that's how James is. He brings me back surprises when he goes out. They're thoughtful. You'd think I'd be used to it by now, but it's always a treat and it catches me off guard. Today was an oversize muffin. The other day it was an acai bowl. A few weeks ago it was a plant that I've already killed because I forgot to water it. Another time it was a charm for a necklace.

"I don't get it either. Seven tests, and I'm pregnant but not pregnant." I pause then say to James, "Can I sue for emotional damages? Those tests are faulty."

"No," he says without looking at me.

As soon as I woke up, I peed into another plastic cup then dipped the rest of the pregnancy tests into the urine. Just like the night before, they gave me mixed results. It was too early to call my doctor, so I called Natalie first thing and told her what happened. She couldn't believe her ears and said that would only happen to me. I've been on edge ever since watching the clock strike nine so I could make an appointment. I haven't been able to think about anything else for more than a few minutes before it's back on the fact that I might be pregnant. My thoughts are consumed with this.

"Remember when you were a nanny and babysat little monsters? You already know how to change a diaper," Natalie says.

"I know the basics, like how to survive on minimum wage and make buttered noodles for dinner. I don't know the first thing about raising a human or balancing two lives."

"Oh, you should get a puppy!" she says excitedly. "That would be good practice. A lot of married couples start with an animal before they have a kid."

My brows rise and my eyes shift toward James again. I sort of like the idea.

"James, Natalie said you should buy me a puppy so I could practice."

"Except you have me, and I don't need practice. I'll teach you everything you need to know. We're not getting a dog. You may not even be pregnant, and then you're stuck with a dog."

"James is a bore," Natalie says jokingly. "Go out and buy one without telling him. You can't return dogs."

"Hmmm," I muse, chewing the last bite of the muffin. "Not a bad idea."

"Don't even try it," James says, and I frown. He folds the paper closed and places it on the table. His gaze meets mine. "I bet she told you to buy one anyway and not tell me." My frown deepens, and he answers the look on my face. "I know how my daughter thinks. She brought home one of those huge rabbits when she was in middle school without telling me. It was the size of a cat, and she hid it in her closet. My allergies were awful. I couldn't figure out why it was happening until she was at school one day and I heard a noise coming from her room and found the thing. I almost had a heart attack when I saw it. She'd hidden it for six months. I'd been to numerous allergists to be tested. I even ripped up the carpet downstairs and put down tile, thinking it would help."

My eyes light up and I laugh. He shakes his head in an attempt to suppress a grin. This doesn't surprise me. It sounds exactly like something Natalie would do. When she has her mind on something, nothing and no one can tell her no.

"What happened to it? Did you get rid of it?" I ask, curious.

He shakes his head. "We kept it until it died. She was in high school when that happened. I had to take three types of allergy pills if I was going to be in the house. I could barely breathe."

"He's so extreme," Natalie laughs. "It wasn't that bad."

James says to me, "You complain every time the neighbor's dog barks. How are you going to handle our dog barking?"

"That's because she has one of those tiny toy dogs that has a Napoleon complex. Ours wouldn't be like that," I say.

"You're so sure?"

"I'd want a German Shepard. They're guard dogs and don't bark at the sound of the leaves swaying on the tree.

His brows shoot up to his hairline. "In case you forgot, we live in the concrete jungle. Are you going to take a taxi to a dog park? Those dogs are large and probably wouldn't fit in the back seat comfortably." Before I can respond, he says, "You love to travel. What are you going to do with a dog when you want to go to Belize for two weeks?"

"Board it? Bring it with us?"

"Sweetheart, I love you, but we are not bringing a dog with us on vacation. I'll pay for the best dog sitter money can buy."

My mouth forms an O. That makes the most logical sense.

"What time is it for you?" Natalie asks. "Is it time yet?"

The clock on the stove reads twenty past nine. My stomach sinks. "Yeah. Let me hang up and call them. I'll text you later when I know more."

"Luca has some dinner I have to be arm candy for, so if I don't respond, then you know why."

Natalie pretends she's dreading it, but I know her better. She loves to get dolled up any chance she gets.

"Don't act like you don't love attention," I tell her.

She snickers, and it confirms that I'm correct. "Fine. Whatever," she says casually. "I just like the jewelry he gives me when it comes to one of these things. He spares no expense. The man has good taste, despite his flaws. Last time he gave me a ruby necklace. The gems were the size of my eyes."

I smile. I can't wait for the day Natalie admits she likes her husband.

"Send me a picture so I can see it too."

"Will do. Text you later, bestie," Natalie says then hangs up the phone.

I exhale a heavy breath and look at James, who is already looking at me. "Ready?" he asks.

"No," I tell him. "Maybe I'll wait a little, like closer to lunch. They're probably bombarded with more important calls first thing in the morning."

"If you make the appointment now, I'll take you puppy shopping."

I sit up quickly. My back goes ramrod straight. "Really?"

James nods.

"Don't lie," I say.

"Would I do that to you?"

I flatten my lips. He has a point. I pick up the phone with shaky hands and scroll.

My stomach is in knots as I scan my contacts and locate my doctor's number. Bringing the phone to my ear, I look for my husband, needing his strength. We don't break contact until my appointment is scheduled and I'm ending the call with a date with my OBGYN.

Chapter 14

My mind has been on my doctor's appointment since the moment I woke up.

I'm antsy. Nervous. I can't catch a good breath. I can't think about anything else. I've tossed and turned in bed all week and hardly slept. I keep checking the clock. Only a couple of minutes pass, and I get annoyed with myself for checking again.

You'd think I was going to court to hear my prison sentence, not to the gyno to get bloodwork.

I blow out a strenuous breath, trying to calm my racing heart. When I made the appointment earlier in the week, I asked a bunch of questions at the time. The receptionist was kind and answered them. She told me it's common for pregnancy tests to give mixed results. She sees it all the time. I learned that I won't be doing an ultrasound just yet and the lab results will take at least forty-eight hours to get back. If I'm positive, then I will have to come back to do the ultrasound to see how far along I am ... and what I decide to do.

I reach for my cup of tea and dip the bag a few times in the hot water. Tea doesn't hit quite the same as coffee, but I'm trying to be healthier and not ingest copious amounts of caffeine at the moment. I'm sitting at my desk at Sanctuary, reviewing the paperwork from women applying for a place to live. For years I always told myself that if I got pregnant, I wouldn't keep the baby. James and I had agreed to not having kids. He's too old, and I don't have a maternal bone in my body. But now that I'm faced with the possibility, I don't know what I would do.

Would we have this baby?

I curse to myself and flip the folder closed, feeling defeated. There are only so many beds available at Sanctuary. I can't give everyone a place to sleep. So many people are homeless, hungry, in need of a shower and a safe place to sleep. It breaks my heart that I have to turn women away. I want to help everyone. I try to take in as many children and mothers as I can, but I can't single out the solo women either. It's tough, and the decision isn't an easy one. I wish I could buy a huge piece of land, build a compound, and give everyone a place to live to restart their lives. I've considered opening a third Sanctuary. James offered to help, but the demand is steep. It's a vicious cycle.

I shoot a glance at the clock again and realize that it's finally time to go home. There's no way I'm going to the gynecologist without taking a shower first. Not that it matters or that I'm not clean. I'm sure the doctors see much more on a delivery table.

Grabbing my purse, I tuck a couple of the files in my arm to review at home tonight. I leave the bland tea on my desk. Next time I need to add honey. Turning the lights off, I shut the door to my office and say goodbye to my team then make my way to the subway.

**

I peel off the tape and remove the cotton ball where the blood was drawn earlier and throw it out. The appointment took all of ten minutes. I didn't even need to spread my legs and get prodded. I begged my doctor to call me as soon as the results come in, and she promised she would.

Leaving the ladies room, I find James waiting outside for me. We just had lunch at Balthazar, where we shared a couple of dishes and then ended our lunch date with a cappuccino. James had one too. I was craving coffee and missing it big time.

James takes my hand in his, and we begin walking down

the block. The cool air awakens my senses. There's still snow on the ground from the last fall. Surprisingly, I'm not as tense as I was prior to my appointment. The anxiety is gone, and my chest doesn't feel like it's closing in anymore. The way I see it, what's done is done. I'll have real results in a few days.

James wraps his arm around my shoulders. His presence comforts me. I lean into his side, and he kisses the top of my head.

"Have you noticed how many people are pregnant?"

He lets out a little huff of a laugh. "Yes, I did, actually. Funny how you don't notice that before."

"Right? I swear it's all I see now."

Big bellies are popping at every corner. Backs arched as they waddle. My brows bunch together as I try to imagine myself like that. My frown deepens when I can't.

"I know I said I won't what-if until the results are back, but what if I really am pregnant? Would we have a change of heart? I keep asking myself, and I don't have an answer."

James kisses the side of my face as we walk together. "We'll decide once and for all when the results are in. I can't say I don't want to see you pregnant with my child. Big and round, needing your feet rubbed, midnight runs to fill your cravings. It's adorable. If I let myself dream, I'd have multiple kids with you. But the reality is, I know what it takes to raise a child, the responsibility that it comes with, and I don't know if having a child fits our lifestyle." He pauses. "I'm getting older."

I'm partially relieved his views on children is in line with mine. The other part of me says it's wrong to be happy.

"Do you feel guilty for thinking that?"

I bit the inside of my cheek as I wait for his answer. I'm supposed to want to have a baby because I'm a woman. But I don't want kids. I never have, and yet I feel selfish for my choice. All my grammy wanted was to be a housewife and mother. It was her only goal in life, and she got it. She loved having kids and being pregnant.

The thought gives me hives.

I remind myself it's okay that I have different aspirations. Some women are meant to get pregnant and raise kids. I'm not one of them.

Then again, I didn't see myself getting married either.

"No. I'd feel guilty for bringing a child into this world that I couldn't dedicate my time to again. I did that once with Natalie and am still facing the consequences to this day. Just because we lived in the same home doesn't mean I was a good father. It requires more than just physical effort."

This was also a thought in my mind—not having the time to raise a child given how busy my life is.

"Do you think you could love another? That you have the love to give?"

"Yes," he says without a second thought. "You would too. It comes more naturally than you think. The moment Natalie was born, it was a love like no other."

I consider his words and wonder if the same would happen with me.

"Is something wrong with me? Shouldn't I want to be pregnant? Shouldn't I want to have a baby? I don't know what I want."

James shakes his head. He adjusts his black sunglasses on his nose then says, "You're being too hard on yourself. Pregnancy is tough, and a child is a lifelong commitment. There is nothing wrong with not wanting either."

"Do you think it's easier for you to decide since you are already a parent?"

"Possibly. But life then was very different than life now. I think it would present more of a challenge now."

We turn left and continue walking. James quietly leads, and I follow. The icy-cool breeze billows against my cheeks. We stroll three city blocks before he speaks again.

"I can feel you overthinking, sweetheart. I'm going to remind you of the two centers for single parents you own and operate full time. They're strangers, but you care for the people like they're your family." When he puts it like that, tears immediately climb to my eyes. "They look up to you like you're their mother. You already have what it takes. Stop questioning whether you would be a good parent. If you need further evidence, didn't you take care of your grandmother before she passed away? Let's not forget about Lucy and how you spoil her. Love is a two-way street."

I'm leaning into James as he wraps an arm around my shoulders and kisses the top of my head. I'm trying to fight back the onslaught of emotion coursing through my heart, but his words choke me up. I hadn't viewed Sanctuary as my child, but in a way, Sanctuary *is* my child. She is my baby. I care for the people who live there unconditionally.

I think back to Grammy. "*Give love toward anything that has a beating heart,*" she used to say to me.

Sniffling, I tip my head back and take the night sky, wishing again she was here.

I think she would be so proud.

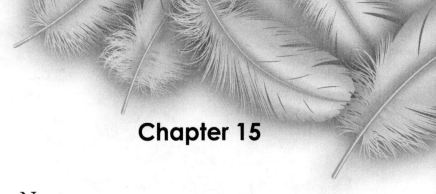

Chapter 15

Natalie should never have suggested getting a puppy.

It's all her fault that I've become obsessed with looking at them online. I've scoured countless websites and followed so many social media pages. I want to adopt every dog. I'm partial to the ones that've been abused or need extra love and attention. Like the one with its tongues hanging out one side of its mouth with hair standing straight up, looking like it's been electrocuted. I want to save them all. Thankfully the search has kept me busy the past couple of days while waiting for my results.

"Babe, look at this one!"

James walks over to where I'm sitting on the floor and squats. We scheduled our lunch breaks together so we could meet at one of the pet rescues I found this morning while scrolling my cell phone in bed. His dress pants stretch over his knees as he balances on his toes. He's rolled back his crisp white long-sleeved shirt to his elbows and loosened his tie. I get a hint of his cologne. The peppery lavender and leather make me want to pucker up and kiss him.

He looks at the Papillion puppy I'm holding and squints. All its bottom teeth but two are missing. I nuzzle my face in the dog's, and it gives me kisses.

Now I know why Grammy loved cats. I still have hers. I don't know what I'll do when Lucy crosses the rainbow bridge.

"How old is it?" He bunches his brows together.

I turn back to the dog. "Eleven."

"Sweetheart, if you're going to get a dog, wouldn't you want a puppy instead? That way you can train it and it doesn't come with bad habits. You don't really know what you're getting with an animal this age." He pauses. "Isn't it a little old?"

"I could say the same for you." The wispy hair around its ears reminds me of my frizz in Belize. "Maybe I have a thing for the elderly," I say.

James chuckles as he pets the top of its head. "Why is it missing so much hair? I feel like I'm rubbing its skin."

"Why is yours turning gray?" I rebut, feeling defensive for the dog.

"You can't save them all, even though I know you want to."

He's right. I can't help that my heart breaks for the lovable little creatures. This poor dog looks like it's had a rough life. I want to make the remainder of his years happy for him.

I pucker my lips and turn to look at James. "What if I open an animal shelter?"

"Are you going to be able to let the animals get adopted?"

I turn my attention back down at the dog I'm cradling. It's falling asleep in my arms. "No," I say softly.

He laughs lightly. James kisses the side of my head and stands. His knees pop as he stuffs his hands into his pockets.

"You know I don't like to say no to you, but I may have to draw the line at an animal shelter."

"I know. I just feel bad. I want to love them all. Are there any that you like more? That you're partial to?"

The fact that James has come around to the possibility of a puppy means the world to me. He loves my cat, even though he swore he wouldn't. We've messaged back and forth tons of pictures during the day, talking about what we like and don't like. We agreed to a smaller or medium-size dog, as long as it's not a teacup. James doesn't like toy pets.

"I think you have puppy fever. It'll pass in a few weeks."

I shake my head, adamant he's wrong. "Not a chance. There's

no going back. I'm all in. It's just a matter of when and which one." I pause. "Unless you've been leading me on this whole time. In that case, expect two dogs. And for them to sleep in our bed."

My cell phone rings in my purse on the table, but I'm too far to reach it. I need to get back to the office, but this particularly miserable-looking dog I'm cuddling was calling my name when I was scrolling earlier. Then there was the black and white puppy with two different-colored eyes.

"Can you grab that, babe?" I jut my chin in the direction of my phone.

He reaches inside my bag and fishes it out, muttering under his breath that I need to clean my purse. I bought a small purse for the sole purpose of not being able to carry much, but that didn't work out to my benefit. It's stuffed with receipts and miscellaneous things I don't need any more. James reads the screen. He stills, and my stomach drops.

"What is it? What's wrong?"

"Your doctor," he says. His voice is steady as he shows me the screen.

The smile fades from my face, and paranoia sweeps in. Our eyes meet. My heart is pumping a little faster, and the noise around me fades away. I snuggle the dog closer to me.

Either I'm really fertile or I'm as dry as a bone.

I swallow back the knot in my throat. "Will you answer it?"

***

James places his hand over my bouncing knee. "It's going to be okay."

I blink rapidly. I don't understand how he can remain calm all the time. It's a moment of truth, and deep down, I don't know what I want.

I thought I didn't want to be pregnant, but after the last couple of days, my views have shifted. Now I'm torn.

James's fingers overlap mine. We're sitting in my doctor's cold office, waiting for her to see us. When the doctor called earlier, it was actually the nurse, and she told me the doctor could squeeze me in between appointments if I came now. I said goodbye to the cute dogs I was playing with, and we left. The office is halfway across the city. We got here as quickly as New York would allow us to.

A million thoughts have passed through my head since we got the call.

On one hand, I hope the test is negative. Guilt swarms me for the thought alone. I feel like scum for wishing this. I should be happy, even grateful, that I can get pregnant.

On the other hand, there's an unusual seed of hope that I am pregnant.

Would I have the baby if the test is positive? My heart is abundant with the love I have for James. I'd do anything. If he wanted a baby, I'd give him one. And if not, then we wouldn't have a child. But do I want a baby with him? I go back and forth. My heart says yes, but my stomach just gives me knots. As much as I say I don't want a kid, I don't think I could give up the chance to not have a child with him. I guess I would have his baby.

There are two knocks at the door before it's being pushed open and my gynecologist waltzes in, her white coat trailing behind. The door shuts with a click.

"Thanks for waiting," she says and pulls her rolling chair under her to take a seat.

She places the manila folder on her desk. "How are you feeling?"

"Like a nervous wreck," I answer honestly.

She chuckles under her breath then scans the paper in front of her. She flips it over and then speed reads the other side. The dense silence ticks slowly by. I'm high-strung and just want her to blurt it out already. James places his hand on my bouncing knee.

His touch soothes me. I wish I had the composure he has. He's as cool as a cucumber and way more collected than I'll ever be. If there was something plaguing him, you'd never guess, judging by the look on his face.

"Thank you for seeing us early," James says.

"It's my pleasure. I'm glad you guys could make it in on such short notice," she says.

My doctor closes the folder and pushes it up her desk. She leans on her elbows and levels James and me with a look. Only, she doesn't say anything. She just studies us. There's a pounding in my ears that the moment is here.

"I ran a whole panel on you and did two types of blood work to test for pregnancy. One detects approximately how far along you are, and the other detects the presence of the hCG hormone. It'll tell me if you're pregnant as early as six to eight days after ovulation." She pauses, and I swear my blood pressure is about to cause a vessel to pop in one of my eyes. "Your tests are negative. You're not pregnant, Aubrey. Not even close enough to warrant retesting you."

A gush of air expels from my lungs. James gives my fingers a tender squeeze before he lets go. My shoulders sag, and it feels as if a weight has been lifted from my chest. Leaning forward, I rest my elbows on my knees and take a deep breath, relieved and saddened about the results.

"I'm going to kill Natalie for this," I mumble under my breath. My doctor's brows bunch together, and I answer her questionable look. "My stepdaughter."

She shoots James a brief look then looks at me. "I suspect you weren't ovulating when you had intercourse."

"I never know when I'm ovulating."

"Most women don't unless they track it. However, let this be a lesson learned about birth control. No contraceptive is one hundred percent. The next time you switch to a new one, no intercourse without a condom for at least seven days. I always say give it two weeks just to be safe."

"Trust me. That will never happen again. I think this moment scarred me for life."

"The only alternative is a vasectomy," the doctor says. She stands. "Otherwise, play it safe."

"Thank you again for seeing us," James says to the doctor. She leads the way out, and we follow her to the front, where we pay for the visit and then see ourselves out.

James hasn't said anything since we left. His stoic features give nothing away. Not even during the car ride back to Brooklyn does he speak. He just stares out of the passenger window while holding my hand. I can't take how many knots have formed in my stomach since this whole ordeal began. Now his silence is tightening them until I'm cramping.

Trepidation creeps in, and I second-guess the past few days, wondering if I misread him and his desire for another child.

Chapter 16

"You haven't said anything," I say as James unlocks the front door.

"Just processing it all."

We walk into our home, and James makes a beeline straight for his homemade bar. I shut the door, but my legs feel like tree logs and keep me in place. He uncaps the crystal decanter and pours himself a tall glass of cognac then pours me one. He reaches out blindly. When I don't take it because I can't seem to move, he turns around and spots me across the room. He rakes a gaze from head to toe, and it makes me shiver.

"Come here."

I swallow thickly, but I don't move. "You're upset."

"Come here," he says again, this time firmly stating the words.

My shoulder leans against the doorframe. I cross my arms and shake my head. My elation caused him sadness. He won't tell me that, but I can read him like a book.

James places both glasses on the marble countertop then strides to where I'm standing. The closer he gets, the tighter my throat feels. He scoops me up and carries me to the couch. He sits and places me in his lap.

"I'm sorry," I say, my voice muffled.

"What are you sorry for?"

"You wanted a baby, didn't you?"

He hesitates, and my gut sinks. I'm queasy.

"Sweetheart, look at me."

I bury my face into the curve of his neck and shake my

head. We're quiet. He brushes my hair back and allows me to cry softly without responding. I don't even know why I'm crying. I'm relieved, but I'm not. I'm happy, but I'm sad. I'm all over the place. I cry for today, and I cry for what will never be.

"I don't want a baby," James says quietly after some time has passed. "The other day when you asked me, I told you how I really felt. I was honest with you. I'm too old, Aubrey. I'm not trying to change diapers at three in the morning or build a volcano for the science fair. But had the results been positive and you wanted to have a child, I would've loved it just as much as I love Natalie."

"But you would eventually come to resent it and me," I say.

He shakes his head. "I wouldn't. When you hold your child for the first time, your feelings change. It's like an out-of-body experience, and you'd have a change of heart. That got me thinking. Today and the last couple of days really put life into perspective for me. There's so much time that spans between us. I feel like I'm taking away the opportunity for you to be a mother. That hesitation you felt is because I want to give you everything you want, and if you want a baby, we'll have one."

Confused, I sit up and meet his gaze. "You're not taking motherhood away from me. I never really saw myself with kids. I still don't. It wasn't my dream to be a mom. I mean, if it happened then it happened, but I'm not secretly yearning for it." My heart is pounding with what I'm about to admit next. "I love my life, our life. I don't want to change anything about it. But there was a very small, tiny part of me that may have wanted the test to be positive." I lower my eyes.

James tips my chin up and forces me to look at him. "Remember when I told you that I liked the idea of you pregnant? It's just a short-lived feeling. It's new and exciting, but the excitement will eventually die down and reality will set in. Sort of how you want a puppy."

One corner of my mouth lifts into a sad smile. "You'd give me a baby if I wanted it, even though you don't?"

"Yes, I would. Ultimately, I want what you want. Your happiness matters most to me," James admits, nodding. He's making me look him in his eyes.

"I've been indecisive about everything. I thought I knew what I wanted. I've given myself whiplash so much, I'm exhausted from all the thinking."

"What do you feel in here?" he asks, taping the center of my chest. "When we got the results, what was your first thought?"

Tears well in my eyes, and my chin bobbles again. "Relief." I sniffle as the tears climb faster and fall down my cheek. "I felt relief. But then you didn't say anything, and I was so ashamed. I don't know why, when I got what I wanted."

James wipes my tears away with the pad of his thumb. "Sitting in the office made me reconsider a vasectomy."

My brows lift. "What? Really?"

He nods then exhales a breath. "Yes, as long as you're okay with it. That, and I should stop being stubborn and visit my daughter in Italy." He pauses. "We should go to her home."

This time my jaw drops, and I bounce on his lap in excitement. I can't believe my ears. "Are you serious?"

"Yes. I have a great daughter already and need to show her that before I could ever consider another one."

I throw my arms around James's shoulders and squeeze him. I'm so glad he came to his senses about Natalie and that I don't have to ask him for this favor. Relief courses through me for the second time today. Pulling back, I palm his jaw in my hands and stare at the man who has my heart completely. His beard has grown in a little more, and the hairs are almost all silver now. I like it, and it suits him.

James doesn't say anything, and neither do I. He guides me to his mouth, and my eyes fall close. I lean into his kiss, not realizing just how desperate I am for it. James takes it slow. His free hand runs up my thigh to cup my ass cheeks. He rubs circles and surges ever so gently against my hips. I deepen our kiss and run my tongue along the roof of his mouth. He moans deep in his throat, and by God, how I love the sound of it. James sinks farther into the couch, taking me with him. He fists my hair, holding my mouth to his. His tongue strokes mine with precision. While his kiss is unhurried, his erection pushes against me. We make out like two teenagers in the back seat of a parked car.

James tears his lips from mine. He's breathing heavy as he says, "Take your pants off now and then sit on my cock."

James unbuckles his dress pants and pulls the zipper down. His movements are rushed. He lifts his hips and pushes the waistband to his knees, not bothering to remove them completely out of need to be inside me. I tug off my pants and panties in one swift move then straddle his hips. I'm eager to feel every inch of him stretch me open. James spits into his hand then wraps it around his cock and strokes himself. He squeezes, twisting his thick length from base to tip. I get such satisfaction out of watching James pleasure himself. It's such a turn-on. I scoot forward on my knees and position his tip at my entrance.

"Fuck me like you want to get me pregnant."

James laughs. His glittering eyes meet mine as we share a moment. I bite the side of my lip, grateful to call James my husband.

"Do you know how much I love you?" he says.

I nod, feeling my stupid emotions tiptoe in again.

"I'd do anything for you."

James places both hands on my hips and eases me down onto the crown of his cock. He thrust up as he shoves me down his length. I bite into his lip and hold my breath. No matter how many times we have sex, I never seem to get used to his size.

James doesn't slow his pace. He guides my hips up and down, thrusting hard and deep so I experience every inch of his cock. He turns me over onto my back and climbs on top, surging in quickly like he never left.

James drives into me, tapping my clit like he's teasing me each time. I chase the desire. He ravishes my mouth, teeth gnashing mine. He's hungry, and I can barely breathe as he takes and takes and takes. Sounds lodge in his throat and turn the heat between us higher. My fingers dig into his ass as I hold on. James deepens the kiss, propelling his body forcefully into me as the couch shifts under us. I'm not sure what possesses me to do so, but I slap his ass cheek. The tip of his cock prods the back of my pussy.

He breaks the kiss, gasping. "Fuck. Do that again."

"You like that?"

He nods, seizing my lips. James surges in deep and holds himself there. I slap his ass, and my pussy floods with wetness as the tip delves deeper. He doesn't pull out but does these little fast pushes into me until I'm breathless and my heart is racing. The way he's hitting my clit and stroking me with his cock is all I can focus on. I fist the hair at the back of his neck and chase the orgasm that's on the horizon.

"Oh, I'm so close. Don't stop. I want us to come at the same time," I tell him. I can barely get the words out.

"Wouldn't want it any other way," James says, looking into my eyes.

His gaze drifts down to my lips that feel swollen from his attack on them. He kisses me slow, like he's making love to both my mouth and my pussy at the same time. The sensations are all too much. My breath hitches in my throat, and my thighs begin to quiver. James circles his arms under my body and cages me to him. He drags his tongue along the roof of my mouth as he grips the back of my neck and drives us over the edge. We both moan, coming together in a wave of ecstasy that somehow gets better and better every time.

James rests the side of his face on my chest, listening to my heartbeat that is his only.

Chapter 17

"Do you want the good news or the bad news first?"

"The bad news," Natalie says.

"You would," I say, smiling over the phone as if she can see me. "The bad news is that you're not going to be a big sister. You're going to be an only child for the rest of your life."

"You got the results!" she yells into the phone.

"I did. I got them yesterday afternoon. I'm not pregnant. Not even remotely close."

"So why am I just now hearing about it?" she retorts.

My eyes shift to James, who's sipping his coffee. I love our chill mornings before we leave for work. It's our special time. I didn't want to put a damper on the moment.

"I had a mini meltdown when I got home, and then I got dickmatized, and you know how that goes."

I see James shakes his head from the corner of my eye. We made love three more times, each one more intense than the time before. Our connection strengthened, and this morning I feel closer to him than ever.

Natalie chuckles. "Was it the result you were hoping for?"

"It was. For a moment there I was sort of hoping I was pregnant, but at the same time I'm glad I'm not. James reminded me that Sanctuary is like my child, so that helped."

"Aww, that's true. You basically already have one hundred kids. I still vote for you to get a puppy. I like the one with the blue and brown eyes," she says. I'd texted her pictures of the puppies at the adoption clinic before I got the call from my doctors. Before

I can respond, she says, "Does this mean we get to start planning our girls' trip?"

With everything going on, the Australia trip slipped my mind. "Yes! I can't wait to do that. We're overdue for one. I desperately need bestie time."

"What do you think about going during the summer? I want to sip drinks from a coconut and lounge on the beach. And I want a guy in a paper skirt with nothing on under it to bring them to me."

I frown. "We have to wait a whole year for that? I don't want to wait that long. Let's pick a different place so it's only a couple of months away and not eleven."

"Shoot. I forgot Australia summer is our winter. What if we go to Antigua? They have adults-only resorts, so no screaming babies will be around. I need some peace and quiet. Luca's family is so loud."

My bestie's aversion to children always cracks me up. Watch her end up pregnant one day.

"Sounds like a date on the beach," I say then stuff the top of a muffin into my mouth.

"I'll start planning! You know I have nothing else going on in my neck of the woods but to drink homemade wine and look fabulous. Luca doesn't want me working, and I'm not going to argue with that. Leave the itinerary to me. Okay, what's the good news?"

I shift my gaze to James. I'd never force him into something he wasn't comfortable doing, but I'm glad he came to his senses. I could tell the pregnancy scare shed new light on his relationship with Natalie, so I decided not to say anything just yet. While I had every intention of telling him that my barter for a night with Valentina and Reece was mending his relationship with Natalie in Italy, I'm relieved I won't have to.

James misses Natalie. He wants to bridge the divide her

surprise marriage put between them. The problem is James resents Luca with a fiery passion. To see Natalie, James would have to face Luca.

James is still hurt Natalie didn't tell him about the engagement until the marriage was already complete. She hadn't even told me. That stung, but I didn't give her shit like I wanted to. I have no room to talk. I dated James behind her back and got paid millions to fuck him.

"James wants to visit you in Italy. You just have to tell us what works for you and Luca."

It's all I say. Natalie is quiet for so long that I pull the phone away to check the screen. She hasn't hung up on me.

Natalie clears her throat. Her words are raspy when she replies. "Yeah, ah, I wasn't expecting that." She pauses then says her question like she needs clarification. "So my dad is willingly coming to my house? The one I share with Luca? Like ... he wants to?"

"Yes."

She's quiet for another moment. Her soft breaths on the other side of the phone sound like she's trying to keep her emotions intact. "The pregnancy possibility scared him straight, didn't it?"

"It put a lot of things into perspective," I say, reaching for my coffee mug.

"I almost don't know what to say. I wish you would have gotten a false positive sooner. This is good news. Really good news." Her words crackle with emotion.

"Are you okay?"

"Yes. I'm okay. I'm more than okay. I know it doesn't sound like it, but I'm happy. I just wasn't expecting that. I don't know if I'm more excited you're not pregnant or that you're visiting me. I thought maybe you were going to say James is getting his nuts snipped so you never have to go through a pregnancy scare like that again."

A laugh I can't control escapes me. James watches with perplexity. "Oh, yeah, he's doing that too. He's agreed to get a vasectomy."

"You're kidding me," she replies, astonished.

"Nope. He's going under the knife as soon as we can plan it."

"Holy shit."

"I know," I say in agreement. "I could come off birth control too, but I think I'll stay on just to be safe."

"This is a lot to take in. I'm going to need Luca to open a real bottle of wine from the eighteenth century, and not the kind his grandparents make in the shed."

I giggle. "You're so dramatic."

"I'm actually not for once. Luca will probably think I'm lying when I tell him the news. How is your puppy going to fit in with all of this? Maybe you should consider getting one after your trips."

I hadn't thought that far in advance. I bite the inside of my cheek, wondering how I could make it work. "Good thinking. I guess I'll have to wait. I don't want to board a dog for two weeks."

James nods quietly, silently agreeing. At least he didn't say no to a dog.

"Get the procedure done before you come to Italy. I don't need you having another false scare, and then we can't do wine tastings and the whole trip is ruined."

Natalie is ridiculous, and I love that about her. My eyes light up. I've done plenty of wine tastings with James, but never with Natalie. I already foresee lots of laughing and memories in the making.

"A double date wine tasting?" My focus is on James. I know he's listening. He resent Luca, but I'm holding out hope he softens a bit toward him when we're there. "Let's hope the wine calms their raging testosterone and doesn't make them to fight."

"I'll have Luca rent out the vineyard just in case." I chuckle, thinking Natalie is just being funny, but then she says, "I'm not kidding."

"He can do that?" I ask curiously.

Her voice lowers. "He has a lot of power here. He can do anything he wants, get away with anything he wants."

She trails off, leaving the statement open. My brows rise. I'm about to delve deeper into the meaning behind her words, but she continues.

"Let me talk to Luca and see what his schedule looks like. He travels a lot. Mostly to Sicily, so it's not too far. I'll have him bring cannolis back for you guys. He swears they have the best ones. I told him to get me a vegan one, but he refuses, says there is no such thing. I know he's lying because I've had them." She quiets again then says, "I'm really happy James had a change of heart. Thanks, Ram Jam."

A massive smile spreads across my face at the nickname she created long ago. "Me too. Life is too short not to enjoy it."

Natalie and I hang up shortly after discussing all the places we want to visit together. I think I'm more excited about seeing her in Italy than going on a girls' trip. I know how much it would mean to Natalie for James to visit and accept Luca as her husband.

"You made her day," I say softly.

James folds the *Wall Street Journal* and places the newspaper on the little glass dinette he's sitting at. His eyes meet mine, and his look of affection has me standing up and walking over to him. He uncrosses his knee and reaches for my waist, tugging me into his lap. I nestle into the crook of his arm, and he rubs the outside of my thigh. He releases a breath, and it soothes all the feathers inside me that I didn't know were ruffled until now. James is my peace, my sanctuary. I rest my head in the curve of his neck, and he twirls the ends of my hair around his finger.

"Do you still want a puppy?"

I nod against his chest.

"We don't have to wait until we get back from Italy to get

one."

I sit up and look at him. My eyes widen to saucers. "Really?"

"Yeah. It doesn't make sense to wait. It's not like we're never going to travel again."

He's got a point. "What caused this change of heart? The puppy, Italy ... Was it really the pregnancy scare?"

He shrugs, clearly unsure. "My whole life has been about making moments. Collections filled with laughter, adventure, people, food, places. Life is so short. I don't want to lose out on seeing my daughter any more than I already have. That's not a collection of moments I want to remember, and I have many of those from when she was younger. The regret eats away at me. I want to be part of her life, and right now it doesn't feel like I am. How could I bring another child into this world and give it attention when I didn't give the one I have now the time she deserves?" He studies the finger that's twirling my hair. Melancholy surrounds James but I don't intercede. I can sense these things have been stewing inside him, and I want him to get them out. "Things happen for a reason. Maybe these last two weeks were supposed to be a wakeup call. We're not getting any younger. If a puppy makes you happy and fulfilled, then we'll get one. I want to see you smile every day."

He pauses to look at me then cups the side of my face. I lean into his touch.

"You would've made a great mother, Aubrey. But you don't have to give birth to be a mom. You already are one to all the people you care for at Sanctuary. You were to your grammy. You are to her cat. Even my daughter. Never forget that."

Tears blur my vision. I blink rapidly, hoping they don't fall. His words are sweet and hit me right in the heart. I try to smile, but my jaw trembles. I hadn't considered myself a mother until James pointed it out that day. And now that he has, the thought of missing out on motherhood dissipates.

"Looks like we're going to Italy. Are you going to play nice with Luca?"

"I never said anything about that."

James pulls my face down and kisses me softly. How I love this man.

Time moves fast. Moments are forever, but we never get the same moment twice.

THE END

About Lucia Franco

Lucia Franco has written over a dozen romance novels. Her emotional stories often include an age gap and forbidden love.

Her novel *Hush Hush* was a finalist in the RWA 2019 Stiletto Contest. Her novels have been translated into several languages.

Lucia resides in South Florida with her husband, two boys, and five pets. She was a competitive athlete for over ten years – a gymnast and cheerleader – which heavily inspired the Off Balance series. When she isn't writing, you can find her at the beach getting slammed by waves or wandering through her butterfly garden.